The Seven Rays

JESSICA BENDINGER

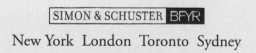

SIMON & SCHUSTER BFYR

New York London Toronto Sydney

SIMON & SCHUSTER BFYR

An imprint of Simon & Schuster Children's Publishing Division
1230 Avenue of the Americas, New York, New York 10020

SIMON & SCHUSTER BFYR is a trademark of Simon & Schuster, Inc.
Tarot Keys used with permission by Builders of the Adytum, 5101 North Figueroa St., Los
Angeles, CA 90042, http://www.bota.org. Permission to use Builders of the Adytum images
in no way constitutes endorsement of the material presented in this work.
For information about special discounts for bulk purchases, please contact Simon & Schuster
Special Sales at 1-866-506-1949 or business@simonandschuster.com.
The Simon & Schuster Speakers Bureau can bring authors to your live event. For more
information or to book an event, contact the Simon & Schuster Speakers Bureau at
1-866-248-3049 or visit our website at www.simonspeakers.com.
Also available in a SIMON & SCHUSTER BFYR hardcover edition.
Book design by Lucy Ruth Cummins
The text for this book is set in Garamond.
Manufactured in the United States of America
First SIMON & SCHUSTER BFYR paperback edition October 2010
2 4 6 8 10 9 7 5 3 1
The Library of Congress has cataloged the hardcover edition as follows:
Bendinger, Jessica.
The Seven Rays / Jessica Bendinger.
p. cm.
Summary: Brilliant, seventeen-year-old Beth's newly acquired psychic abilities lead her to
uncover secrets about her past, bond her to an attractive young man, and send her from
Illinois to New York to rendezvous with six similarly gifted young women.
ISBN 978-1-4169-3839-2 (hc)
[1. Psychic ability—Fiction. 2. Identity—Fiction. 3. Mothers and daughters—Fiction.]
I. Title.
PZ7.B43153Sev 2009
[Fic]—dc22
2009000150
ISBN 978-1-4169-3840-8 (pbk)
ISBN 978-1-4169-9739-9 (eBook)

To You

To Your Shine

To Your Light

To Your Spirit

To Your Fight

To Your Heart

May You Live It

To Your Love

May You Give It

CHAPTER 1

*T*HERE ARE SOME THINGS YOU CAN'T UNSEE. I DON'T know when I started seeing things. I don't know exactly when the little flickers started popping up, demanding my attention, mucking up my vision. I really don't remember. Which is annoying, because you think you'd remember the first time your life was about to change irrevocably. But you don't. When your personal cosmos explodes, you don't remember precisely when the match first strikes the tinder. Or when the wick on the TNT gets lit. Me? I just remember pink dots. Stupid pink dots.

The only dots I'd seen previously were dotted lines, where I signed my name: Elizabeth Ray Michaels. Beth to those who knew me. Elizabeth to those who didn't. I'm the only child of divorced parents, who neither speak to each other nor interact. This is a fact my overprotective, hardworking mother assured me was better than dodging my father's fists and his screaming. It is also a fact I've learned not to question. In my seventeen years I've mastered one thing: the art of staying out of trouble, and a knack for insanely good grades. That's two things. Two things that were about to change faster than a fourteen-year-old boy's voice. And a hundred times more awkwardly. But I'm getting ahead of myself.

I don't remember if my eye-flashes first started when my mom blew a gasket over the fact that I didn't ever cut or style my long hair. Don't get me wrong: I brushed it and loved it. I had been growing it since I was seven. It was dirty blond, long and shiny, and the only thing I appreciated about my looks. Ever since reading that guys preferred long hair, I'd been growing mine. Superficial and shallow, I know, I know, but my hair was like my beauty raft: I clung on to it for dear life. Once Mom had tried to trick me into cutting it by giving me a certificate to a salon in Chicago. When I used it toward a mani-pedi? She ragged on me, and there was a red flashing dot. Like a flashing red smoke-alarm light that didn't stop for several seconds. On her head.

The second visual flare was when my bestie Shirl wouldn't admit she'd lost my favorite bag. She'd borrowed it. And failed to return it. Period. Okay. So, second to my hair? I loved my stuff. I didn't have a lot of it, but what I did have, I adored. My old stuffed animals, my clothes, my books, my shoes, my bags. We couldn't afford much, so I treasured everything and took good care of it. I guess I took "pride of ownership" a little too seriously at times, because I began naming things. Betty was the name of my favorite bag. So, when Shirl lost Betty and wouldn't admit it? This blast of dots went off. "You treat your stuff like it's alive, Beth." She was railing on me like she always did when she'd messed up. "Who names their stuff? You'd think they were pets the way you dote on them; it's ridic. And who do you think you are? Are you really accusing me of lying about something I could totes incredibly easily replace, anyway?" My things were like my pets. Betty was my fave and she was gone. And I was pretty sure Shirl was lying about it.

But that was all eclipsed by the fact that Shirl was covered in pink dots: tiny dots, pancake-sized dots, quarter-sized dots, nickel-sized dots, penny-sized and micro-sized dots. She was covered in all sizes and varieties of translucent, Pepto-Bismol pink dots. I was blinking so much at her she asked, "Are you developing eyelash Tourette's, or what?" Then the dot-o-vision got all fuzzy and stopped. Sadly, eyelash Tourette's was not to be the diagnosis. Or the live-agnosis.

Weird crap began popping in, out, and around people in my field of vision every day for weeks. I was terrified to tell my mother (who had a tendency to become *hysterique* about anything and everything), so I kept my mouth shut. I was tripping. Tuh-ripping. Although I knew there had to be a logical explanation for what was happening, I probably wasn't going to discover it in my crappy high school's version of AP Chem. Which wasn't actually a class at my school, but (drumroll, please) . . . a college-level course at the fabulously craptastic local community college! In fabulously craptastic New Glen, Illinois! Having sailed through high school with a 4.1 GPA, I finished junior year as a senior. The faculty decided my time was better spent off campus in college-level classes than repeating classes I'd already straight A-ced. I'd be spending most of what would have been my last year in high school as an exotic export: a New Glen High School senior dominating the academic scene at NGCC (otherwise known as No Good Criminal College). By the way, there is no one less popular than a high-school kid in a college class crammed with college-aged underachievers. I was an inter-loper doing something my classmates had never dreamed of: graduating early.

It was the only thing I'd ever done early. I'd developed late, shot up late, and shot out late. Shirl and I were the last girls in high school to have chests that weren't concave. We were never the cutest girls or the hottest girls or the most popular girls, the weirdest girls or the most annoying girls. You'd have to matter to someone, somewhere, to be any of those things. And we didn't matter. To anyone, anywhere. Not when we met at New Glen Elementary, not at New Glen Middle School, and not at New Glen High. We were pretty much invisible.

In private, Shirl was a drama queen, constantly battling the nonexistent five pounds she had to lose, or complaining about her bad skin that was perfectly clear. She did it to combat her biggest fear, which she vocalized regularly: "We are becoming snore pie with yawn sauce, Beth! C'mon, let's do something spontaneous and unforgettable!" Which usually involved the exciting rush of mainlining coffee at the local mall.

Shirl's hobby was the cool kids. She pined for invitations to their parties, shopped where they shopped, knew where they hung out and where they worked. She studied them like they were constellations in a telescope: She understood what they were and how they behaved and could forecast their movements better than an astronomer. The difference between me and Shirl was simple: She wanted to be a part of their solar system. I wanted to get the hell out of that universe. And into university.

There was, however, one particular planet that Shirl revolved around: Ryan McAllister. Ryan Mac was the younger half of the lethally gorgeous, perpetually delinquent Mac Brothers. Stunning and troubled, athletic and not so bright, Ryan and his older brother, Richie McAllister, were legends around New Glen. They had dreamy hair, dreamy eyes, and the kind of sad family story that let them get away with anything. I didn't know the details, but Shirl swore their father had abandoned the family under some kind of mob death threat involving guns and gambling debt. Their mother was in and out of rehab, and the boys were given the kind of free pass that is handed out to heart-stopping hotties with tragic life stories.

And how Ryan worked it! Ryan McAllister was the sworn nemesis of promise rings anywhere in a hundred-mile radius. Reputed to have deflowered bouquets of virgins, Ryan was legend. Arrested at fourteen, illegally driving an old motorcycle at fifteen, all-state in soccer and basketball by sixteen, Ryan Mac was drunk with power by seventeen. By his senior year Ryan had plucked more local buds than the horticulture industry. This naughty fact was how Ryan McAllister got his very naughty nickname: the Hymenator. His conquests were legendary, and were usually followed by the unfortunate and very public dangling of an unwrapped condom on the victim's locker. Needless to say, Shirl would've willingly offered her rose to him without hesitation.

"I'm feeling thorny" was her whispered giggle every time we'd cross Ryan's path.

"Hey, Charlene." Ryan always got Shirl's name wrong, and this didn't deter her.

"A rose by any other name would still smell as sweet?" I squeaked out, trying to protect her fragile ego.

"He knows I exist. I'm making progress." She was so gleeful about it. It was as if he'd just asked her out.

"Please don't lose your V to Ryan McAllister," I'd beg, rolling my eyes out of worry more than anything.

"He'd have to find it first," she'd laugh. "Unless I lost it already. Do you think my virginity is in the lost and found box in Principal Tony's office? I haven't seen it in a while. . . ." She'd joke about her total lack of sexual experience. But despite Shirl's self-deprecating humor, I worried about the truth: She'd do anything for Ryan McAllister.

I reluctantly indulged her fixation by hanging out with her at the Bordens Books at Glen Valley Mall. Ryan worked part-time at the sporting goods store next door, and I could at least study and drink coffee while Shirl obsessed and memorized Ryan's flight pattern.

There wasn't one cool kid who Shirl didn't know something about. Grenada Cavallo—the style icon of New Glen—never wore the same thing twice, and her luxury Vuitton bags were way beyond what most kids could afford. Shirl would speculate relentlessly about their origin. "Do you think Grenada is a master shoplifter or master Web-shopper and deal-finder?"

"I no know," was my constant refrain. "They are your specialty, not mine." I needed to nail my physics test, and she was not letting me master Newtonian mechanics.

Shirl was sucking down her fifth coffee. "She says it's a wealthy aunt who works at Bergdorf's in New York."

"I didn't realize the wealthy worked in retail."

"I know, right? Lucky her." Shirl was buzzing. "Did you see Jake's new tattoo"—she knew I hadn't—"on his lower back?"

"He got a tramp stamp?" I asked, incredulous. "How tacky

and how tragic!" I detested tattoos. "Why not just wear a sign that says, 'Please think I'm cool. I'm begging you!' How'd you see Jake's lower back, anyway?"

"He took off his shirt in PE."

"Did the angels sing?" Shirl liked Jake. And by that, I mean Shirl liked all boys.

"Don't mock me. You're missing a lot, you know." Shirl said it in a resentful voice, like I'd abandoned her and made a horrible mistake by investing in my future. "And now that you're gone, he's probably going to be valedictorian."

She was trying to rile me up, and I wasn't biting. "I have to take as many college classes as possible. I can apply them as credits next year and save money. Gimme a break."

It took a second to process what Shirl had said. "And since when is Jake Gorman smart?"

"His grades turned around after he was diagnosed with ADHD. They put him on Adderall, and he's like an academic rock star now." She was sucking on a straw, flattening the end and picking something out of her teeth with it. "You are so out of it! You can always make up college credits. But you will never make up lost time in high school. Jenny Yedgar is gaining weight. None of her clothes fit, and I have to sit behind her triple muffin top every day in Trig. There's some supercompelling drama unfurling. Especially if you find back fat riveting."

"You are the most compassionate person on the planet." I laughed.

"Jenny Yedgar is a bitch. And the weight has only made her meaner. She's gone, like, all mad cow."

I had to get some studying done, so I pulled out the big guns. "Was that Ryan?"

'Twas a lie. But predictably, Shirl was out of her chair in his phantom direction at light speed. I took a deep breath to focus. I loved Shirl, but sometimes being friends with her was one-sided. In her favor.

As she ran toward her Ryan-stalking ground, little blobs of squiggles were streaming behind her, blurring like runny ink. *Mine eyes are filled with eye mines!* I said to myself as I tried rubbing them away. It didn't work. The act of blinking was becoming dangerous, setting off explosions without warning. I snuck home early and climbed into bed.

The next day at No Good Criminal College, the eye-bomb really dropped. At 11:33 a.m. in Chemistry, I thought my eyeballs were playing tricks, for sure. Because Richie Mac was smiling at me. Richard McAllister. The Richie Mac. Brother of Ryan. In all his nineteenly glory. Eyes of an angel. Body of a god. Smile of death. He waved at me and I looked around. Nobody moved. I looked back. He waved again. At me. He shook his head as if to say, *Aren'tcha gonna wave back?* As I was about to catch my breath and wave, some weirdness said hello. I mean, it's not weird at all if the sight of dots animating before your very eyes is something you see every day. This time, the dots did something. They became giant fibers. Giant fibers braiding as they moved toward me. If the sight of three imaginary strands of nonexistent thread interlacing in the air is normal, forgive me. They didn't cover that in my SAT prep course. Fortunately, my unexpected encounter with Beauty and the Braid got all fuzzy and blurry and disappeared in an instant.

"I think the word you're looking for is 'hello'?" Richie said.

"Uh, hi-llo, I mean, hello," I blurted out as my cell began vibrating. My hello to His Royal Mackness was interrupted by a text. From my mom. DINNER 7:30. CHICKEN? It's like she knew I was lusting after a boy who was completely inappropriate for me in every way, so she was busting my nonexistent flow. I resisted the urge to tell her to stop ruining my first taste of human eye candy when Richie spoke.

"It's rude to take a text message in the middle of a conversation. . . ." He grinned. Shirl would've died. He was so beautiful I lost the power of speech.

"Sorry—my mom—" *And that phantom braid,* I thought.

"Is she as pretty as you are?" Richie said, without a hint of irony in his voice.

My blood pressure reversed direction, pausing briefly in my throat before flooding my cheeks and ears with heat. *I don't know, do your teeth actually sparkle?* was my unspoken reply. I knew he wanted something, and I couldn't risk speaking with all the blushing taking place on my face.

"I was wondering if maybe you might wanna possibly join our study group? It's usually after class." I noticed two college girls loitering nearby. They seemed less than thrilled with the prospect of me joining their band. "I'm Richie." Even his voice was beautiful. How was that possible? I couldn't speak for a second, and he beat me to it.

"Do you want me to guess your name? I enjoy games," he joked.

"I'm Beth," I finally squeaked out.

"Hey, Beth"—he pointed his enormous hand at the duo, and I wondered how he could pick his nose with fingers that large—"that's Elena and . . . ?"

"It's Marin, Richie. My name is Marin," the girl who was not Elena practically spat. Richie looked at me like, *Sorry about her*. He added a shrug that said, *How can I be expected to memorize names? I'm way too yummy for that.*

I pointed to my phone. "My mom is expecting me."

"I hope we'll see you after the next class, then?" He must've been six foot four, and he leaned on my table for emphasis, twinkling his freakishly long lashes at me. I felt him towering over me, pausing before saying, "Beth?" My legs went numb. I could've wet my pants and never felt a thing, my body was that paralyzed by his appeal. I wasn't hypnotized. I wasn't magnetized. I'd been Mac-netized. I barely mustered a nod as he walked away. There I was. In Richie Mac's Chemistry 101 study group. As my Mac-nosis wore off, I nervously slapped myself on the leg for being susceptible to his infamous charms. Maybe Shirl wasn't crazy after all.

Before heading home, I had to pick something up at my

future alma mater, New Glen High School. The sign outside read THE RIDE OF ILLINOIS, the P in front of RIDE stolen long ago and never replaced. I texted Shirl to meet me in our fave spot: the girls' bathroom near the teachers' lounge. Other kids hated it because of its location. We loved it because it was always empty.

"What do you mean Richie Mac asked you to be in his study group?" I shouldn't have told her. She had that tone friends get when they are jealous, and I hadn't thought this through.

"Um, he says hello and that Ryan wants to marry you. I accepted on your behalf. I hope that's okay," I joked to ease the jealousy whammies coming my way. "You'll be honeymooning in Cabo."

"As long as the family doesn't mind if I don't wear white at the wedding. I'm planning on having a lot of sex before my wedding night, FYI." Shirl was joking. This was a good sign.

We'd each had our share of odd make-outs and exploratory sessions over the years, but we were both virgins. This drove Shirl crazy. "I'm just going to sell my virginity on eBay. It's such a curse. How much do you think I can get for it?"

"On the free market?"

"EBay is not a free market. You have to put down ten percent of your reserve price, so we really need to think this through. I'm thinking a million dollars." I spit out my latte.

"We could totally get a cool mill for your trampoline." The word trampoline was our synonym for the revoltingly unsexy word "hymen." I mean, a word that sounds like "Hi, men!" seemed like a funny thing to call the membrane that separates virginity from sexual experience with actual men. Don't get me wrong, I loved men and I loved my hymen, but we preferred "trampoline."

Whenever either of us said it, that was our cue to do a lame sing-along dance we'd made up in seventh grade. We'd cover our crotches with one hand, point our fingers sternly with the other, and chant, "Cross this line and you're a tramp! So do it while you're off at camp!" Then we'd shake our butts and marvel at how stupid we were.

"How did we start calling hymens 'trampolines' anyway?"

"I think you'd heard some story about a gymnast busting hers doing tumbling—"

"Oh yeah, and how trampoline starts with the word 'tramp' and is a giant elastic thing everyone always wants to bounce on—"

"But no one wants it to break—"

"—without protection!" we'd say in unison.

"Would anyone get that but us?" I asked.

"Of course not. No one's as cool as us. Except the Mac Brothers," Shirl cooed. "So what are we wearing to our double wedding?"

It was time to jet, and so I grabbed my stuff. "We really need to see the world, Shirl. There's a sea of guys beyond Ryan McAllister."

"We'll see the world on our double honeymoon. We'll wear matching outfits." We low-fived a good-bye, and I had a weird feeling she wasn't entirely kidding.

The school had called that morning and said I had a package waiting in the main office. When I got there, I was promptly lectured by Mrs. Dakolias, the school secretary. The moment she started speaking, her body grew something around it. I blinked. Out of thin air these gross knotted braids sprouted around her in every direction. Like I was hallucinating.

"We're not a post office for students. We're not supposed to accept your mail," she chastised, as she presented me with a trashed FedEx envelope. The braids evaporated into nothingness before my eyes.

"They had to send it twice," she whined. "The first time they spelled your name wrong. We couldn't even pronounce it, let alone think it was you." The original addressee's name had been crossed out and replaced with the following: ELIZABETH RAY MICHAELS, C/O NEW GLEN HIGH SCHOOL. I squinted at the newer Sharpie lettering, trying to decipher what name was underneath.

"What was the other name?" I asked, genuinely curious.

"I don't remember. It was some odd typo. We didn't sign for it the first time—there was no name like that in the roster. We sent it back." For someone who obviously disliked kids, Mrs. Dakolias had picked a strange job.

I nodded while staring at the envelope, pondering the return address. It was from a company called 7RI, with an address on Fifth Avenue in New York City. I didn't know anyone in New York City. I didn't even know anyone who knew anyone in New York City. It suddenly felt kind of glamorous to be getting a FedEx from the Big Apple. I hoped it was scholarship money. *Please, God, let it be enough for Columbia,* I said to myself, *'cause you know Mom can't afford it.*

I didn't want to open the letter in front of anyone. "It's probably some scholarship information, or something. I'm sorry for any inconvenience, Mrs. D. Thank you for your help."

"Don't let it happen again," she grumped before returning to her filing.

"Beth?" It was Principal Tony, leaning out of his office and motioning for me to step inside. He was stuck in the seventies and was the kind of guy who you called Principal Tony. He broke up fights, and students liked him because he wasn't a total dick.

I really wanted to open my package, and I was getting impatient. He extended some paperwork my way.

"I called NGCC. I need some signatures on these," he lectured, "or you can't graduate early, Beth." I snatched the papers. Graduation—early or on time—could wait. I couldn't wait to open my package.

I headed to the restroom, entering the big handicapped stall. I hung up my bag, put a thick layer of paper toilet-seat covers on the lid, and sat down. I couldn't take my eyes off that Sharpie lettering. There was an energy coming off the envelope that gave me a big feeling. Not the creeps or anything, but just like an anxious feeling when you are not expecting mail from a company called 7RI and they've sent something to your school. It was disconcerting and kind of thrilling. I prayed for big bucks. *Big Educational Bucks, por favor!*

I pulled open the tab. I closed my eyes and took a deep breath. Inside was another envelope. Gold and small, like an invitation. On the front of the envelope, in very careful lettering, was the name **Aleph Beth Ray**. Odd typo indeed. It didn't even look remotely like my name, and I started to doubt it was for me. I rechecked the packaging. That was my name on the outside, right?

I flipped it over and saw a beautiful, antiquated wax seal. I carefully peeled it back so I could do forensics later. I extracted this heavy piece of pulpy, old-fashioned paper from the envelope. The message was written in block lettering. Only eight words. Eight words that read **YOU ARE MORE THAN YOU THINK YOU ARE**. I flipped it over. That was it. Eight words, eight words that couldn't possibly be for me.

THE KEEPER

*Y*EAR AFTER YEAR SISTER MARY PERFECTLY TIMED the mailing of the gold envelopes, patiently sending them on precise dates from the headquarters of 7RI. The process was always the same: Mail a gold envelope with a specific message and wait for a response. Replies could take days, months, sometimes years. Sometimes they never came at all.

Mary took in the unobstructed view of the East River through her large office window. The new decorator had painted the walls an expensive shade of slate. The floors were polished to a high shine. The archives were securely protected by both manual lock and digital code. Fingerprint and voice recognition had been installed, and Mary delighted in the ease of inserting her finger and saying her name versus the cumbersome use of key and code. These precautions were there for a reason, and she had nothing but the greatest respect for protocol. But Mary was tired of waiting. Someone's life was in danger.

As she made her daily journey across the river to All Saints Hospital, Mary fidgeted. One of the biggest alignments in centuries was just around the corner. The legacy of the Seven Rays—an inevitability that had been promised before promises existed—was finally about to play out. She peeked out the back of her chauffeured town car, hoping the sunlight would relax her. Mary didn't get giddy, but this excitement was positively overwhelming to her. Nothing short of everything was at stake. Mary needed Sarah to hang on.

All Saints Hospital was not renowned for its successes. A small, private hospital serving up third-rate care, it employed an underpaid staff and served dissatisfied patients. The facility had faced bankruptcy on more than one occasion. All Saints didn't fit anyone's idea of first class, and it showed. Which is why it was so surprising when the cancer ward started releasing cancer patients. Without cancer.

Word about the "miracles" at All Saints spread quickly

through the Catholic community. Some claimed there was a weeping Madonna in the mosaic tiles; others said the hospital had been built on a sacred burial ground. Some said it was the nun in the plain brown habit who sat with Sarah David every day.

"Good afternoon, Sarah," Mary cooed. "How are you today?"

"Sister Mary. Thanks for coming. I'm tired."

"I know, dear. But we're getting closer. Any day now."

"I don't know. If I can do it—" Sarah had survived months of IV feeding tubes, mechanical respiration, dialysis, and several bouts with deadly infection.

"Come now. Recite for me, dear." Mary took out her large knitting needles and began knitting a purple scarf.

"'Canst thou bind the sweet influence of the Pleiades, or loose the bands of Orion?'" It pained Mary to hear the effort in Sarah's tone.

"Silly girl. You know I prefer the Tennyson, my dear."

"'Many a night I saw the Pleiads, rising thro' the mellow shade, glitter like a swarm of fireflies tangled in a silver braid.'"

"Lovely. Thank you." Mary noticed some unfamiliar faces outside the intensive care unit.

"They're from the Department of Health," Sarah wheezed. "Verifying the remission statistics."

"Again?" Mary shook her head. "Scientists hate the unexplained. I don't know why they get so worked up."

"They think the staff is fudging the figures." Sarah's voice was evaporating. Mary let her rest a moment, considering what lay ahead for the Seven Rays.

"List the names for me, Sarah."

"Matariki, Makali'i, Tianquiztli, Kilimia, Subaru, Krttika, Al-Thurayya." Sarah's accents were perfect.

"Always so good with languages," Mary purred. "The sites, please."

"The Temple of the Sun in Teotihuacán, Chichén Itzá in the Yucatán, Machu Picchu in Peru, the Great Pyramids of Giza, the Parthenon in Greece, Mateo Tipi . . ."

As Sarah recited the list, Mary nodded to herself. *The seven days of the week, the seven colors of the rainbow, the seven seas, the seven major planets, the seven notes on the scale, the seven glands in the body . . .*

Sarah's lists all owed a debt to the Rays. One or more of the Seven Rays had always been murdered or slaughtered before the Great Work could be completed. Destiny always had its detractors. The Rays were no exception.

The Music of Sevens was about to be played again. For the first time in centuries these human stars were aligning, and providential dominion would be reclaimed. The imbalances and atrocities from centuries of patriarchal rule were about to be righted. The masculine had grown out of control. The feminine was about to take its rightful place. This planet was called Mother Earth for a reason. Yes, the Seven Sisters had been born before. This time they'd be protected. Mary was startled out of her contemplation by a familiar orderly.

"How are you, Sister Mary?" She loved the sweet Catholic boys. They were so respectful.

"Vince. If the doctor asks me to sign that do-not-resuscitate order again, the answer is still no."

"I don't know why they bother you, ma'am. The bills are paid; she's not hurting anyone. I guess it's the rules, when . . ." Vince trailed off, embarrassed.

"When what, Vince?"

"When patients are in, um, a persistent vegetative state, ma'am." Vince quietly adjusted the tubes coming out of Sarah's otherwise motionless body. A body that had not moved, blinked, or taken an unassisted breath in more than eighteen months.

"Vegetables are alive, Vince," Mary said sweetly, as Sarah's machines clicked, pumped, and beeped, "and so is Sarah."

| 0 | THE FOOL | ᛋ |

STARED AT THE GOLD ENVELOPE IN A TRANCE. As I rode the metro bus home, I decided I would not share the letter with my mother, who would surely decide I was the victim of a stalker and was in some sudden, creepy kind of grave danger. I also decided that whoever Aleph Beth Ray was, she might want to know that she was more than she thought she was. Or he. So when I got home, I did what anyone would do. I Googled Aleph Beth Ray. And I discovered something. That name, the name Aleph Beth, was also numbers. Aleph was the number one in Hebrew (pronounced "al-eff" or "ollif"), apparently, and Beth (pronounced "bet" or "bait") was the number two. I had to laugh that someone would be named Number One and Number Two, and wondered if their nickname would be PeePoo. I was cracking myself up over my golden note to PeePoo when I started wondering if there was an Aleph Beth or if the note really was for me. After all, the package had been sent to my school twice. The gold stationery and wax seal didn't seem to fit the profile of a crazy stalker with a malicious plot to kidnap and fillet me. Or maybe that was part of the seduction? Fake 'em out with some nice handwriting before tossing 'em in a hole. Or—in the case of my new friend PeePoo—flushing 'em down a toilet?

I studied the address on the front of the envelope. I Google-mapped the address and studied the image on my old laptop for quite some time. I Googled 7RI and found some paper for the American Mathematical Society about "noncrossing partitions." I did a reverse address search and couldn't find out anything without paying twenty bucks, so I tried searching "free reverse address search," and those results led me to a different site that wanted ten bucks. I called directory inquiries in New York City, requesting a business number for 7RI on Fifth Avenue. Nothing. I studied the wax seal as if I were a crime scene babe: It was an intricate decorative symbol with a bunch of interlocking rings. This was going nowhere. I needed to get more info without alarming my mother. I picked up the phone.

"Carleton and Company Health Insurance—your health is our business. May I help you?" I felt so bad for receptionists who had to repeat things like that all day long.

"Jan Michaels, please. It's Beth." My mom disliked calls at work and preferred texting, so I braced for the tone.

"What's wrong?!" My mother was exceedingly predictable. She catastrophized everything, especially unexpected phone calls. The unofficial verb form of "catastrophe" is "catastrophize," meaning to assume the worst. It fit Mom well. I figured it came from looking at medical claims all day long: She anticipated disaster.

"The registrar's office needs some paperwork completed for my diploma, and they need two forms of ID, so I guess I need to know where I can find a copy of my birth certificate. I also need my eyes checked. I've been having issues with double vision and stuff."

My mom's voice pitched up in that mom-alert way when you ask something out of the ordinary. "Birth certificate's buried in some files—can you wait a day or two? I'll need to move some boxes." A day or two in Mom time meant two or three weeks. Possibly months.

"I can look for it myself if you want," I offered.

"Why the urgency?"

"I was thinking of getting some fake IDs made, and I need to screw around with the original documents so I can commit fraud. Preferably on some kind of national level involving a media circus that will embarrass you and Grandma, forcing you to relocate and change your names."

"Do not go through my file boxes, Beth. Not if you want to live." She wasn't the greatest, but she wasn't the worst either. She was, however, super annoying.

"But what if I could find it faster than you?" Two could play the whining game.

"If you can decipher that mess, Beth, you should join the CIA."

"The CIA are notorious for making messes, Mom, not cleaning them up."

"Stop being so smart. Now, let me figure out your eye appointment."

"Okay. Thanks." I wasn't thankful for what was sure to be an interminable wait, but annoying her would never expedite things. I hung up and felt relieved to get the eye monkey off my back. And then I wondered something. What if I *could* find it myself? I couldn't resist.

I walked down the hall of our teeny two-bedroom ranch house and yanked the garret stairs out of the ceiling. I carefully climbed up and pulled them behind me. I looked around, and it was pretty clean in the crawl space. There wasn't that musty, dusty smell that most attics have. It smelled like my mom had been up here cleaning recently. I could smell the citrus cleaner; I could smell that vacuum-bag smell. How the hell did she get the vacuum up here? There was no dust anywhere. In fact, it was the cleanest I had ever seen our attic. It wasn't that disorganized, actually. There were my old toys, some old track trophies of my grandfather's, my mom's big box with her wedding dress in it, and tons of other boxes and chests of various shapes and sizes. After a bit of digging I found some accordion files and legal boxes. They were filled with tax records and financial files going back about ten years, but then they stopped. I dug around some more and found a box with stuff from fifteen years ago: divorce documents and letters, notes, or cards. I looked around the room, and all this static started forming around my head and in my eyes and in my ears, and—damn, it was getting hot up there—everything got filled with white noise, and I couldn't swallow or breathe or smell, and then everything went soft and dark and black. That's the thing about a blackout: You don't see it coming. If you could see it coming, they'd call it something else.

When I opened my eyes, I was in an empty room. Empty except for seven chairs in front of a blackboard. Behind the chairs were seven perfectly drawn chalk symbols: an ox, a house, a camel, a door, a window, a hook, and two swords. Above the first chair was a crude drawing of a house with a bull standing in the doorway. Over the second chair was a drawing of a camel. Over the third, a door. The fourth picture was a window. The fifth had a shape like a bent nail or a hook, while the sixth seat was paired with a sketch of two swords.

The seventh seat had no drawing. Just blank space behind it. I got up and looked at the first drawing, leaning in to see the crude outline. I licked my finger to smudge the chalk, when I noticed that the eyes of the bull were real, not drawn. These eyes were looking at me. Except they were my eyes. My eyes were bull's eyes. I heard someone yelling "ALEPH BETH! ALEPH BETH!" and getting louder and louder, all frantic. I woke up, and the syllables changed as I came to. It was my name: "Elizabeth!"

It was my mother, screaming from downstairs. I coughed and heard her swear and pull down the attic steps, screaming my name. I sat up, shaking off the heat. My eyes landed on the open file box, and when I reached to close it before Mom found me, I saw something. A section in the file box labeled 7RI. What? I grabbed it and shoved it under the back of my shirt, slamming it shut before Mom's head emerged from below.

"You scared the bejeezus out of me! Are you okay? What happened? What are you doing up here?" She was beyond irked.

"I guess I fell asleep." My cheek hurt. *Damn, I must've fainted hard.*

"Up here? What are you doing up here? You're beet red! It's boiling hot, and you're probably dehydrated. Let's get you downstairs."

"What's a bejeezus?" I was suddenly very eager to get the tone lifted.

"Don't be a smartass."

"I'm being serious. How do you spell it?"

"G-O D-O-W-N-S-T-A-I-R-S." My mother was annoyed.

"Fine. But I'm pretty sure there's a *b* in 'bejeezus.'" I ran downstairs and slipped the file in my room before facing her wrath in the kitchen.

I drank some Gatorade at the kitchen table, feeling pretty light-headed. This didn't stop me from being desperate to get into that 7RI file. Then my mother slapped an envelope in front of me. "Here you go!" I opened it, and there it was. My birth certificate. In black and white: Elizabeth Ray Michaels, 7 pounds 7 ounces, February 23rd, 1992. St. Joseph Mercy Hospital. In Ann Arbor, Michigan?

"I was born in Michigan?" This was news. Huge news.

"You knew that." My mother was annoyed, and a flicker of something like a rope knotting in thin air blurred my vision.

"No, I didn't know that." I rubbed my eyes.

"Your father and I lived in Michigan until you were three months old. He loved it up there. Probably moved back there to find new punching bags, for all we know." As I looked at my mom, suddenly these weird tendrils came out of her head. They were about an inch in diameter, and they were knotting as they moved toward me, like some kind of live-action boy scout test. I felt these hungry stomach pains sink in my belly. Watching her talk about my nonexistent dad gave me pangs, but then it all hazed and vanished in the flip of my eyelid. I figured it was my ailing eyes and shook it off.

"Michigan? Huh. I remember that. His family was from there,

right?" She rarely told me anything about him, so I pretended like she already had in hopes I could get more info. It didn't work.

My mother grabbed the birth certificate and put it back in the envelope. I wasn't really done looking at it, but she was annoyed with me, and I didn't want to push it. My dad was not in the picture for a reason, and any reminder of him turned my mom to acid.

"Don't look around in my stuff, Beth," she said, and she looked like she meant it. "It's not respectful."

"I'm sorry I scared you." At that moment I was glad I hadn't told her exactly how gnarly my vision was getting.

"I called the ophthalmologist, and you're on the waiting list in case something opens up this week. They suggested you keep a record of anything unusual that might be happening." By unusual, I was pretty sure they didn't mean sci-fi. But I wasn't "pretty sure" of much right then. I wasn't sure of anything, and it definitely wasn't pretty.

I was desperate to open the file, but my mother was watching me like a hawk, rendering my desperation futile.

I decided to write down all my eye symptoms thus far, and it helped to distract me from the fact that sneaking into my room and reading the file from the attic was momentarily impossible. So I wrote three things in my notebook that night: dots, ropes, knots. As soon as I could, I pretended to get tired early, and I snuck into my room for privacy.

I opened the file's clasp and dumped a pile of gold envelopes onto my bed. The envelopes were all addressed to Aleph

Beth Ray at our old house in Glencoe. We'd moved six years ago, and ever since then my mother had kept a post office box, since we had lived in a series of apartments. Some of the post-marks were more than ten years old. My heart raced as I flipped through the envelopes: different addresses, different forward-ing addresses, with certified mail and registered mail stickers. I arranged them chronologically and carefully sliced open the earliest postmarked letter with scissors. Inside, there was a card with an old-fashioned drawing of a young man. A young man about to walk off a cliff. It read THE FOOL at the bottom of the card, with a zero to the left of the writing, and some symbol to the right. That was it.

The next six envelopes had similar old-timey cards with different pictures, numbers, words, and symbols. The next one chronologically (sent a year later) was called THE MAGICIAN. He had a sideways eight over his head, and the card also had a number one on it and another symbol. The next card had a two on it and was called HIGH PRIESTESS and featured a lady on a throne sitting between two pillars, each with mysterious sym-bols on it. Number three was named THE EMPRESS, number four was THE EMPEROR, number five was something called THE HIEROPHANT (a pope-looking dude with two guys kneeling at his feet), and the sixth was called THE LOVERS. This last card featured a butt-naked guy and a butt-naked gal looking up at an angel. I laid them out in front of me and studied the seven pictures, flipping them over, holding them under the light, and looking for more clues. There was a blue plaid on one side, and the images, numbers, names, and symbols were on the other. They were clearly drawn by the same artist and meant to be a series, but I didn't get it. At all. What were they, and why was Mom keeping them from me? Visions of those characters danced in my head. All night long.

1 THE MAGICIAN

WOKE UP WRECKED. MOM DROPPED MY TIRED butt at NGCC the next morning so I could deal with my signatures. Anything that moved me toward a new life was fine by me. I stuffed all the envelopes and cards into my bag and checked my reflection before heading to Chem. And all things Richie Mac. I wasn't his type. I wasn't his type. There was no way I was his type, and I resisted the urge to put on lip gloss as if it might matter. And then put some on. Okay, I wasn't his type, but maybe I wanted to be.

I quickly sat down and got busy taking notes, when I caught Richie looking at me out of the corner of my eye. Did I have something on my face? When I looked back, he looked straight at me and laughed. What was going on? After class Marin and Elena were nowhere to be seen, and I prayed like a little kid that he wouldn't bail on study group. *Study group for two! Study group for two, please!* I ranted internally as I waited to see if he'd join me.

"C'mon, Beth." He smiled. I sat there frozen. "I finally have you all to myself!" That's how he was. Everything that could be loaded with flirt juice? Was. I was going to drink it in, even if "finally" was a gross exaggeration that I couldn't trust but wanted to believe.

Our maiden voyage together involved copying my Chem notes on a copier, and his expression of disbelief about how much I managed to transcribe over the course of one lecture. "You like a stenographer or what? I can't even read this—what's the three-dot triangle thing?"

"Shorthand for 'therefore'?"

I didn't really believe he was that interested in me or my shorthand, but he smelled incredible, and I didn't care about his motives. His hands were as big as my notebook, and I doubted that they could hold a pen. Maybe that was why he'd never been a great student—his hands were too big! He must've caught me staring, because he set down my notebook self-consciously. "These hands are better for lacrosse."

"Lacrosse your heart and hope to die?" What did I say? I swear, it came surging out of my mouth before I could even stop myself. I wanted to lacrosse *my* heart and die. It was so dumb. And then Richie said, "That is so stupid it's funny," and he let out this low-pitched grumble from the back of his throat. His eyes got wide, and he ripped out with a booming laugh. God, he was the hotness.

I pretended to study with Richie Mac in the totally uncool Community Coffee Haus after class. I'm sure I spoke words, but it was a blur as we talked about nothing and I tried to retain feeling in my legs. My stomach was twisting into a complicated ice dancing routine when I noticed his energy getting more and more focused on me. He was staring at me. It wasn't manipulation anymore, and it was making me blush.

"I can't believe you're only seventeen. You seem way older than seventeen, you know." There was light refracting off his eyelashes, sending my internal tummy choreography into some kind of triple axel.

"Well, you don't look fifty-eight. So we're even." What? Me and my mouth needed lockdown. Richie snickered and then bit his lip thoughtfully. How could he look at himself in the mirror without falling in love? It was ridiculous. I felt the region between my knees and my belly jellify.

"Happy Birthday, Beth."

As it wasn't my birthday, this left me and my jelly belly completely confused.

"You must be confusing me with some other girlie. Because it is really not my birthday." I tried to sound all cool, and I was anything but. He leaned in, looked me right in the eye, and moved his mouth toward my ear.

"Then consider it a belated birthday kiss. Or an advance birthday kiss. Whichever you prefer." He whispered so softly that the words floated me up to the ceiling.

Without hesitation Richie Mac did the unthinkable. This gorgeous, perfectly lipped nineteenish man-boy tilted in and kissed me. Suddenly and masterfully, he planted one. On my mouth. With tongue. For a while.

As my face flushed and I forgot we were in a public place, time stopped. Not in the way that it felt so amazing or anything (it did), but because the silky smoothness of his mouth completely consumed me. Each moment felt stretched: all soft, all wet, all lips. His kiss swirled itself around me like fresh cotton candy, the nerves of my entire body funneling into one incredibly sweet point.

I briefly opened my eyes to make sure it was real, and I saw Richie surrounded by ropes. Long white ropes with knots all over them. I opened my eyes again. He was—ropeless. I closed my eyes and opened them again, and they were still there—clear as day. Richie was surrounded with more knotted ropes than a pier during a sailing festival. Ropey tentacles. Floating out in all directions. Into infinity. I blinked them out of existence. I didn't want to stop kissing. Richie began caressing my head with his hands, when an explosion happened. Dots burst into an internal jumble of images blasting through my mind. I felt and saw Richard McAllister's entire life flash before my eyes. I felt his father gamble everything away and his mom drink herself sick and his brother cry. I felt the crying and fighting from the medical bills and the humiliation of the foreclosure on their home. I felt his dad leave and their shame about a move into a tiny apartment. I felt Richie and his brother working odd jobs to help their mother, and I felt Richie Mac feel so powerless that flirting and smiling made him feel in control. I felt how he felt nothing anymore. As I felt something like sadness flooding through the kiss, it all got very hot. Like, scalding hot. We both pulled away and said, "Ow!" Simultaneously.

I must've seemed stunned, because Richie couldn't stop looking at me, disoriented. "That was—are you okay? I'm sorry—was that uncool? Did you—Beth—it was just meant to be a kiss—I'm sorry—" He was horrified. "Did you—?"

"Just have my first public kiss? Maybe." I was covering, sipping some water to cool my flaming mouth. He had the strangest look on his face before grabbing all his stuff to leave.

"I'm not eighteen yet, but you won't go to jail or anything. For underage kissing."

Richie wrinkled his brow and touched his mouth before waving good-bye. Then he walked away. I didn't want him to. I didn't know what to do. My heart was pounding. I closed my eyes as elation surged inside of me. *Richie Mac just kissed me.* I wasn't sure who was going to die harder: me or Shirl.

I raced home on the bus, reeling from the kiss-tastrophe but determined to get upstairs and into the rest of the file before my mom got home from work. I couldn't get that little gold letter out of my head.

YOU ARE MORE THAN YOU THINK YOU ARE.

What if I wasn't more than I thought I was? What if that wasn't even the question? Considering how blurry my vision had become, I wondered if it was impacting my ability to reason. I covered my eyes and felt my stomach lurch and realized the card should have read "You are not who you think you are." I had to get home and get upstairs.

I was a stealth speed demon about racing and sneaking upstairs to open the file. The attic was quiet and still except for the citrus cleaner scent. I dove into the file box. There were two manila envelopes in the 7RI section, and I grabbed the bigger one and left the other one there, just in case Mom was checking it. As I went downstairs, I realized I should've taken everything and put fakes there instead. A noise came from outside. I jumped and quickly put the stairs back into the ceiling, rushing to my room.

"Beth! Come here!" Mom was home, and I couldn't believe I hadn't heard her car. I shoved everything back into the envelope and under my bed. When I got to the kitchen, my mother sat with two huge bags of takeout, which was code for "special occasion."

"Did you get a promotion?" I asked, trying to cover my irritation about the fact that she was fully hiding stuff from me.

"Nope. But this came for you." She tried to conceal her smile, but she couldn't. It was a very thick packet from Columbia.

"That's fat." I was beaming. It was like winning the lottery and getting a ticket out, all at once.

"Yes, it is." Her eyes were twitching like she was about to start crying, and she hastily unpacked the food.

"Do you think I got in?" I already knew the answer. I just gazed at the logo, wondering if I'd ever have a sweatshirt with one of those logos on it. I was smiling so hard and was so happy; for one brilliant second I forgot about all the crap that had been going on.

Mom burst into tears right then and there, nodding. I got choked up looking at her and ripped open the packet. Inside was an early acceptance letter from my top choice. I was ecstatic, but I was pissed off at her for the mail that I wasn't supposed to know about, and I was scared to be too excited, because clearly she hadn't processed my imminent departure completely.

"I'm happy for you, honey," she squeaked before she ran out of the room, howling uncontrollably. It was kind of a killjoy, but once she was gone, I got up and did a little shimmy. Despite the drama, I was thrilled that I'd been admitted—birth certificate, weird visions, gold envelopes, hot kisses, and all. If

I got a birthday kiss without a birthday, imagine what I might get for getting into college. I pictured kissing Richie again, wishing that feeling back into my body until I was buzzed. My inexperience felt nonexistent when our mouths met. His mouth was so skilled there was nothing to do but relish it. That kiss swept over me like a wave, and I laughed as I realized that meant that I'd surfed Richie Mac's mouth. Or boogie-boarded? I didn't know what I'd done, but it was watery and swell and made me glide on the surface of time. I turned the kiss over and over in my mind, spinning it on my thought rotisserie until it was scorched.

In one day, I, Elizabeth Ray Michaels, had kissed Richie Mac and gotten into college. Unreal.

And despite two unexpected packets, I was still who I thought I was. But all the college acceptance letters in the world wouldn't explain why I was still seeing things I shouldn't be seeing. Things I couldn't be seeing. Things that were not there, but were right before my eyes. Or, or, or, or . . . maybe there was no "or." Maybe it was all in my head.

"I got you in to see the eye specialist tomorrow; his waiting list opened up. Can you get downtown tomorrow?" my mother yelled out while blowing her nose in the bathroom. My continuing attic shenanigans would have to wait till later. "Yes! Thanks for doing that, Mom!" I yelled back, suddenly hopeful. Maybe there was an explanation for my eyes. Wasn't there? I ripped open the takeout and began setting the table. When Mom said she wanted to lie down, I ate in the kitchen alone. I stared at my admission packet, wondering if I'd be eligible for a decent financial aid package. And who on earth was sending me those gold envelopes? Was it my father? All the more reason to keep it from *mia madre*. Would I see/kiss/touch/taste Richie again? Was he thinking about me at all, or was the player playing me? My brain ticked from one tock to the next. The food stung my burnt tongue as I chewed, and I wondered if Richie Mac's mouth was scalded too.

THE KISS

ICHIE MAC HAD BURNT HIS TONGUE BEFORE,
but never like this. He was in the dingy bathroom
he shared with his brother Ryan, staring into the
crooked mirror on the medicine cabinet. The top hinge was broken, so Richie lifted the lower corner of the mirror with one
hand, peeling his lips back and holding his mouth open with

the other. He stood there for a while, staring inside his mouth in pain, horror, and amazement. A thin sheet of skin was dangling off the roof of his palate, completely intact: a membrane floating like a wet sheet on a laundry line. Inside his mouth. It looked bad. But he couldn't believe how good it felt.

Driving home, he couldn't recall anyone who'd felt like Beth. He was filled with the urge to be around her. Constantly. He wanted to kiss her again, feel her again. Something in her scent pulled him in. Her eyes, the way she looked at him. He'd never been interested in anyone like her. She was the opposite of girls he'd dated before. There was nothing obvious about her. She didn't try too hard. She seemed to be thinking, always thinking. She was smart. He dug how her bottom lip plumped bigger than the top. He pictured clearly the light pink against her fair skin. He liked all that she wasn't: Her brows weren't overplucked; her hair wasn't dyed; she wasn't spray-tanned; she wasn't putting on makeup or lip gloss all the time; her clothes weren't too tight. She was real. By the time he got home, Richie was aware of an uncomfortable fact: He wanted Beth Michaels. For breakfast, lunch, and dinner. He got hunger pangs every time he thought about her. His mouth was toast, yet he was full of longing. What the eff was going on? His sweaty hand slipped off the mirror, and Richie sat down hard on the edge of the toilet, dizzy. He looked down at his T-shirt: It was soaked. Front and back. His pants were stuck to his skin. The sweat wasn't beading; it was slicking off his pores like he'd just gone swimming. He reached the faucet and splashed water on his face, pulling off his shirt to get cool. The fabric stuck to his skin. As he wrung it out in the sink, he noticed something against the yellowed porcelain. The fluid dripping out wasn't clear like sweat. It was pink, as if small traces of blood were sweating out of his body. Weirder still was that he didn't panic. He felt too good.

Richie jumped into the shower, ice cold water pummeling his increasingly heated body. As the cool rolled down his skin, a delicious burning sensation seared him from the inside. He swayed against the shower door as if he were drunk. He could barely think. Grabbing a frayed white towel, he yelped as he dried the blood-tinged sweat and water off his body. The terry fibers blushed pinkish red, and Richie tried to say "wow," but nothing came out. His throat was parched dry. Naked, he lurched for the bathroom door and noticed something under his skin: small bubbles raising and moving the hairs on his arm. Paralyzed, he watched—almost detached—as the spheres pushed against his flesh, popping and bursting at the skin's surface like small blisters. He slipped on the wet floor, swaying toward the phone in his bedroom, as he watched his skin froth open like foam. Richie's body gave out to sweet sleep as he reached the bed, collapsing before his fingers could dial for help.

While Richie passed out, the flesh foam turned into a seamless crust, forming a thin, hard shell over his skin. He slept hard, feeling and dreaming nothing but numbers. His brain was silent, but for a woman's voice repeating numbers as he slept: "Five five five. Seven eight three. Four seven eight six. Five five five. Seven eight three. Four seven eight six," over and over again during his motionless slumber.

By the time he woke up almost eighteen hours later, he was dozing in and out of bliss. When he finally got up, his eyes couldn't fully open. His lids squinted against a thick glue, trapped shut under a thin veil. He flailed his hand to his face, unable to open his lips for air. His nostrils and mouth were covered in a slight scab that covered every inch of his body. He scraped at his face, scratching off the layer with ease, sitting up as the veil crunched into sharp crumbs under his rear end. His thighs and calves told the same story: His skin was peeling off and crackling like delicate candy brittle. Richie swatted the fragments off like unwanted insects, thrashing around his small bedroom as if covered in spiders.

Dehydrated and disoriented, Richie fumbled to the bathroom for water, bending under the faucet and letting the water flow into his mouth for ages. His mother called out from her bedroom, barely coherent. "Y'all right, darrrrlinnn'un?" Her slurred speech meant "darling one," and he responded quickly so she wouldn't freak out. "Great, Mom, everything is great!"

And it wasn't far from the truth. Despite the dehydration and the flaking skin, he felt amazing. He was excited to see Beth again, and was still buzzing from their kiss. He hummed to himself as he looked in the mirror: Everything was fine. Flicking off some stray pieces of mystery crust, Richie opened his mouth and looked inside: No more blisters, and the tent of dangling skin was gone. Upon examining his hands, he saw no scabs. His skin looked perfect, in fact: softer, clearer, healthier. He dismissed the episode as a weird reaction to scalding hot coffee. He felt fantastic. If the kiss with Beth was that good, he could only imagine what more would feel like. What more was in store? The idea of more got him excited, and he took a shower. Richie rinsed off all evidence of his excitement, along with the remaining flakes of dead skin. Would she be in class today? He couldn't remember her schedule. He had to see Beth. He was never like this, but he didn't care. It felt too good.

As he dried off and opened the medicine cabinet to grab his toothbrush, Richie's finger impulsively wrote ten numbers on the steamed surface of the mirror. Dropping the towel, he rushed to find the phone and dial before the digits evaporated. After two rings, someone answered.

"7RI. Mary speaking." The woman's voice on the other end of the line sounded incredibly familiar.

"Is this 555-783-4786?" Richie tapped his foot nervously, wanting to be sure.

"Yes, it is." Her voice was kind. He splashed faucet water into his mouth as quietly as possible, hoping the liquid would help him form words. He didn't have to.

"So, then," the woman continued, "how can I help you, Richie McAllister?"

CHAPTER 6

I AWOKE THE NEXT MORNING TO THE SOUND of my mom's car heading out of the driveway. I had to get up to the attic.

I yanked down the stairs, raced up them, and grabbed the second manila envelope out of the 7RI file, and rushed back down again, my pant leg catching on the stairs and nearly tripping me. I was panting, willing myself to calm down as I carefully opened the flattened metal clip. Inside was one more gold envelope addressed to none other than Aleph Beth Ray. The postmark was dated several months earlier. It contained a white paper cutout of a large key affixed to the gold note card. Typed onto the key shape was a rhyme called "The Seeing Key."

THE SEEING KEY

If you see ropes, you are seeing connections
From this life, between folks of every complexion.
If those ropes have knots? Lies and harm are
    energetic.
When ropes double-helix? Correspondence,
    genetic!
If it's braids that you see? They're from karma
    descended.
From past lives to present, there's wounding
    untended.
If harm is repaired in this life with deeds sweet,
The braid comes undone, and the karma's complete.
Rays—those bright rays!—pure forgiveness and
    love.
If rays you do see, this is work from above.
When you see more—as you will—there is work to
    be done.
Chart a course! Stay on track! Your journey's
    begun!

I read and reread the rhyme with a sense of panic and elation. Even though the envelopes had been unopened, I was
panicked that my mother had been keeping them from me, or
keeping them from Aleph Beth Ray. Who I was beginning to
think might be me. Whether it was me or not, I was elated that
someone, somewhere, knew what I was seeing. And apparently
knew what it meant.

I transcribed the poem into my notebook and tried to figure
it out.

> *If you see ropes, you are seeing connections*
> *From this life, between folks of every complexion.*

I'd seen ropes, alright. But what did "from this life" mean? Were
there other lives? Past lives? Simultaneous other-dimensional lives? I
drew a little doodle of the kinds of ropes I'd seen and moved on to
the next couplet.

> *If those ropes have knots? Lies and harm are energetic.*
> *When ropes double-helix? Correspondence, genetic!*

I had seen a knot on the rope when Shirl claimed not to
have "borrowed" my bag. If knots meant lies, then she was
lying about losing it. I hadn't seen the double helix yet, but I
imagined that would happen between relatives or something.
Shouldn't I have seen that between me and my mom? I'd have
remembered that! But no, no double helixes yet.

If it's braids that you see? They're from karma descended.
From past lives to present, there's wounding untended.
If harm is repaired in this life with deeds sweet,
The braid comes undone, and the karma's complete.

I remembered the braid with Richie! The braid that waved hello! It didn't explain why my visuals came and went with Richie, but it was something! The braid did that weaving dance toward me when we first met. So Richie and I had "karma" and "wounding untended"? I wasn't sure what that meant, but I liked the idea of sweet deeds. Sweet dude deeds.

Rays—those bright rays!—pure forgiveness and love.
If rays you do see, this is work from above.
When you see more—as you will—there is work to be done.
Chart a course! Stay on track! Your journey's begun!

Okay. This seemed instructive. Couldn't hurt to test how and when the visions happened. Maybe it would help me see if this Seeing Key was even in tune.

I went outside and walked down the street. Sure enough, visual chaos swarmed over everything. There was Mrs. Janowicz and her four kids under the age of five. She was covered with ropes, dots, and swirls of colors, textures, and shapes. I took in an ocean of breath and closed my eyes. Mrs. J was covered in ropes. Knotted ropes! She embraced her smallest child as she lifted her out of her car seat, and I noticed double helixes between the little girl and her siblings and Mrs. J. That was it!

I was so distracted I barely made it to the bus in time for my date downtown with the eye doctor. I reread my notes about my sight: dots, knots, ropes. I tried to find words for the Richie kiss—feeling and seeing someone else's life? I knew my eyes had been closed while it was happening, but I still wanted the perfect word, a shorthand so I could remember what had happened. The feeling of seeing. Or seeing a feeling. Feelseeing? Seefeeling? A feelsee. Yeah, that described it. It was a case of the feelsees. As I rode up the elevator to the ophthalmologist's office, I had no intention of sharing that. That was between me and the Seeing Key. And whoever wrote it. I couldn't help but wonder if the author was my father. And by wonder, I mean hope.

Dr. Rigtonio's office was not the ode to pasta one might expect with a name like Rigtonio. It was very streamlined and high-tech, and I was in the examination room within minutes. I reported the basics of what I'd been experiencing, and the doctor took notes and quickly placed me behind a giant Phoroptor: an elaborate mask of lenses that looked like a facial microscope.

"The flashes you are describing sound like floaters, but we'll check for astigmatism first. But floaters can look like cobwebs, threads, spots, or squiggly lines." I'd never been so happy for a diagnosis. Sounded like dots, knots, and ropes to me! I was starting to feel better. Maybe I wasn't crazy! I gave an internal shout-out to Dr. Rigatoni, yo!

"It's uncommon in people your age, but the vitreous can pull the fine fibers away from your retina, creating flashes of light. We call more extreme cases retinal detachment, but yours appears to be relatively mild."

"Can you relatively mildly fix it?" I asked.

"We have an opening tomorrow. You are going to be good as new."

Boy, did I want to believe him. But I also wanted to understand the Seeing Key. If it wasn't real, why did it all line up?

I raced back to school. I may have been cruising for Richie Mac out of the corners of my floater-filled eyes, but he didn't have to know that. Or that my mouth still felt a little sore from the kiss-burn. Or that I was preoccupied with thoughts about him, praying I'd bump into him. Or plunge into him, whichever came first. I would resist the urge to swan-dive into his mouth, and pretend like I wasn't consumed with craving. I wanted nothing more than to soothe my crush burn with some Richie balm. My brain was a revolving turnstile with three parts: my eyes, the envelopes, Richie. My eyes, the envelopes, Richie. Like there wasn't enough going on in my life—I needed to be obsessed about a guy who was wrong for me in every conceivable way. I was screwed. Or wanted to be.

With all the eye-tivity, I realized I'd miss class the next day with the flame kisser himself, and that gave me the idea to leave word with the Bio TA. My request was simple: Could he give Richie Mac my number so I could get class notes and be caught up by the following lecture? I didn't want to miss a chance to connect with Richie, even if it meant living in the torture of waiting until next week. Even if the whole thing had been a fluke chemical reaction involving toothpaste brands and saliva. I had no other way of contacting Mr. Mouth Burner, so it was worth a try. After my nonchalantly strategic loitering, I left a carefully worded note and a voice mail for the Bio TA. I prayed a silent prayer that it would work. I had one more thing to do, and I was dreading it. I picked up the phone and braced myself.

"What do you mean you kissed Richie Mac?" Shirl was indignant.

"What do you mean what do I mean? He kissed me." I had debated sharing the truth, and I couldn't contain it anymore. I was spilling over my edges with him, and I needed to tell someone. "And this is weird, but our mouths got really hot."

"You were kissing Richie Mac! Of course it was hot!" She was almost mad at me.

"No, yes, it was, but—my mouth was physically burning from it."

"Were you drinking hot coffee? Hot soup? Did you have a hot, soupy make-out with the brother of the love of my life?" It made me glow to remember it, and I could feel my jelly belly returning.

Shirl was immediately on it. "Did he have a cold sore or something? Do you think Ryan gets them? Would you kiss me with it so I could get Ryan cooties? That's how far I'd go, Beth. I'm not kidding." Shirl was losing it. "Wait. Why did he kiss you? This is so unfair!" I could hear her get up and start pacing. It was her stress tic, and I changed my tactic. I would downplay it.

"No, no—we were studying and talking, and he kissed me good-bye and—it's not a big deal . . ." This wasn't going well.

"I don't understand, Beth. Why would you get to kiss Richie

Mac? You don't even care about the Mac Brothers. Wait—do you like him?" Shirl's volume went up. "Do you like him?" Her voice cracked. I didn't know what to say. She did it for me.

"I gotta go." Her voice got tight and mean, and I felt like she hated me. She didn't hate me, but she wouldn't be able to control her jealousy. That was Shirl.

"Why? Wait—I need you to help me tomorrow. I'm getting laser surgery on my eyes. Please come over."

"Fiiiiiiiiiiiiiiiine." Shirl hung up, still annoyed. As I splashed cold water in my mouth to cool it down, I almost wished she'd been the one to kiss a Mac brother. Almost.

Later that night, as I cuddled in the curve of my old twin bed, Mom knocked on my door. "Hey, hon. Are you nervous about the surgery?" She walked in and sat in my desk chair. I wasn't, actually. I probably should have been, but I was relieved. "I guess I should be, but . . . I'm happy I can get rid of these floaters. They've been kind of annoying." Since she was there and seemed in a chatty mood, I really wanted to figure out a way to learn more about the gold envelopes without alerting her anger or suspicion.

"Shirl's coming over to be my nurse tomorrow," I began.

"That's hilarious."

Even my mom knew Shirl was not the most nurturing soul. And without thinking, I went there: "Do you think there's any chance that Dad had this kind of eye condition? Like, maybe it's genetic?"

She gave me one of those condescending parental looks

that said, *There's so much you don't understand, and it would only hurt if you knew the truth,* but she answered: "Not likely. I wish he were more interested in you, baby. I'm sorry that he isn't, and he's missing out, but you are better off. I know that's easy for me to say—"

"A birthday card every now and then would've been nice." I gave her an opening, and it was her chance to explain it. Maybe he had sent the gold envelopes.

"You're right. There are a million things he could've done for you that would've been nice. That would've been, well, normal. But he's a jerk who likes punching things more than he likes people. You know I had to leave to protect us both." She hugged me before closing the door. "Sweet dreams, hon."

I was exhausted, and passed out with dreams of the Richie Kiss dancing in my head.

| 2 | HIGH PRIESTESS | ב |

IMMI'S BOOTS WERE STARTING TO WEAR THIN. The studs were falling off the insteps. It was either from the studs rubbing together when she walked or from the metal footrests on her chair. Gimmi had had the boots for years and was not inclined to replace them. People commented on the boots as frequently as people mispronounced her name. They pronounced it like Jimmy, with a really soft *G*, but it was a hard *G* as in "gimme some." And she did give people some. Piercings. Tattoos. You name it, Gimmi did it. She was hard to find and harder to book, but Gimmi Ray was the most sought-after tattoo artist in twenty states. Her escape from an unstable adoptive home in Wyoming at too young an age precipitated her immersion in a trade. The only trade she knew: skin.

Latex, rubber, studs, and blood. These were Gimmi's tools. She didn't look a day over sixteen, even though on paper she was twenty-six. All those hours indoors had protected her skin, and she was whiter than white. She was practically translucent, with sapphire eyes that glimmered pure indigo. Under certain lights, her skin appeared lighter than the latex stretched onto her small hands. She'd been wiping blood off new ink since she was twelve. Gimmi Ray wasn't just a prodigy. Her tattoos were reputed to be the most elaborate and expensive work in the world. Working freehand, Gimmi didn't use patterns like most artists. She worked entirely by inspiration. Inscribing messages from the divine onto skin. Not that many people knew what they meant. But they did know one thing: Tattoos from Gimmi Ray had power. A tattoo from Gimmi could make you, break you, heal you, or destroy you. Her tatts were reputed to have healed everything from cancer to Parkinson's, Alzheimer's to MS, AIDS to a bad personality. Gimmi's ink was no joke.

The coolest thing about Gimmi's studio was the motto inscribed on the ceiling. She'd transcribed it from one of the many gold envelopes she'd received over the years. Handwritten in UV black light ink were these words:

> I am the one who creates intensity of experience and sees intensity of colors, who marks energy on the cells with precision and blood. I extract meaning from ether and scar it onto flesh. I take the canvas of man and mark it with the infinite. I raise the vibration of the individual through color, blood, and ink. I return lost tribe members to the homeland of their soul.

Gimmi kept the gold envelopes safely hidden, but she had written the message in plain sight. But unless you had a black light, you were totally out of luck.

CHAPTER 8

TRIED TO KEEP TRACK OF WHAT WAS happening in my trusty notebook as my mom drove me to the surgery. I wanted a clear record of before and after. Whenever I was with Mom, Shirl, or Richie, the visions were triggered but got blurry or fuzzy, then vanished. Did my emotions have something to do with it? Because when I was around strangers, the images were clear. Writing in a moving car exacerbated my eyes: The floaters were happening nonstop. Eyes open, eyes closed. It was constant. And I couldn't help but feel that the floaters were trying to tell me something. If the Seeing Key was right, they were talking to me—okay, not talking to me, but like they had a story to tell. Everything seemed to be a code. I know how this sounds. Delusional. I know because we covered delusions last year in Psych 101. It might be a cool story, but I just wanted them gone.

We got to the laser eye center and my mom signed a bajillion forms, and I was finally led into the outpatient surgery room. The drugs—an Ativan and some local anesthesia for the eye—were pretty good. I felt terrific as this giant machine lowered over my eyes and the doctor and the nurse pried my eyelids apart with some device so I wouldn't blink during the surgery.

"The human eye is a powerful, beautiful thing, Beth. And your eyes—in the scientific, objective sense—are quite extraordinary. There's violet everywhere. It's like hazel, but with a violet tone infusing the iris instead of blue, green, brown. It's quite . . ." He trailed off and began working. I drifted into a zone of pure focus, determined to have my eyes back. It was over before I knew it.

The nurse was emphatic about my instructions: "Keep the eye shields on. No rubbing, no swimming, no water on the eye from the shower, and no mascara or eyeliner for one week.

Wear your sunglasses over the eye shields. Keep the eye shields on for the next two hours, and then use the eyedrops four times a day in each eye, and wash your hands. If you're a restless sleeper, please continue to wear the eye shields at night. Rest today; under no condition should you do anything straining, okay?" My mother grabbed the large bag of drops, leading me out of the office and to the car like I was a blind person. It was really bizarre—getting in and out of the car, driving, walking into our house with zero vision.

"Hey, Mrs. Michaels." It was Shirl. I couldn't see her, but I'd know that voice anywhere. I prayed she wasn't still mad at me.

"Thanks for doing this, Shirl. Let me give you money for that." I wasn't sure what my mom was referring to, but I figured it was food of some kind.

I was touching the edges of my superstyley eye shields and fingering the wads of cotton wrapped around my eyes. I couldn't see a thing. And it was a total relief.

"You look like Bono," Shirl snarked, but she was joking, which meant she'd forgiven me for the Richie kiss. "I decided that you kissing Richie is a good thing," she added, "because it'll get me closer to Ryan." I heard Shirl rustling something like plastic bags and cardboard. "I brought you your favorite," she said, and I could smell it before my hands could grab the gooey, dreamy, cheesy glory that was a double pepperoni slab from Pizza and Oven Grinder. I didn't need to see it; my mind knew what it looked like, and my mouth didn't care. I was starving.

We'd been eating for barely two bites when I seized up. My mind's eye raced with dozens of random images, and the pizza congealed in my mouth. Best as I could figure, I was immersed in pictures of anything related to the pizza. My body was "feelseeing" everything. Like TV channels changing in my body, pictures switched and I could see and feel the dairy cows hooked up to these mechanized udder squeezers to produce milk to make cheese; their nipples were in agony from the forced milking. I saw the pizza-making kid sending his parents in Bogotá money every month. I felt the pepperoni when it was alive, but I didn't just hear the livestock; I could feel it being killed. I tried to scream, but there was blood filling my throat, gurgling . . . choking me. I was completely helpless to do anything. You don't want to know about the slaughter. Trust me.

I must've started shaking, because Shirl put her hand on my arm. "Beth. I know you love pizza but the shaking is freaking me out. Are you okay?"

I showed her my teeth, convinced my mouth was filling up with blood. "Did I bite my cheek?" I lied. "Is my mouth bloody?"

I could feel Shirl lean in. "I can't tell if it's tomato sauce or blood. Here, swish some Mountain Dew." And I did, and the Mountain Dew did the same thing—I felt every worker who'd touched the beverage from inception to distribution and suddenly I could smell the infected tooth of the delivery guy and feel the searing pain of his tooth deep into his jawbone, and

I almost puked in my mouth. I forgot I was blindfolded; the images in my head were so real. The smell of the infection hit the back of my throat. I didn't quite make it to the bathroom, but I quite puked. All over myself. The Seeing Key hadn't mentioned this.

"Mrs. Michaels!!" Shirl shrieked and ran to get my mom. Or so I felt. I sat there, clothing splattered, and took a deep breath. This was more intense than the kiss, and certainly more disturbing. I was terrified to move.

My mom hated barf. I could hear the two of them making grossed-out noises as my mom handed me a towel. "I can't see where I barfed, Mom, but maybe this should be my talent for Miss Universe. Blindfolded Barf Clean-Up on Command feels like a real winner to me."

"Go outside, Shirl. Let me get her cleaned up." My mom's disgust was not comforting, and I needed to hear her laugh. This was too freaky.

"Just call me Barfing Beauty. It's probably the anesthetic. It can be hard to keep food down. Or maybe it's some weird vertigo from being in the dark . . ." I could feel my mom relaxing a bit, so I kept going. "I mean vertigo is usually inner ear, but inner ear, inner eye, what's the difference? They're the same thing when you're covered in puke." My mom laughed. Finally.

"Beth? I'm gonna take off now!" Shirl was thoroughly grossed out. "You know how I get!"

"Have fun stalking Ryan!" I called out, as my mom called work to tell them she'd be working from home that day. I sat in the room alone, smelling the pizza. Feelseeing the thud from when the pizza delivery guy had run over a raccoon the night before. You couldn't be mad at him; he felt really, really bad about it.

Two days later I was still refusing to leave my room, and my mother was livid. "Honey, I called the doctor, and he says you have to take the eye shields off!" I'd been sleeping with them on for days, scared to get out of bed. Scared to smell, touch, or eat or drink anything but water.

"I'm really okay, Mom; I'm just not ready to take the shields off. I'm having some sensitivity and corneal discomfort, and it's my body." I sounded really calm. But it was either that or admit that I was terrified I would spend the rest of my life feel-seeing things that weren't there. I didn't even care that Mom was keeping stuff from me anymore. I was more concerned that I would spend the rest of my life in a straitjacket. And never go to college. Ever.

"The doctor said if you won't take them off, I have to bring you in. You leave me no choice."

She sprayed me with body spray and made me gargle mouthwash (feelseeing the mint leaf cells exploding as they were pulverized was new). As we drove to his office, my eyes were feeling pretty crusty from the shields. By the time my mother had led me from the parking structure through the lobby and into the elevator to Dr. Pasta's office, I didn't have to see the looks in people's eyes to know what they were thinking: *That girl is losing it.*

I was ushered into the office of Dr. Rigatoni, yo! Away from everyone, including my seeing-eye dog mommy. We were alone.

"Change can be uncomfortable, Beth, but having clear vision is going to be a good change. I promise. I have a feeling the shields are actually exacerbating things. But tell me"—I could feel him cutting the gauze—"why aren't you eating?"

I stayed very still with my eyes closed, and I laughed. "I like food way too much to not eat it." The bandages slowly pulled off all that dried goop that had accumulated on my eyes. Pasta King was waiting.

"Open your eyes, Beth." I tried to think of some funny way to stall, but I realized it wasn't going to work.

"You'll be able to see clearly." He sprayed some saline stuff in my eyes, and this, of course, forced me to blink and do the one thing I was terrified to do. Open my eyes. See.

It was blinding white at first. Like the sun flaring, or a flash going off at close range. Everything was bright. Too bright. *Go to the light,* I said to myself, and laughed.

"What do you see?" The truth was, it looked like I was facedown on an ice rink. An illuminated giant ice rink. It really did look like those scenes in movies where people go toward the light when they die or have a near-death experience.

"I see"—I tried to focus, but it was still just blazing whiteness, a loving burst so strong and sweet my heart filled up from it—"white light. Everywhere." Dr. Rigtonio seemed okay with this and slid a pair of special sunglasses over my eyes. I closed my lids.

I didn't want the sublime whiteness to end. It felt like a clean slate, like things would be different from this moment on.

"Open your eyes now." I opened my sticky lids. And in the blink of my eye an explosion happened. A psychedelic kaleidoscope of color, shape, and texture—purple jags, red blobs, orange streams, green rays, yellow sheets, blue rain—all of it screamed throughout the room. Moving so fast and so intensely that I convulsed, and flailed the glasses onto the floor. I covered my eyes, hit the fetal posish, and shook my head in a fit that from that moment on would be known as my super hiss. That's short for super hissy fit, the likes of which I'd never thrown before.

I guess it was pretty bad, because they gave me a sedative. Dr. Pasta rebandaged my eyes and informed my mom that I was experiencing corneal sensitivity and needed to wear sunglasses to protect my eyes. My mother informed Dr. Pasta that I had better not be experiencing malpractice. Mom immediately called her insurance company for a second opinion with some big muckety-muck. This was my mother at her worst: frantic, fearful, shrill, and impolite. My mother was in a lather.

Once we got home, I climbed into bed and told her I was going to sleep and she should go back to work. I was fine. I could feelsee tornadoes of static electricity swarming around her body like bees, and I prayed she wouldn't hug me goodbye. As I heard her shut the front door, I exhaled for the first time all day.

Once her car was out of the driveway, I bolted upright. I knew I had to open my eyes. I could handle it. I had to handle it. Everything was going to be fine as soon as I could open my eyes and keep them open. This was the solution, the answer, the moment. I sat up, faced the direction of my bedroom mirror, and clumsily pulled the glasses off. I felt for the edges of the gauze and slowly peeled it from my eyes. I kept them closed, reaching for the drops Mom had placed on my nightstand. I squirted them recklessly into each eye before opening. I blinked. I was scared to open them fully, so I blinked again. In the blink of my eyes another sight-storm whipped around my room, sending me under the bed for cover.

In my hysteria I knocked a bottle of Ralph Lauren perfume to the floor. Did you know that Ralph Lauren's real name was Ralph Lifshitz? I didn't either, and this was the kind of info that poured through me as I surveyed my room. It was like what had happened with the pizza, only now I was beginning to understand what it meant: Info about whatever I was touching or seeing unfolded within my mind. I looked at my DVDs of *Freaky Friday* and *Mean Girls* and saw a feedback loop between the boxes and knew they were directed by the same person. I flipped them over and there it was: DIRECTED BY MARK WATERS. Same with *Mr. & Mrs. Smith* and the X-Men movies—a green line connecting the boxes. Both? WRITTEN BY SIMON KINBERG. How did I know this stuff? Mother Teresa, I was losing it. Or did she answer to Agnes Gonxha Bojaxhiu? That was Mama T's birth name. This was bananas.

I sat perfectly still and closed my eyes, catching my breath. Random snippets of *Access Hollywood* and Trivial Pursuit played out in distracting, fascinating, and terrifying high-definition around my entire bedroom. I felt like a time-traveling fly on the wall of life. It felt so very fly-on-wall I called it a FOW because it sounded like "Ow!" and felt like being punched. FOW was like wearing an all-access pass that was totally out of control. Smell, touch, taste, sight, sound? You name it, it triggered the FOW! My bed? Made in Wisconsin. Kenosha, Wisconsin, to be exact, and the factory was near a brewery. My sheets? Woven in a place called Perugia (a city where they also made chocolate, apparently). I took twenty deep breaths and tried to figure out what to do. My mind was racing, so I did what I always do when my mind races: I put on my iPod.

With the first few chords of my playlist, the unthinkable happened. I was sucked into the song. Sucked into the life around the song. The life, I could only guess, of the songwriter, or the performer. I was accessing FOW and feelsees in someone else's life. FOWsees of the rich and famous!

I took a breath or thirty and slowed myself waaaaaay down. Hang on. This was kind of amazing. Maybe there was a silver lining here. Maybe this could be interesting. I slowed down my breathing and placed my attention (my ear-tention) on specific parts of the music. I gradually discovered a way to navigate the music and the feelsees. When I focused my attention patiently, I started accessing something unspeakable, unthinkable, and unfathomable. I was accessing something musicians had a lot of. Sex.

To say this excited me would be an understatement. There were gory details, to be sure. Imagine getting launched into something like a roller coaster hooked up to an electric chair and that's what happened to me, on me, and, yes . . . there, too. After four or five hours of listening to my iPod and getting X-rated video-on-demand in my head and body, I was exhausted, but I'd been "exposed" to quite a few tricks. This was life-changing. This was addictive. This had to be illegal. Especially for a virgin and a minor.

I had my first orgasm by proxy. I had girl-gasms, boy-gasms, he-gasms, she-gasms. After experiencing my third or fourth vicarious guy-gasm (thanks to a certain former boy-band singer, now legit musical talent), I could honestly say it *is* different for boys. Not just physically—testosterone is powerful stuff, whoa—but emotionally. It was like this: When the girls were attracted, it filled my belly and my heart and then went warm and fluttery. As for the guys? That warm flutter of the heart may have been there somewhere, but it was eclipsed by the strong thud of blood rushing between the legs. My first guy-gasm was so real, so shocking, that I was fully expecting to look down and be covered in boy goo. Worry not. I was goo-free.

There were occasional moments when I got the feeling

that what I was doing was pervy, but I couldn't help myself. I figured if I was going to be cursed with this new existence, I might as well get something out of it. And I got more than Celebrity Sex Ed, believe me. I got some Addiction Ed, to boot. It was amazing how many people just had random sex, thinking they wanted to feel good but feeling pretty bad afterward. Addict Ed. It was dizzying to feel how eagerly people abandoned their lives in pursuit of the thing we all crave: that kiss, that feeling, that . . . release. But it wasn't really the release people craved. It was love. The oxytocin and dopamine produced during sex mimicked that feeling of love. So, despite my previous inexperience, I now had a virtual PhD about why people chased sex down. The temporary rush equaled temporary love! I was suddenly a genius in things I knew nothing about!

But pursuing anything to the exclusion of everything else isn't healthy. I couldn't stop, and I was getting a little too athletic, kind of bouncing off my bed and my walls in an iPod-gasmathon frenzy.

Suddenly, I saw someone peeping in my window. I screamed. Whoever it was began banging on my window, waving at me behind the open blinds. And when I realized who it was, I screamed again. Dear Lord, no. It couldn't be. It was. Richie Mac.

After calming myself down, smoothing out my lunatic hair, and going to the front door, I let him in. He was amused, but he also seemed different. I couldn't put my finger on it (although

I wanted to!), but his skin looked really clear, almost newborn. As if he'd done facials and body scrubs. He had a glow.

He was trying not to laugh. "I tried calling you, and pounding on your door, but . . . well, now I can see why you didn't answer. Sorry to, uh, interrupt your, uh, dance routine?"

"You weren't interrupting . . ." I wanted to die. My death wish was eclipsed by my total excitement about seeing him. In my house! Alone! I wasn't having any visual storms, and this was annoying. Richie was the one person I'd actually want to have a feelsee with, and it wasn't happening.

I took a deep breath. I had to calm down, lest I finally take that swan dive into his mouth.

His eyes were kind, even while he was smirking at me. Wait—did he—he looked like—was he happy to see me, too?

"I come bearing homework," he said, his teeth blinding me with that smile. He was carrying a notebook. I led him into the kitchen and offered him something to drink.

He sat down abruptly, asked for water and opened his notebook. I stood behind him, admiring his hair, when I took one glance at his work. It was a mess. I tried to think of something to say, when he moved his leg. He was pressing his thigh against my knee, and a rush sailed through my body. I didn't move, focusing on his notebook in case it was an accident. The current between our legs was buzzing me dizzy. I took a deep breath and leaned on the table so I wouldn't pass out, as my hair fell forward from behind my ear. My mane curtain was totally blocking him from view. I felt like I might start shaking. "Your hair smells really nice," I heard him whisper, as he shifted his leg again so his entire calf was touching mine. The heat was incredible, and I was ecstatic to feel skin without a feelsee.

"You don't dye your hair, do you? So many girls dye their hair. I don't think I've seen real blond hair in a while."

Nervous now, I was about to push it back, when his hand moved. His fingers were near my cheek suddenly. I didn't dare move. He tucked a finger under my chin and softly pulled my face toward him. "May I?" My knees were buckling, and I nodded, completely unsure about what I was agreeing to.

Very gently he brushed the wall of hair back over my left shoulder. He moved his face closer to mine.

"Do you always put it behind your ears?" His voice was full of breath, hot on my jawline, the moisture landing on my earlobe. I felt dizzy, but I nodded and put the stray strands behind my left ear. My cheeks were burning up. I didn't dare look at him, but he pushed my chin back so I was looking at him. My heart racing. I couldn't control my breathing. His cheeks were flushed pink, and his eyes were incredibly focused, gazing into me and peeling my layers off.

"Your skin . . ." His index finger grazed across my top lip, circling around and brushing my bottom lip. My back arched involuntarily, and my eyes closed. "I can't stop thinking about your mouth, Beth. . . ." It was so direct, so unfiltered, it flooded me in every direction. His fingers delicately sweeping my lips, his face barely touching mine. His lips met my ear again, his voice lowering. "I can't stop thinking about you. I can't stop thinking about you since we kissed—" He kissed the words into my ear, and I wobbled, suddenly incredibly thirsty. On cue, Richie gently held up the glass of water to my lips and tilted it into my mouth. I sipped, staring into his eyes the entire time.

My mouth was dripping. Richie took a sip from the other side of the glass. We sipped back and forth for a long moment, and all gravity left my body. Our mouths were wet, and my chest was ripping heartbeats into my ears. He stood up, his eyes locking me in a gaze so strong I couldn't move. We were about to swan-dive into something incredible.

"I think it's time for your friend to go"—but it wasn't Richie speaking. It was my mother. The water crashed to the ground, and our hands dropped our clasp as wet glass shattered at our feet.

"We'll clean that up," she ordered. "Please go. Now."

"Mom. He brought me notes from class. Give us a minute."

"Sorry," he said. "I should go." He walked out of the house so fast I didn't even have a chance to say good-bye.

"Why didn't you tell me you were seeing someone? What's been going on?" She had the nerve to accuse me of being secretive? That did it. How dare she keep stuff from me and act like she should know everything. I couldn't see anything around her, and that infuriated me too, but I held it together. My mom out of control was not going to help things.

"I'm not 'seeing someone.' We're in a study group together.

We're getting to know each other. It's not a big deal. I mean, you've been keeping things from me, right?" I bit my tongue when I wanted to bite her. I hated her for hiding the envelopes and for eavesdropping. "You didn't have to be rude to Richie."

"Has anything else been going on? Is there anything else you want to tell me? Now is the time, Beth. If someone you don't know has been trying to talk to you"—Was she asking about the envelopes? Was this my opening?—"or pressure you into taking drugs or doing things, you know, now would be a good time to let me know."

I shook my head no. I was scared to tell her about the gold envelope I'd gotten at school, since I hadn't finished looking at the file in the attic. I didn't want her hiding more before I'd had a chance to look at it. "No, Mom, " I lied. "But is there anything you want to tell me? Is there anything you've been keeping from me?" I knew she would dodge the question, and every time I got angry at her, a visual fuzz of bees would swarm around her. In and out of focus, completely confusing me. I took a deep breath to keep that from happening.

"I've been very worried about you. I spoke to Dr. Rigtonio at length, and it's his opinion that your eyes are fine but your brain may not be. I'm inclined to agree with him, so we're going to see two more doctors. A neurologist and a psychiatrist." We stood staring at each other, arms crossed. It was war. I could've sworn schools of static fish were swimming around my mother. I tried to see something that would convey the truth, but it blurred as quickly as it swam into view. I didn't want to look at her anyway.

There was nothing I could do but storm to my room and slam the door.

I was fuming as I got ready for bed, and eye demons spooked in and out of sight. Dots on toothpaste, tails from towels. It was lifestyles of the inanimate. It was the only thing that could distract me from the rage I was feeling from the mom-us interruptus. I wanted to flail her into submission for letting my watershed moment slip away. Grrr. If there was this veil between reality and pretend, it was suddenly lifted or had giant holes in it. I wasn't sure. Whatever the rabbit holes were, I wanted to fall into them with Richie Mac. As I burned with questions and sexual frustration, I took no solace in the fact that people who are crazy don't often wonder if they are crazy.

CHAPTER 9

THE NEXT FEW DAYS WERE ALL ABOUT GETTING MY head examined. Dr. Milton worked in an empty office with bad lighting, two chairs, a couch, a clock, a phone, and a box of tissues. When he shook my hand before we got started, his hands were clammy and moist. His touch filled my mouth with a bad taste, but I used the contact to focus. It might come in handy.

I gave him the simple version of what was going on, but as Dr. Milton took notes, a taste like old pickles crept onto my tongue, puckering my whole body.

"We're going to put you on some meds, Beth, and see if we can't get these visions to settle down."

Fine by me, I thought. Then, "Doctor . . . ?"

He looked up for once. "Yes?" I took a deep breath as dots swirled into an image, alongside his head, of a woman in a green dress showing me movies of his life. She wore a name tag that read, MY NAME IS JOANIE.

"Beth, are you alright? Is something happening?"

"Who's Joanie?"

The doctor coughed. "I don't know what you're talking about." This made Joanie irate, and she addressed me directly from the projection. "Doesn't know? I was his mistress for six years! For six years that weakling told me he'd leave his lunatic wife. Oh, his dog was named Benzo. After Benzedrine or something. He loved that dog. So I killed it." I could feel how much the doctor loved his dog, and I felt sad for him suddenly. For one second I realized that maybe I wasn't crazy. Maybe this was really happening.

And with that, I went for it. I needed answers, and I was tired of screwing around. "I'm sorry Benzo died."

The doctor tried to cover his shock with his training and asked, "Who is Benzo?"

"Your dog? Benzedrine? A woman named Joanie told me about your Benzo. She's wearing a green dress—" Dr. Milton's face couldn't hide anything anymore; his eyes widened. "She also told me she was your mistress for six years and thinks your wife is a lunatic but you stay with her because you're weak." And with that? The doctor stood up and vomited. I was just glad someone besides me was barfing for a change. At least he used a trash can.

My mother was waiting in the reception room when I came out. I waited outside as the puking shrink spoke to her in somber tones. "She is at high risk for schizoaffective disorder, Mrs. Michaels. I'm afraid that teenagers are the highest-risk group for schizophrenia. If she were older, I'd be less inclined to diagnose. The chances of developing it past the age of twenty-five are almost nil, but she's in the target age group." My mom started crying. "I wish I could be more positive. I'd recommend that another neurologist run some CAT scans and MRIs for a second opinion." I heard the sound of tissues and nose-blowing from my mom. This was bad. "If her visions continue and there is no evidence of a tumor or nerve damage, I'll prescribe haloperidol." My mom freaked at the suggestion of drugs, her emotional meltdown taking on more volume. The more she cried, the worse I felt.

As we walked to the car, a whirlpool of static surrounded my mom. Tongues of static leaped at me when they weren't blurring into oblivion. I was determined to stay calm and see what my mother knew, but she cried the whole way home. It was impossible to see anything. I slumped in the backseat, feeling her pain and how it came out of love for me, and I noticed that when I focused on the love, things calmed down. Not entirely, but they became manageable. Manageable enough for the blurry, static tornado whirling around her skull to quiet. My mom was picturing some future version of me in a straitjacket, which I saw to the right of her head. It was hard to focus, but to her left was a four-year-old me with a bloody nose, crying while she was yelling at me. That's when it hit me. I had to try and act like these things weren't happening to me. I had to try and act normal. Or my life was about to get much, much worse.

In an attempt to get the sensations down, I cultivated a plan. I decided that a hat, sunglasses, and gloves would be my new fashion trend. Over the next few days I practiced avoiding things and looking at the ground while I moved. If I didn't touch them, taste them, or smell them? Nothing got triggered. It took some practice, but I was gradually getting the hang of it. I worked out a walk where nothing would touch me or trigger the unforeseen—or the feelsees. If I felt loving thoughts about whatever I was eating, I could swallow food without catastrophic results. Frozen veggie burritos and frozen yogurt were safe. I smiled and reassured my mother I was feeling better.

Touching food was one thing, but touching people was a different story. As I was subjected to CAT scans and MRIs, it became abundantly clear that my proximity to a person determined how much I knew about them. So I was avoiding people like the plague. My tests came back clear as a whistle. My brain was fine. But my physical encounters were traumatizing: I could see someone's entire life simply by brushing up against them. The longer they were near me afterward? The more I could see. I couldn't control it, but I had to try.

When I got home, I called Shirl and asked her to bring me to school the next day. I needed to turn in my forms and graduate. I was going to will this away. Everything was fine. At least that's what I told myself as I tossed and turned all night long.

CHAPTER 10

I AWOKE THE NEXT MORNING TO THE SOUND of my mom's car heading out of the driveway. I dragged my butt into the kitchen. The smell of my mom's coffee took me to the jungles of South America for some impromptu coffee bean harvesting. I opened a box, figuring plain crackers were safe, when the smell of vegetable shortening nearly blew me over. I really didn't need to know how it was made (vegetable lard grossness!). Or was it the body odor of one of the cracker employees? The feelsees had me seesawing. Teetering or tottering, I was not going to be deterred: I had to get it together.

I grabbed all the gold envelopes and put them in my bag before Shirl arrived. Shirl seemed nervous to see me, but my attempts to see things around her failed. "I was so glad you finally returned my texts!" she said. "I've been dying to talk to you! I felt lame about running from your house. I'm sorry I had to flee the scene of the vomiting—do you forgive me?"

"You? I'm sorry to have made you an accomplice in such a violent crime!" I smiled, willing things back to normal. She was relieved, but a little distracted.

"If I'd stayed, I would've started puking on you, setting off the largest reverse-food heist in history. I'm already on parole for petty bulimia, so I would've gotten a stiff sentence." Shirl parked her car in her fave spot off campus.

"I couldn't let you go back to the big house for barfing, Shirl. Not after all the time you did for farting under the influence . . ." We always picked up on each other's jokes and ran with them. It was good to feel quasinormal for a second.

"Well, we don't want to be late to the pokey." Shirl laughed as we arrived at our personal jail: New Glen High School.

"I gotta run drop something off quick, but I've got major developments to download. Like so major, they're practically a four-star general!" Shirl bolted toward the entrance ahead of me. "I'm so glad you're okay, Beth. You scared the poop outta me." "Okay" was not exactly the kind of perfume I was wearing. But Shirl thought I was okay, which meant I didn't smell crazy. And that was progress.

I braced myself as Shirl took off and I stood alone in front of New Glen High School. I blinked and the dots appeared as Shirl vanished. The dots funneled into clear pictures. What emerged before me was enough to make anyone turn and run. The exterior of the school was a seething hotbed of colorful shapes and slithering ropes. As students bumped into me, the plot thickened: Myriad little movie screens began projecting everywhere and overlapping and collaging like some obsessive kid's bulletin board. It was a menagerie of flying movie kites with thick strings, chains, or tentacle-like threads connecting every image to the person who "owned" it.

I winced. If every picture told a story? This was a teeming, squealing vortex about how much crap people carry around. At least I wasn't alone. Something told me it was alright to go inside, while confirming what I already knew: Teenagers were insane. I could look around at my hallucinations and see everyone was scared like me. I closed my eyes, ducked, and moved into the flock of fleck.

En route to the principal's office I noticed something interesting about the ropes (which were everywhere now). Some people had these thick hose-like projections with suction disks on them. Grenada had quite the vacuum hoses emerging off of her, sucking energy off the people she was talking to. When

Grenada called Libby Mueller a "biatch," two knots formed on the rope between them, and a static cloud of white noise smooshed around them. Grenada got some attention for this from some jocks, and her hose unfurled and sucked in their stray energy like a sponge.

When a fight broke out moments later? The same thing happened to the skate kid and the burnout from their impromptu smackdown: Cracks of light broke into shafts around them. Then, as two new knots tied between them, a boatload o' static fuzzed around their bodies and the shafts of light.

Not surprisingly, adults in the administration office weren't any different. The ropes between the staff were forming knots like suspended crochet, binding each staff member to another in choke holds. The Seeing Key was starting to make sense, but the chaos was agitating me.

"Beth! How nice to see you—come on in!" It was Principal Tony. I practically dove into his office for refuge. He was very peaceful, and I was grateful for the visual vacation.

I noticed a shimmer of light over his head and saw very clearly something I hadn't seen before: a simple cord, about three inches in diameter, rising out of his head. It came in and out of focus and radiated flares of light off of its sides.

I relaxed and felt very comfortable with him. "I got into Columbia early decision."

"That's terrific! Are you kidding me? Why didn't you say so?" He stood up and came around his desk with his arms extended. I stood up and he gave me a warm back slap.

"Congratulations, Beth! You've been a rock star. You worked hard to finish high school early. You got into your top choice early decision. Is there anything you can't do, my dear?" He was genuinely happy for me, and I could've sworn his cord of light grew into a halo that enfolded both of us.

"I hope you know you are welcome to attend commencement services next year. If you haven't already moved to New York City! Just let me know . . ." I had forgotten about graduation ceremonies. Given how out of control the world looked to me, parents and teenagers in the same space would be Armageddon. "Thanks," I lied as I flashed on that apocalypse, "I'll let you know."

Principal Tony beamed proudly. "Then let's get you graduated, shall we?" He signed a form that said I was a graduate of New Glen High School and told me my diploma would be in the mail. "Remember: Your community-college classes don't count toward graduation anymore. I know you want to use them toward college credit, but you could take it easy." I had bigger problems than classes, but he didn't know that. He stood up and extended his hand. "Toss your invisible graduation cap in the air, c'mon, now." I played along, removing my "cap" and tossing it in the air. "Now, please spray your invisible can of silly string at me." I sprayed it at him and he pretended to get hit with it. It was lame, but kind of sweet. He really seemed to care.

"Elizabeth Michaels. You are done with high school. Graduated. Finished. Kaput. Now get outta here." He smiled and whacked me on the back again. I had to admit, I was completely elated.

I hoped I could catch Shirl before first bell, and ran toward her locker through the web of kaleidoscopic chaos. That's when I saw a crowd clustered and laughing, assessing something. People were snickering.

"Shirl? Did you—?" I stepped to her side, my back to the crowd.

Before I could ask what was going on, I saw the answer hanging there, for everyone to see: an opened, unused condom hanging on the front of Shirl's locker. Shirl stood there, staring at it.

"I'm sorry I didn't tell you," she whispered really quietly. "I tried, but I was embarrassed." She didn't move to take it down. I remembered her saying she needed to download something major, and I felt like a bad friend.

"Do you want me to get rid of it?" I looked in my bag for tissues as the buzz of students got louder.

"Yes. Thanks."

I reached up and pulled the condom off with a tissue. It had a slippery surface, and I noticed it left an oily, reflective sheen on the locker. In the shape of a condom. I crumpled it up and could feel it sliding around inside the tissue.

"Are you saying you slept with Ryan Mac?" It was Jenny Yedgar, the mad cow. "Because putting a condom on your locker and pretending to sleep with someone is pretty lame, dumbass."

"I didn't say anything—" Shirl was humiliated. I tried to see Shirl, but the visions were blurry. I looked away to clear my eyes, and everything came back full force around the crowd gathered by her locker. I couldn't stand it. I pulled her arm to get her away, but our exit was being blocked by the mass of bodies.

Grenada and her crew were chuckling particularly hard, and I was getting really irritated. Jake Gorman only made things worse, yelling like he was selling hot dogs at a ball game, "Liar for sale! Come and get your red hot liar here! Get your fresh, hot liar here!" I wanted to kill them all. As I tried to pull Shirl past him, my arm brushed against his. Four or five movies were playing around his head. All the strings carrying his movie kites were leaking something like light.

"I don't know where any of you get off calling her out for anything." I couldn't believe I said it. Jake's movie was clear: He wasn't on Adderall; he was on drugs. And he was having sex. With men. Hoses were coming out of his body and attaching themselves to Shirl. They were starting to suck on her. I had to do something.

"Jake. Just because you like guys is no reason to get jealous of Shirl," I said firmly. "There are enough men to go around." My body got weak as I said it, but it seemed to work.

"What? What are you saying?" he said defensively, his vacuums retreating. They were moving toward me. His movie showed him making out with Mr. Cochran, the married chemistry teacher.

"Don't yell at me about your sexuality. Or should we go talk to Principal Tony about which teachers you're bonking?" His hoses pulled back, as Jake scoffed and backed down, shaking his head like I was nuts. He flipped me the bird so he could save face, but he was spooked. "Nobody cares that you're gay, Jake," I added. "They just care when you lie about it."

"I don't have time for this," he said nervously. "I don't know what you're talking about." I watched as his pictures and strings pulled into a tight barrier around his body as Jake slinked away.

"Where do you get off making stuff up about people?" It was Grenada. "You and your lame friend Sheryl? What right do you have?" She was trying to intimidate me with her arms crossed. I intentionally let my arm bump into her, but her movies were blocked by giant tentacles. Extending from her head in four directions, coming straight for me.

"Making stuff up is gossip, Grenada, and that's your specialty." I dodged an invisible octopus. It was spraying ink in my direction. "Don't worry, I'm not trying to steal your territory." I brushed her arm and saw a giant leak in her. Stuff was leaking out of Grenada in every direction.

"Do you want me to kick your ass? Because I won't do it myself; I'll get people to do it for me. And it'll suck. I promise you." Grenada took this really annoying, holier-than-thou tone that she must've learned on TV.

"Well, do you want to tell everyone how you afford all your clothes, or would you like me to?" There were kite movies of her shopping all around her head. And how she paid for the clothes, which was surprising. "Because, while you tell people you're going to visit your sister for long weekends, you're doing something else, aren't you?"

Grenada's face melted into fear. "No, I'm not." The quivering of her upper lip was obvious to any untrained eye, but the tentacles trying to strangle me were visible only to me. I flinched and forced my arm to brush hers. Her movie got huge, and I saw more than I wanted to see in high-def. I saw Grenada taking off her clothes. I saw Grenada dancing. Naked.

"Unless by visiting your sister you mean stripping in a nudie bar. In which case, forgive me. You were telling the truth." The crowd was silent with some gasps and whispers: "Is it true?" "How does she know?" and "What?"

"Does the owner know how old you are, G?" I asked, using the nickname only her clique used. "If you're too scared to tell him, I'm happy to call on your behalf."

Grenada eked out a lame "You're ridiculous," before walking away. Jenny Yedgar wasn't done, however. She was up in Shirl's face like she wanted a fight. I was exhausted, suddenly, just drained of all energy, but Shirl looked terrified. I had to help.

"You didn't answer me! Why are you lying about sleeping with Ryan?" Jenny shoved Shirl, knocking her down on the ground. I stepped in between them and grabbed Jenny's arm. With my touch I saw—clear as day—why Jenny was upset. There were moving pictures of Jenny having sex. Lots and lots of sex. I couldn't see with whom, and then it became crystal clear. Different outfits coming off, different hairstyles, and different locations. But all with the same guy. Ryan.

"You aren't the first girl to have a lot of sex with Ryan McAllister, Jenny," I said loudly enough for the remainder of the crowd to hear. I dropped her arm, but she grabbed me by the elbows with every intention of hurting me. New movies extended from her like puppets on strings. Her whole body pressed against mine, and I had a feelsee from her stomach. There was something in there. A baby something.

I stepped back to dodge two spongy vacuum cords, which were spiraling out of her and trying to get up my nose. She wouldn't let go, so I blurted out the only thing I could think of: the truth. "Just because you're pregnant doesn't give you the right to hurt me!" Shirl's eyes widened, and the gasps from the crowd were huge. A buzz raced through the halls: "That's why she's fat!" and "I knew she was pregnant!" No one questioned what I'd said.

Before Jenny could respond, her tears got the better of her. Jenny shoved my arms down and plowed down the hall, sobbing. Jenny's bestie, Libby, stood there with her mouth open. "Nobody was supposed to know that. That wasn't very nice." It was true. The cat was out of the bag about Jenny's bun in the oven.

I extended my hand to Shirl and pulled her up to her feet as the bell rang. She hugged me as the remaining looky-loos dispersed.

"Thanks, Beth. I think." Shirl was breathing heavily.

"No problem." Dots swirled around her like a funnel. I couldn't focus on her. A tsunami of exhaustion descended on me. It felt good to tell everyone off in the moment, but now I was drained.

"Look—I'm sorry I didn't tell you about Ryan. But how—when—how did you know all of that?" Her voice cracked like a wrong note, high and off-key. She blinked away tears with a mixture of admiration and fear. I didn't know what to say.

"Beth. How long have you known all that?"

"Less than two minutes," I admitted. Which was the truth.

"But how?" Shirl could tell something was wrong. I had to get out of there. I felt terrible about what had just gone down. I didn't want to explain.

"I heard a rumor," I lied. "Meet me at Bordens later? I gotta get out of here." I summoned what little energy I had and walked toward the exit doors of New Glen High School, touching them for the last time. "Happy graduation to me," I said as the first bell blared. "Let freedom ring?" I didn't feel very free. I felt weighed down by a ball and chain heavier than anything I'd ever experienced.

3 | THE EMPRESS | ⁊

OLLY HAD ACCUMULATED ALMOST ALL THE charms she needed for completion. It was her twenty-fourth birthday, and that would require precisely nine more wrist blings for a total of twenty-four charms. The Tiffany "If Lost" charm, the tiny golden H and Birkin charms from Hermes, the 24-karat gold Chanel flower, the Van Cleef & Arpels trefoil, the miniscule Louis Vuitton purse, the Bucelatti star, the Bulgari ID tag, the Gucci dog tag. All of them hung around Dolly's wrist, sparkling in her emerald eyes. More than seven thousand dollars in charms. All of them stolen.

The kleptomania started harmlessly enough. Dolly didn't even realize she'd done it. She was trying on a ring, and the salesman got distracted. It wasn't until she was home that Dolly realized she hadn't taken it off. She even went back to the store to see if she could turn it in. The salesman said hello and spoke with her as if nothing had happened. That's how it always happened. It was like the universe wanted her to have these things. No one ever got mad or chased her or banned her from the store. Why would they? They didn't even know anything was amiss.

Cartier was a new spot. Dazzling cases. Impeccable staff. Dolly wore her bracelet like a weapon, daring any salesperson to question her shopping power or prowess. She never got intimidated by the gatekeepers. Quite the opposite. Dolly dazzled them. Not all of them. All she needed was one. Preferably near her target of choice. And today? Dolly's bull's-eye consisted of an eighteen-karat pink gold heart padlock with diamonds and rubies. Cartier was famous for its lucky charms: the scarab, the four-leaf clover, the Queen of Hearts, a lucky 13, a horseshoe. And today would be the beginning of Dolly's next level of acquisition. It wasn't like she was going to keep them all; she'd pawn the ones she could and dispense the cash to the needy. But she was going to have all of them. By the end of the hour.

Dolly's salesperson couldn't have been more perfect. A middle-aged woman with bifocals, an ingratiating stare, and perfectly coiffed short hair stood before her. "Welcome to Cartier. I'm Nanette." Dolly knew she could trance her, but she did a test just to be sure. Locking eyes, Dolly exhaled through her nose and into the woman's pupils, holding her gaze until the woman blinked.

"What's your name?" Dolly asked sweetly, exhaling again and watching the woman relax into her breath.

"Welcome to Cartier. I'm Nanette. What can I show you?" Nanette smiled like she might be high, which was what always happened. Dolly could get people stoned with her jade eyes. She called it trancing; some would call it hypnosis. But with Dolly it was so strong and so natural that her mark had no idea anything was happening at all. By the time the lucky charms had been cleared off the black velveteen display tray, Nanette was turning around to fetch a tissue, blithely unaware that the entire collection had just been pocketed.

"Nanette? Are you going to show me the lucky charms collection? I'm sorry, I'm in kind of a rush."

Nanette apologized, "Oh, I'm so sorry. This case should have been restocked last evening." And Nanette simply went to the stockroom to refill the tray. Dolly waited patiently for Nanette to return with the items, oohing and aahing over the dazzling craftsmanship and miraculous metalwork. Dolly said she'd drop hints with her boyfriend, and was it okay if he asked for Nanette when he stopped by? Nanette agreed to push the fictitious Romeo toward the eighteen-carat pavé diamond charm, and even winked at Dolly as they said good-bye.

When Cartier's security team played the tape back later, nothing out of the ordinary could be detected. It would take an expert to see the small pulse of energy rippling through the electromagnetic field, time-lapsing the recording into an imperceptible fast-forward. That was the beauty of Dolly's trancing. It didn't just work on people. It worked on entire buildings.

It wasn't until Dolly started receiving the gold envelopes that she even knew she had this gift. But there it was, written on a gold card someone had sent her when she turned seventeen. It read:

I am the one who drizzles with the stolen gems of the earth. I steal what is stolen and return what was taken. I shoplift these trinkets and wear them like armor, dazzling you like a tree at Christmas. I trick and I treat. I teach the adoration of adornment without end. The icon. The status. The label. The dazzle. These are the false gods of a culture lost. I parade these false idols and let worship adorn me in excess. My gift is to teach you what you don't need. I give the pearl of great price by taking it. In consuming me, you return to the perfection of yourself . . . without embellishment.

She wasn't entirely sure what it meant, but she loved it.

CHAPTER 12

MY BODY COLLAPSED ON THE BUS-STOP BENCH. Exhausted from my psychic cage fight, I was reeling from what had gone down. Shirl lost her virginity to Ryan? Jenny was pregnant? Grenada was stripping? Jake Gorman was gay? And all of it was true? I was happy no one had kicked my ass, but my energy was toast. I felt like

I'd been squeezed through a pasta maker and was fettuccine afraid-o. Somebody would retaliate; of that I was confident. It was just a question of where and when.

As I waited for the bus, I debated whether the library or the bookstore would be the best place to research the mysterious cards. I chose our hang, Bordens Books. Shirl wouldn't last long in class after the morning's hoopla, and she would meet me there later. There was much to download, and I had no idea what I'd tell her about how I knew what I knew. It was going to be sticky.

The metro bus ride downtown was a sticky adventure in and of itself. Much like high school students, people who ride the bus have a lot on their minds. I was getting quite the visual thought feast. As I boarded, I had the misfortune of brushing legs with a lady whose thoughts consisted entirely of alcohol. Bottles of it, glasses filled with it, ice cubes clinking in it. I settled in a seat down the aisle and decided to practice: I tried to see if anything else popped onto a screen around her head. I thought, *Show me why she drinks.* Suddenly all these leaks appeared on her body. The leaks streamed into ropes attached to several suitcases. The cases opened, revealing empty bottles of vodka. *Very funny,* I thought.

I didn't know who I was talking to or asking specifically, but the instinct overtook me. *Why does she drink?* I stared intently. Nothing happened. I asked again, *Why?*

Out of thin air a car appeared to crash into her. First it hit her from the front. Then the same car hit her right side. It crashed into her from behind. Like a crash-test-dummy movie, the car crumpled into her from every angle. The car rammed her and rammed her and rammed her, twisted metal balling around her entire body.

The bus driver hit the horn and jerked us to a stop. Something fell out of Car Crash Lady's bag and rolled toward my seat as the bus started moving again. Rolling, rolling, landing right in between my feet and lodging there. Whatever it was, Car Crash Lady wanted it and wobbled up out of her seat, looking like she'd already downed a few. As she was weaving toward me, I froze. I looked down at my feet for the first time and saw what it was: a full bottle of alprazolam, the generic for Xanax. The bottle had a sticker warning: AVOID ALCOHOL. And here she was, right over me, looking at the prescription bottle between my feet. Pleading with her eyes that I pick it up and hand it to her. I didn't move. I looked in her drunken, zombie eyes. I took a breath and got a whiff of hers, which was intensely alcoholic. I was revolted and frightened.

"Give it to me," she slurred.

I couldn't move. Car Crash Lady looked at me, her eyes searing me with hatred. Her energy went darker, leaking out of her like arms . . . trying to grab me. Before I could think, she cleared her throat. Like, hock-a-loogie cleared her throat, making a sound worse than ten boys at recess, and then she did it. She spit. She spit the thickest, most disgusting-smelling blob of cigarette-soaked, vodka-tinged mucus I have ever smelled. In my face.

"Screw you, you lazy bitch!" she yell-slurred at me. Her energy arms were like an octopus, sliding around me, sucking me dry. I had every urge to move, but no oomph to do it. Was her misery like a virus, infecting me? I was pinned to my seat and could do nothing to get away from it. Misery encased my entire being, and I felt depressed and incredibly alone. I wanted to sob.

"Leave her alone," someone called out. Just as other passengers were about to protest, the bus stopped. Car Crash Lady stumbled, grumbled, and flung herself off the bus. Fast.

A nice mother with two scared kids handed me some Wet Ones, asking if I was okay. I watched Car Crash Lady flipping me the bird and walk-flailing down the street. I felt bad for her, but was relieved she was gone. I could breathe.

The bus moved, and I felt something between my feet. I looked down. The Xanax was still there. I picked it up, reading: RX FOR: ALICE KIMBALL. *Thanks for the loogie, Alice.* I put it in my knapsack and would toss it first chance I got.

I desperately wanted a shower. Or ten. But the public restroom at the mall would have to do. I remembered my mission and sighed. Psychic cooties were exhausting.

By the time I got to the mall, I was pretty worked up. I couldn't wait to wash my face in the bathroom. There had been so much coming at me; had it overloaded my circuits? The ooze gripping onto people was alarming. Gripping ooze. Groping ooze. Grooze. Since it made me woozy and groggy afterward, I named the adverse effects "grooze grog." It felt like a bug you could catch: "Look out for the grooze! It gives you the grog!" Or something like that. I was beat down.

I grabbed a coffee and headed to the bookstore. It was pretty quiet on a weekday afternoon. I figured I'd take advantage of the optical serenity and hightail it to the information desk. Even the goth guy behind the info desk didn't appear to have any additional color forms dancing around him beyond his tattooed arms. I showed him my old-timey cards from the gold envelopes and asked if he had any books that might explain them.

"Books on tarot cards are in the back and to your right. Aisle seven." He returned to his superthick book.

"These are tarot cards?" This was news to me.

"Pretty much. Aisle seven." He barely concealed his eye roll and pointed me toward a direction that gave him no pleasure. I guess if goth guys ever took pleasure in anything, they wouldn't have gone goth.

"Have a goth day," I joked, and he scowled. I gazed around, watching other customers as I headed to aisle seven, and noticed that light was streaming from the books they were selecting as well. "Screwy decimal system," I thought out loud, and saw a flash of something around an engrossed reader's head. There was a feedback loop of energy between her and the book—a cord of light extended from the top of her head and looped into the pages and back to her head. A little figure eight circuiting between the open pages and her cranium. She had a look of wonder on her face, and I was thrilled that a lightbulb moment looked more like a beautiful waltz of light.

I looked back at Goth Guy, hunched over his large book.

There was no firestorm over his head. Thick grooze poured out of his feet, running up his sides and back and out his ears and eyes, the weight of it pulling him down like gravity. There was no sign of light. He wasn't just under a dark cloud; he was in one. "Not again," I groused. Grooze was definitely starting to gross me out.

The book gave him no joy, and he appeared to resent it. He kept going over two pages in a frustrated back and forth, not finding what he needed. He sat, stuck there, for what seemed like an eternity. I hoped he'd find what he was looking for, and as I hoped I saw a stellium of light travel from somewhere behind my head and land around him, instantly straightening him up in his seat. He quickly turned the page, scanning and pointing with an *aha!* motion, and smiled. He caught himself and looked around, closed the book, stretched, and took a deep breath. As he exhaled, the grooze blew away and he stood up. Satisfied.

I could make people feel better with a thought? This couldn't be, but I saw it with my own eyes, impaired as they'd been of late. I made a mental note to try again later, but I had to focus on the task at hand: the cards.

I spent a good hour in the tarot section. My cards were part of a specific deck, and the options were overwhelming. I was over all the whelming. I was flustrated over what to do, when my phone started vibrating. Shirl was here.

When I found her, she was talking to none other than Ryan Mac. They were arguing in front of the new releases. I didn't want to cramp her style, but he looked mighty upset. Dots around Shirl started forming into pictures that blurred. Why couldn't I see Shirl? My flustration continued! I spied on Ryan and focused. The dots streamed into pictures, random movies, none of them containing Shirl. His dots became braids, but there were no braids between them. His braids were groozy, so different from Richie's. I eye-bandoned my eye-dropping and decided eavesdropping might be faster. As I got closer, Ryan was easy to hear, 'cause he was upset.

"I didn't sleep with you, Charlene," Ryan said emphatically. Charlene? Was he messing with her? "I didn't put that condom on your locker. And my friends didn't do it either." Shirl was silent. Her entire being got blurry. I shook my head to try and get the blur to stop. Nope. Ryan was clear; Shirl was a blur. What did it mean? Grooze-icles were extending from Ryan toward Shirl. I didn't wait to see what they did.

"Shirl," I called out, "are you okay?" After the events of the morning, I was gonna nip this funk in the bud. I was tired, but that was no excuse. I had to act fast.

"Leave me alone, Beth," Shirl snarled at me. Snarled!

"What?" Her tone blindsided me. Why would she bark at me that way after this morning? Did she want to be alone? Had I done something wrong?

"What's up?" I'd been through too much to get attitude from her. She shot daggers at me, and I backed off. "Fine, Shirl. Be that way."

"I didn't sleep with her," Ryan pleaded to me. "I don't even know her!" I took a breath. He had tons of ropes around him and his share of leaky garbage, but one thing was clear: Ryan was telling the truth. I hated to admit it, but a new possibility bitch-slapped me: Maybe Shirl was lying.

"Shirl?" I asked, getting more and more upset with her bitchy attitude toward me. If I couldn't trust Shirl, who could I trust?

"Why are you believing him?" she barked. "I'm your friend! You're supposed to be on my side!" As I got closer, I saw it. The same dark mist I'd seen earlier, but this time it was leaking out of Shirl from every direction. Gray grossness seething out of her pores, morphing into creepy feelers. Around her entire body. There was a giant squid wrapping around her collar and extending itself toward Ryan. With every word she spoke, the grooze caboose was sucking energy off of Ryan. And choking Shirl. I freaked.

"Shirl, are you lying? Please stop lying!" I begged. Shirl looked embarrassed and mouthed, *Stop it,* and when I kept moving toward her, she snapped loudly, "This is none of your business, Beth." Her grooze calamari was continuing its dance of death between them, when it turned its suction toward me. Shirl was breathing hard.

I was gonna need a different tactic to save us. In my head I said to the energy, *I hope you find what you are looking for. But not with me or my friend.* The energy loosened its grip before sucking up to me, stronger than before. Was it coming from her? Did Shirl hate me? All my alarms were going off, and my body was losing vitality fast. Something was wrong. I decided to get out of there.

That's when I tripped and fell flat on my face. Hard. As I got up on my knees, I lost my balance again, and *blam!* Right on my stomach.

Ryan was horrified. "You okay?" I pushed myself up onto my elbows and could go no further. The energy was strangling me. I couldn't move. It was as if a giant foot was on my back. Maybe this was it: I was falling apart. Maybe this was what a nervous breakdown felt like. I was nervous, I was confused, and I definitely felt like I was breaking down. I sat up and turned to get my knapsack. And my knapsack flew straight across the room. Far out of reach.

Shirl laughed. "You freakbag. Why would you throw your knapsack? That is so juvenile." The problem was I hadn't thrown it. Something else had tossed it. Something big.

My best friend was laughing at me, and a rage filled me. How dare she laugh at me after all I'd done to help her? She'd bailed on me after I puked, and she was bailing on me now. She wasn't my friend. She was more into saving face than saving our friendship. Eff her.

Now, this looked bad and I knew it. People were staring at me on the floor, and I turned around, trying to compose myself. But I was furious. I wanted to punch Shirl in the face for not helping me and for not telling the truth. And then? BAM. An enormous black cloud of—*God, what is going on???*—swirling black golf balls pinned me down. They felt like static, like sitting in the middle of two guitar amps reverberating. Ungodly, high-pitched feedback was seizing my body and holding me down. I flailed against it, and that was laughable. I tried squirming and wiggling out from under it, but it was still too strong for me, flipping me over onto my stomach. I kicked and thrashed and, yes, I screamed. I let loose the word "help," but nothing could come out. My voice was locked in static. I thrashed some more, noticing a crowd gathering out of the corner of my eye.

I heard Shirl say, "She's a total drama kid. She's been studying improv. This is her idea of a performance piece. Just ignore her." That was a lie. "Your shenans aren't funny, Beth." Shirl was lying about Ryan, and she was lying about me. I was livid. I wanted to kill her.

Finally, a scream ripped out of my throat as I got hurled toward a book display—or should I say through a book display?—books flying everywhere, paper cutting my face, and my leg knocking against another book display. "God, please let them be paperback!" I said as I knocked into a second, larger display. Hardcover crime fiction nailed me in the head, and people started screaming. Which was appropriate, since they couldn't see what was tossing me around like a rag doll. Security was running toward me as I gasped to scream. Finally, some help! The pressure on my back didn't back off, convulsing me again. A security guard grabbed me. I felt his hand on my arm, even though he couldn't lift me up. Another security guard joined him, dragging me up and toward the exit. The static held my legs down, not letting me move. I was in the middle of a security guard/golf-ball-gremlin tug-of-war. The crowd got bigger, and suddenly the GB gremlin released my legs and we went flying. Into the plate-glass storefront of my local mall's Borden's Bookstore. The plate glass won.

As security dragged me out of the store, I saw Ryan flee the scene out of the corner of my eye, glancing at me like I was certifiable.

While the two security guards were busy cursing at me for "fighting instead of cooperating," I looked back and saw Shirl. She was covered in a fog of gray gook. And she had nothing but hatred in her eyes. Goth Guy looked thrilled by the developments and stood next to Shirl territorially. As I got farther away, I could barely make out their faces underneath the groozy blur, which was wrapping around them like an unholy pod. I'd known Shirl for ten years and didn't know her at all.

After two hours in the mall security office, I realized that I might actually be in trouble. Big trouble.

Goth Guy made a statement saying I was "trying to accost" my friend, and Shirl—loving all the attention from a new boy—didn't defend me. It didn't matter that it wasn't true; whatever vampire energy she was working needed attention from guys more than she needed me. I'd risked my butt for her twice in one day, and for what? To get dissed? Shirl was dead to me. I never wanted to see her again.

A police officer arrived and was looking at videotape of the incident. I heard snippets like "prankster" and "drug addict" and "seizure" and "seriously troubled." They were all convinced that I was a troublemaker. I didn't tell them I was an honors student looking for a book when I happened to be pinned down by an invisible static beast. A beast that seemed to come from my lying-ass best friend.

I realized any attempt to try and explain what really happened would sound like lunacy, but unfortunately I was halfway into defending myself when I realized it and tried to course-correct.

"Something was holding me down—I had a disagreement with my friend—I was trying to reason with her—"

But I just gave up. I had no hope. I had less than no hope.

My mother was distraught when she arrived, and her review of the security cam footage did nothing to alleviate her hysteria. She summoned me into the room of security monitors and had them show me the footage. "Do you think this is funny? Do you think it's cute to terrify people with bizarre and destructive behavior?" I watched the tape. There was no golf-ball gremlin pinning me down. No energy swarm stepping on my back. And from the angle of the camera, it totally looked like I threw the knapsack myself. My flip-flopping across the floor didn't look like the result of some battle between good and evil. It looked like a bizarre tug-of-war with myself. I gasped at the images: It was like watching a complete stranger having a completely different experience. Except that stranger? Was me.

In whispered tones they told my mom about the bottle of Xanax they'd found in my bag when checking for stolen items, and they asked if I was using drugs. My mother informed the security guards about my "psychological fragility" of late, and even used the words "schizoaffective disorder." They seemed to understand, and my mother signed some document banning me from the mall. I was banned. And Bordens was reserving the right to press charges against me for aggravated criminal mischief. They'd be sending a bill for the damages to my mother.

I knew how it looked. And the look on everyone's face confirmed what I knew: I was officially crazy.

The drive home was dead silent until we pulled into our driveway.

"Is there anything you want to tell me?" my mom asked, turning off the car. "Are you sure no one has been . . ." Her voice trailed off.

"Has been what?" I asked, annoyed with the question.

"Has anyone been trying to contact you?"

"I got a gold envelope at school." It was time.

"You did? From who?"

"I don't know. The return address was from a place called 7RI in New York City."

"Why didn't you tell me?" She was freaked out. "What did it say?"

"It said, 'You are more than you think you are.' Who is it from? Do you know?" My mother clenched her jaw and didn't speak. "Why won't you tell me? If you know something, I really need to know."

"I don't know what you're talking about." Grooze flared around her before blurring.

I couldn't trust the one person in the world who was supposed to have my back. My insides pumped rage through my veins. I looked at my mother with pure hatred. The pressure exploded into swarms of visual bees that enveloped her. The static between us got so loud that I had to get out of the car and away from her.

I stormed into the house; I could not see clearly. I collapsed in my room, my body exhausted. Kicking off my shoes and pulling off my socks took a clumsy eternity. I didn't have the strength to undress, and I wished Richie were there to help. I felt a pang, hoping Ryan wouldn't tell his brother about my misadventure. If only Richie were there to wrap around me, I could disappear inside his arms and his smell and I'd be okay. I needed him to kiss me again; I needed to feel his mouth again. It was the only thing in the world that would make me feel better. My life was upside down, and I couldn't help but fantasize. Something in his smell courted my brain. His eyes, the way he looked at me. I wanted to absorb it, envelop it, swallow it. I was in the trouble of my life, and there I was thinking about a boy. I hid under my covers, fully clothed. I curled my body into a small ball, my knees near my chin, and rolled back and forth, rocking myself until I passed out.

I woke up a few hours later to the sound of my mother crying in the other room. She was on the phone. I picked up my cordless and eavesdropped long enough to hear Dr. Milton's voice. He was comforting her. "It's just for observation. We'll see what meds work and get her on a program so she's not a danger to herself or to other people."

Observation? I was going in for "observation." I was pretty sure I knew what that meant. A psychiatric hospital. I was swimming in black. I closed my eyes and tried to think happy thoughts that didn't involve psychos and straitjackets. If I was insane? Maybe there was a drug that could make me normal again. Maybe there was a way to make this all go away. But the more I thought of maybes, the more I worried that I had so lost my touch with reality that I was hanging on to false hope. And all the maybes in the world wouldn't bring me back to earth. I'd lost faith in my ability to be rational with myself. Gold envelopes? Tarot cards? Rhymes and visions? I clung to the Seeing Key, reading it over and over again, memorizing it and reminding myself that somebody somewhere knew what was going on. But in my heart I feared the worst: I'd lost it. I'd lost me. And I'd lost all hope of ever being with Richie again.

The next morning my mother looked as if she hadn't slept. Her hair was unwashed; her clothes didn't match. Her voice was hoarse when she finally spoke. "Pack some things. I can't live with myself if anything happens to you, Beth. If this mental ill—"—she stopped before saying "illness"—"if this can be prevented or managed, we have to do it. This is for your protection and for your safety."

In a stupor I quickly packed some clothes, my phone, my iPod, my toothbrush, my hairbrush, and my journal. I looked for the gold cards, but they were gone. My mother drove in silence. The visions returned for a flash, and I saw that straitjackets were dancing in her head too.

"Mom. I'm going to be okay. We are going to figure this out." I found myself saying it, and her straitjacket flashes stopped.

She started weeping. "There's so much we don't know about—" and she stopped herself. To the left I saw a flicker of a baby in a hospital, but that went dark as fast as it appeared.

"Were you thinking about a baby? If you were thinking about a baby, Mom, tell me—because I just saw it. Tell me you were."

She paused, startled. "How did you know that?" But she wasn't soothed; she was scared. "Yes, yes, I was. I was remembering when you were at the hospital, and I realized that the last time I was at a hospital with you was when you were a baby. You've always had insights about things that were beyond your years. But Dr. Milton says it's common in young people with schizoaffective disorders." Oh. The doc with his medical mind was labeling me, putting me in a neat little box.

"What if I'm just special? What if I just have something that is different? Is it possible I'm just having—" and I stopped. I'd taken enough science courses to know that whatever was going on with me? Was beyond the limits of science to explain it. And where the known boundaries ended? That was where my mother's ability to have compassion or insight stopped.

"You are special, Beth. You will always be special. So brilliant. It's such a—" And this time, she didn't mean it the way I wanted her to mean it. She meant it like special-educationally special. My mother now believed I was damaged in some way. She'd lost hope in me too.

CHAPTER 13

*T*HIS REALLY IS FOR YOUR SAFETY" WERE THE LAST words my mother said to me before having me committed to the McCall Psychiatric Institute. And my last words to her were the only ones I could have said: "Safety from what?" I didn't get an answer. I was going to have to get answers on my own.

There was nothing scary about the loony bin from the outside. It was a proper four-story brick building with white trim and "decorative" white grates on the windows. Inside, the linoleum floors were clean and shiny and smelled of pine. The hallways were empty but for staff members in scrubs. The admitting nurse had spoken to the barfing Dr. Milton, and I was taken to a room, where they took my knapsack. My iPod. My clothes. Everything. Despite the alarming discovery of Car Crash Lady's bottle of pills the day before (and the story of how I came into possession of them—which no one believed), they decided I was not a suicide risk. I was allowed to keep my journal (which they checked for razor blades), a T-shirt, my fave sweater, and some sweatpants and socks to wear with my gown. I sat on the edge of my bed. How the hell did I get here? A month ago I was an honors student with some vision issues. Now I was in a psychiatric hospital with issues issues. A week ago I'd had the best kiss of my life with the best kisser of my life. Now I could kiss Richie and his kisses good-bye. And with that I put my head on the pillow, and I cried until I couldn't cry any longer.

"Good morning, Beth. I'm Dolores. I'm here for morning meds."

"Oh. Hi." I was disoriented, wiping drool off my mouth and sitting up in bed to see a massive nurse standing over my bed. Had I been asleep for twenty-four hours?

Dolores laughed, pulling me into a sitting position with her considerable strength. "Honey, you were tired! Or were you fakin'? I like an actress, girl, don't worry. Should I call you MacBeth? Are you gonna get all Shakespearean and stuff? Child, don't sweat it; I've seen much, much worse." I liked that she called me MacBeth, since it was like Beth Mac backward. Then I remembered where I was and I wanted to die.

"Seventeen, huh? I hear we're going to be keeping an eye on you for a minute—seeing what kind of cycle you're on."

I stared blankly. What did my period have to do with this place? "My cycle?"

Dolores snorted. "Not your lady business cycle, although that will get in line with the other patients here soon enough. No, how you cycle through episodes. Schizoaffective cycles are really—we're just going to watch you and see how it comes and goes and what happens. The more you can tell us, the sooner we can get you on the right meds and hopefully get you out of here." Dolores smiled. "We do these on an empty stomach and then feed you, girl. The food here is not bad. It's terrible." She giggled again before giving me my options. "You can shower before breakfast. But I recommend showering afterward. In case of flying food." Ohmigod, I'd almost forgotten: I would be eating eggs with lunatics.

"Do you have diapers? Cause that kinda makes me wanna pee my pants. And not 'cause it's funny."

Dolores howled at that one. "You funny, girl. I hear you're smart. You'll be fine. Just duck." She burst out laughing again. "And if you need diapers? Lord, we got plenty of those to go around." She laughed and then looked at me, and it was as if I could see her thoughts, and they said, *This girl isn't crazy.* I was so grateful I must have sent her a burst of light by accident. I saw it land all over her and just tickle her. As she gave my arm a squeeze, I saw flickers of all these kids jumping on Dolores and hugging her, but they weren't her kids; they were calling her Auntie DeeLee and clinging to her with so much love she was laugh-crying and out of breath. Dolores caught herself and looked at me. "Something happening, MacBeth?"

And I figured I was safe now. "I'll tell you about how cute your nieces and nephews are later, Auntie DeeLee." And as large a woman as Dolores was, you could've knocked her over with a Frito. There was a huge silence, the quiet noise of someone realizing they've experienced something inexplicable and wonderful.

"Oooh, girl." Dolores roared into laughter again. "We gonna have fun! And wait till you meet Nessy. You two gonna love life together, I tell you that right now. Breakfast down the hall whenever you ready, girl. 'Auntie DeeLee'-in' at seven in the morning. Damn, girl." Dolores winked at me before waddling out the too-small door.

The walk down the hall to breakfast was like stepping through a maze. The hallway was virtually empty, but on these drugs it was now full of dots, braids, and ropes playing double Dutch. In the emptiness I refined my technique. I tried an eye-bat switch to double-check: Left-eye closed, no one's there; right-eye closed, party time.

Breakfast consisted of twenty or so patients scattered around a sunlit dining room. With everyone in robes, peacefully eating breakfast, I expected to be called for my lobotomy any minute. This was like a spa from hell, where celebrities suffering from "exhaustion" had been known to check in. I had to hand it to my mom: Working in the insurance biz was a smart move. We had amazing coverage, and there was no way we could've afforded it otherwise. I was scared, but the place was almost nice, painted yellow as if willing people into a cheery mood. With very tastefully appointed cages on the windows. Most of the clients were so drugged it didn't matter what color the walls were.

I got some eggs and toast and a cup of coffee. It all seemed harmless enough. I sat alone, watching the other clients. The drugs were strong, and they were making me sleepy. I had to really blink hard to shift between inner and outer vision, and the meds were making it challenging. Eggs. Whoops, they brought me right back to their coop. I didn't want to swallow.

After a moment, I realized the eggs had been sitting in my mouth. This is how people lose it—they forget to chew, drooling food onto their chin. *Spit them into the napkin, Beth.* I did a double take and noticed the video cameras for the first time. *Be careful,* I said to myself. *They'll notice.* I got up to get some oatmeal instead of scrambled egg feelsees when I saw a girl around my age across the room. I decided to go sit with her.

She extended her hand right away: "I'm Nessa." Her grip

was delicate, and she wore a hoodie that zipped up to her nose, covering her mouth. After shaking, she unzipped it and smiled, only to rezip it so just her radiant eyes peeked out, like some kind of hip-hop urchin. Gorgeous, long strands of dark hair poked out, and her enormous brown eyes had gold flecks in them. She could've been a model.

"Hi, I'm Beth. Can I sit here?" She nodded and slipped a bendy straw through the hoodie opening and took a sip of orange juice. I sat down and realized I was completely disinterested in food.

"Are you a poet? Do you make something with rhymes?" Nessa wondered.

"I'm not very artistic. I don't write or draw, or anything."

"What about that rhyme you practice in your head?" Was she asking me or mind-reading me? "I like that poem. About the key or something." She could hear the Seeing Key?

"Um. I didn't write it. But wow. How do you know about that—?"

"Your radio." Nessa delivered this like it was the most well-known fact on earth. I wasn't sure what she was talking about. She slurped the remainder of her OJ with a loud suck.

"My radio. What radio is that?" I risked sounding dumb for something that was clearly obvious to her, but I had to ask.

"Everyone has a radio. Broadcasting all the time."

"Is mine playing music?"

"No. The radio is the radio of your life. Everything that happens to you lives on you and in you. Everything that has ever happened to you forms a frequency. That frequency plays in you and transmits like a station. We all have a bunch of stations on our dial that we're broadcasting—" She widened her eyes. "Are you following? I can slow down, if you like." I was eating it up. Nessa could've turned me into an information gorger. I didn't want to stop eating what she was serving.

"Keep going" was all I could muster.

"The frequencies we're running give off vibration. Vibration is sound. I can hear the story of your life through your vibration, your various stations, your radio. No big deal. Lots of people can do it. Everyone can do it when they're little; they just get it beat out of them in different ways." I wondered why it didn't get beat out of her, when she answered my question. I brushed my foot against her leg to try and feelsee something, to no avail.

"I didn't lose it!" Nessa explained. "People don't like hearing about their stations. Especially people with lots of secrets. My family has lots of secrets, so it's easier if I'm the crazy one. That's why I'm here, I guess. Everyone's radio playing so loud for me and all. You'd think people would want to know what they're broadcasting, but they don't. Quite the opposite." You could've scraped my jaw up off the floor, I was so stunned at the coincidence. Was it possible? Was it possible that Nessa was hearing what I was seeing?

"Everyone's radio plays all their stations"—she twisted some hair through the eye opening in her hoodie—"all the time. I can, I can—I don't mean to sound arrogant or anything—but

I can hear them twenty-four seven, whenever, and I can spin the dial and go where I want when I want to." She seemed embarrassed, but she didn't have to be. "I mean, you have stuff happening, right? Don't you? Unless my signal is jammed, in which case ignore everything I just said."

I didn't know what to say, so I just started babbling it all out. "Yes, I see things. I started seeing things that aren't there, or that no one else can see, so if yours is a radio, I guess mine is a TV. But I also feel it, and I don't know what device on earth does that."

"Oh. You're clairsentient and clairvoyant." Nessa shrugged.

"What, what? What's that?"

"'Clairvoyant' means 'clear seeing' and 'clairsentient' means 'clear feeling.' In French. I'm clairaudient. That means I hear clearly. Some times better than others. But yeah, I am guilty of clear hearing. They convicted me, and here I am."

There was a name for this insanity that was happening to me? It wasn't a scary mental disorder?

"But you have a funny name for it—you call it something else? Wheelies, or something? No, that's not it . . . reelsies?"

"Feelsees. Feelseeing."

"Oh, you feelsee!" Nessa hit the table, like she was incredibly entertained and excited. "That's so, so cool. Much better than the French crap." She even started playing with the strings on her hoodie, pulling them back and forth like dental floss.

"I gotta go, Olive."

"Olive? Who's Olive?"

"I guess you'll tell me later." Nessa looked at me sympathetically and got up to leave. "See you later, Beth." I nodded and she walked away, suddenly hungry. My oatmeal was cold. My coffee was cold. I turned to get seconds, and there was a man covered in grooze standing there. I did the eye-bat switch to make sure he was real. He was. I felt like he was scrutinizing me, so I blurted, "My oatmeal's cold."

He smiled. "Well, by all means, Beth, get some more. May I join you when you return?"

Sure, I nodded. "Want something?" I asked, which startled him.

"No, thank you, Beth." It always creeped me out when people I didn't know repeated my name a bunch.

"I'm Dr. Duncan." I must've smiled, because he tilted his head into the *Why are you smiling?* position.

"As in donuts? I didn't know you could get a PhD at Dunkin' Donuts." I thought this was hilarious.

Dr. Duncan pretended to think so but didn't. "I'm an MD, actually."

"Oh, sorry," I blurted. "My mother told me how much it bugs shrinks who are MDs when people think they only got their master's degree and PhD instead of the whole med school thing. I was just goofing around."

"It doesn't bother me at all." The doctor was lying. "We're going to have our first session later today, but I wanted to welcome you and introduce myself."

"Thank you so much, Dr. Duncan," I said, sensing that he was a man who enjoyed formality and decorum. "I really appreciate that."

"A PhD in donuts. That's funny, Beth." As he rose to leave, I sipped my coffee and decided from that moment on that he forevermore be known as one thing and one thing only: Dr. Donuts. And I had a feeling he was going to try and glaze me.

I needed to hose the ick off of me, so I took a shower. Nessa made me remember I'd been committing the Seeing Key to memory. I tried summoning some lines of the rhyme, but the drugs were too strong. I let it go. Were the drugs silencing my brain? I needed my neurons to work! As the water poured over my body, I let myself think about Richie. I wondered if he still wanted me as badly as I wanted him, or if he'd written me off as a case of the basket case. I imagined his fingers tracing magic touches on my mouth. I saw his mouth shiny with water as we sipped from the same glass. I remembered the pink of his tongue as he sucked his bottom lip. I relived the kiss over and over in my mind like a hamster on an exercise wheel, racing to the same spot again and again. Until my fingers were pruned. Relieved my brain was still working, I realized that thoughts of Richie were the only thoughts that made me happy.

Afterward I got into my fresh crazy gear: a hideous pair of yucky rusty rose-colored scrubs. I had two things on my mind: finding the TV room and finding Nessa. The TV room was kind of multipurpose: There were books, games, art supplies, and a television. One television. One remote. I could tell by the two people seething behind someone watching a talk show that this lack of televisions was a problem. As the clock struck eleven a.m. and the credits rolled, positions were switched and the new regime turned to their show, *Court TV*. And they lit up. I realized that watching people who were worse off actually made them feel better.

"Time's up!" It was Nessa, who surprised me from behind. She was in a new ski-masky hoodie. How did she get such cool clothes in here?

"They let you wear whatever you want or what?" I was very curious.

"I've been here paying full freight for four years. I'm, like, their best customer! They let me wear what I want, or I pay DeeLee to get it for me online. Let me know if you need anything. DeeLee's a friend of the court."

"Four years?" I couldn't imagine being in the place for that long, and it broke my heart.

"Believe me, it's better than the alternative." She laughed, but I didn't believe her, and Nessa quickly changed the subject. "No. Yes. Wait. But there are more than two. Six? No seven. Who are the seven? You've seen, like, pictures? Yes, pictures!"

Hearing someone speak about something you've never spoken of can make your brain stutter. I felt like Nessa was ahead of me, and I was in her dust . . . trying to play catch-up.

"The tarot cards? I got these cards. I found them, actually. They weren't addressed to me but to someone called Aleph Beth." When I said the words it sounded like "All-Eff Beth."

"Olive! That's it—not Olive, but All-Eff! It's not exactly pronounced like that; it's cooler than that. It's foreign and exotic. Like one of those languages that sound like they're clearing their throat?"

I didn't know and didn't want to lie to her. "Nessa, I have no idea, actually." I really didn't. Then I remembered. "Oh, wait! Is it Hebrew?"

"Yes, yes, yes! Thank you. Hebrew. I don't speak it, but I can hear it. That name is Hebrew!" She was practically grateful and daintily clapped her hands. "Yes, yes, hmmm. And what are the other names?" Now she was talking about the tarot cards! My name? The cards? Where was she getting this?

"High Priestess and Empress? Um, Emperor, Hierophant and the Lovers?" I asked. "The tarot cards?"

"No, no, no—they have names!" She was deeply amused, bouncing her butt in a motion that made her fall out of her chair. I was getting annoyed.

"I already told you the names." People were staring at me talking to Nessa, and as she stood up she motioned at me to move, so my back was to the room.

"Sorry. Radio's playing something else." Her eyes widened, accentuating the point.

"What do you hear? Tell me!"

"That for someone so smart, there's a lot you don't know." *No kidding,* I thought. It was weird talking to someone whose mouth was covered. It felt like her eyes were talking to me.

"I haven't felt smart in . . . weeks." It was true. It had been like someone had scooped my brain out and replaced it with some new substance I wasn't sure how to use.

"Beth, it's time for your tour. Whaddaya say?" Nessa plopped back into the chair. A client across the room waved, clearly in love with her.

"You have a fan," I whispered, and Nessa laughed. She adjusted her zipper, rubbed her nose, and rezipped.

"He's not a fan, Beth. He sees what he wants to see. Just like everyone else in the world. Except for you." Nessa stood up and took my hand. "But right now? We're going to see what I want you to see."

As we stood up to take a tour, we walked right into a giant, doughy man with a big hole where his heart should be. "Hi, Dr. Duncan," I said. He looked perturbed.

"We have an appointment, Beth." I had totally forgotten-slash-avoided it. "Follow me," he ordered, and I gave Nessa a shrug to say I was sorry, but she was already gone.

Dr. Donuts believed he had a very nice office. The furniture was simple, but there were plants and some artwork. I had a feeling everything was plastic or nailed down so it couldn't be thrown. At him. I nudged the planter. It didn't move. I smiled.

"What are you smiling about, Beth? Are you happy to be here?" The word "happy" was monotone.

It's not as bad as I thought it would be, I thought. "It feels like I'm where I'm supposed to be for now. I'm much less anxious here. Although the meds are too strong."

"We'll get the dosage taken care of. The goal is to get you well. You want that, don't you?" I did. But I wasn't sure I was sick. "Believing you are actually seeing things is part of the disease. We're not sure where you are on the spectrum. Yet." Maybe he was right. Maybe I was sick. "I'd like for you to introduce yourself to some other clients here. Get to know some people."

I nodded. "I do feel safe here."

Donuts scribbled. "Safe from what?"

"The unexpected."

"Tell me something about the unexpected."

"Are you going to repeat everything I say?"

"Would you like me to repeat everything you say?" I didn't trust him.

"No. It's irritating, actually. I feel like you are using a technique on me, rather than seeing me as a person. It doesn't feel great, but I'll live."

The doc got very serious. "Beth. You've been seeing things. I'd like to understand what you've been seeing."

And I understood that what I was going through was something he would never understand. I needed to buy time, so I played along. "I understand that what I'm seeing isn't there. I'm hoping you will find some meds that will help me manage the hallucinations, Dr. Duncan."

He nodded. "Good. We're going to adjust your dosage and add another medication. If all goes well, these meds will serve you well at college in the fall. There's no reason you can't have a normal life, Beth. At Columbia or anywhere for that matter."

"I'd like that." My present had been so demanding that I'd completely forgotten about my future. College. The idea actually cheered me up.

"Clearly, you've been having delusions. About someone sending you letters. Do you want to tell me what happened?"

He knew about the letters, which meant my mother was feeding him information. "You don't have to talk to my mother for answers. You can ask me. What do you want to know?"

"Who is Aleph Beth Ray?"

"I have no idea," I said, which was the truth.

"Do you think it might be a character you made up?"

How did he know that name? Had he been listening to me and Nessa? I didn't know what to say, so I said nothing.

"Your mother found these gold envelopes under your bed—were you addressing these to yourself?"

"Those were in my mom's files. They are hers." I was furious now. "Or she kept them from me." He scribbled down some notes, and I realized I really needed to keep my cool.

"I'm going to share some things about schizophrenia, because I believe it is the key to your wellness. Paranoia is a sign of the illness."

"Look at the postmarks, dude. The envelopes all have different dates." Donuts held up a small stack of gold envelopes. The upper right-hand corners containing the stamps had all been neatly lopped off.

"I suppose my mother gave those to you?" I already knew the answer.

"The postmarks have all been removed. Maybe by the person who sent them?" It wasn't a question. It was an indictment. He believed I sent them to myself and I'd cut off the proof.

"Ask the head secretary at New Glen," I offered weakly. "She had a FedEx delivery for me just like it."

"That doesn't mean you didn't mail it to yourself, Beth. As you know, you can easily send something to yourself using FedEx or regular mail."

"It was from New York, in case you were wondering. You know what? Have you heard of Munchausen by proxy? Where the mother is making the kid look sick because she is sick?" I had read an article about a mom who fed her kid poison just so the mother could keep going to the doctor and getting attention. I may have been grasping at straws, but the way my mother had told me this was "for my protection" made me wonder what she was hiding.

"Munchausen by proxy? You think your mother is out to get you? That sounds like another paranoid thought. Who was trying to get you at Bordens?" he asked. No way I could answer that one without proving his point, so I changed the subject.

"Can I see those envelopes? Please?" Reluctantly, the doctor handed me the envelopes. The seven tarot cards were all inside, as was the Seeing Key. And the "You are more than you think you are" note that had set this whole thing in motion. That one had no address on it since it had been in the FedEx envelope, but the corner was cut off anyway.

"Whoever cut off the postmarks cut the corner off of one

that didn't even have a postmark. Look, it doesn't even have an address on it." I held it up for him to see; it just said Aleph Beth on the front. "You know why? Because it was inside a FedEx envelope. Which I still have somewhere, by the way." I shoved the unaddressed, corner-snipped-off-anyway envelope under his nose. Donuts didn't care.

"It's going to be okay. You are having paranoid episodes, and it's a good thing we are catching them before they destroy your life."

I just nodded. I knew it was useless. What I didn't know was why my mother was setting me up.

As I walked back to my room, I wondered which was more lucrative, getting better or staying sick. I wondered what percentage of "clients" ever got healthy. Or couldn't afford to stay. Later that night I asked DeeLee, "What if people can't afford it here? Where do they go?" I wanted to know what might happen to me if my mother decided to really cut her losses and cut me loose.

"Depends how sick they are. There's a county facility, and some other state facilities. This place is heaven compared to those hells. No one gets out of County Psych Hospital a better person. Oooh, doggie, you do not want to end up there. Trust me. And you are not going to end up in one of those places, now, are you? You got college to go to!"

"DeeLee. If someone were trying to see me, or send me something? Would you, could you get it to me? Or let them in to see me?" She studied me for a while before answering.

"That's against the rules. But there is a visitors day tomorrow." She lowered her voice to a whisper. "Otherwise you can talk to Nessa about that and we'll see what we can do." DeeLee finished with a wink before leaving. I fell asleep determined not to end up in one of those awful places. In case they were going through my stuff, I wrote the following in my journal: "Feeling better. Dr. Duncan is fantastic. The drugs are really helping. Yay!" Inside, I was desperate to know if Richie was okay and prayed I'd get to kiss him again. Then I wondered what I'd have to do to get out of there. I didn't know how it was going to happen, but it had to happen. Fast.

| 4 | THE EMPEROR | 7 |

ENRIETTA'S NAME HAD GONE THROUGH SO MANY permutations that she'd given up trying to remember them all. People shortened it, calling her Henry as a kid. By the time she was in her fifth foster home, she was tired of explaining that she had no idea why her skin was so bronze and her eyes were such a yellow shade of brown. It was easier to start dressing like a boy so people would leave her alone. She finally begged the nuns at an orphanage to let her stay and get "aged out" of the system; she was so tired of moving around. She became invaluable to the Carmelite sisters who ran the place, and acted very much like a mother hen herself, and so the name stuck. "Mama Hen!" was the cry used by so many of the kids that most people thought she was a young mother. With her gloriously dyed hair and colorful outfits, Henrietta looked more rooster than hen. But she was no chicken. Hen was like a brave super-hero. The signature pink hair with black stripes didn't scare the kids; they thought she was a real life Powerpuff Girl or beloved stuffed animal. A baby-faced, twenty-two-year-old, gorgeous, live animal girl.

Hen's colorful stripes let the kids know it was okay to be different. And she wore them proudly. When she'd bring toys and clothes for the kids, the sisters would chastise her, "You shouldn't have! How ever can you afford this, Hen?" Which always made her laugh. "I can't afford not to, Mama." Which is what Hen called all the sisters, although none of them were mother superior. Hen knew better than to tell them where the money came from. And as far as she was concerned, it didn't matter. She'd been turning secrets into dollars since she was old enough to get a fake ID and work a pole.

Hen had been dancing since she was fifteen. Illegally at first, so she'd switch up venues, and she was careful to select establishments that wouldn't ask too many questions.

Because they always asked questions. Everyone wanted to know what she was doing that made men cough up so much money. Money they didn't even know they wanted to spend. Let's be clear: The customers thought they'd spend something. They just didn't know what hit 'em when Hen got them in her feathers.

The first time it happened, it wasn't even in a club. Hen was thirteen years old, walking home from school, when a freak in a car pulled up. The man inside had bad things on his mind, and Hen knew it. So Hen just stopped in her tracks and looked at him. She stared at him and these words came out of her mouth: "Give me all your money and I won't report you to the cops." The guy smiled, and before he said a word, Hen continued in the sweetest tone, "I have the make, model, and license plate of this car burned into my memory. I'm studying you now, with your salt and pepper hair and your brown eyes, and I know you are a good man who does bad things. I'm telling you that it's not going to happen. But I will have to start screaming and report you to the cops if you don't give me all your cash right this instant." Hen smiled compassionately as this terrified guy simply opened up his wallet and handed Hen eighty-two dollars.

"Thank you," he said.

"Promise me you're going to stop doing this." Hen leaned in and scorched him with her golden gaze. "You think no one is watching you. You think you are above all things, but you are not." She pointed her small index finger skyward. "They are watching. They are counting. And you must repent."

The man driving the car blinked back tears, knowing she was right. "I swear I'll stop, I promise," he cried before he drove off.

And so it went. Hen could spot a guilty man a mile away. She'd get them to feel guilty and give her their money. Catholicism had served Hen well, and in her the sisters had inadvertently created a repentance machine. Since guilt was a rampant ingredient in the air of exotic-dancing establishments, this fit in nicely with Hen's goals: to earn enough money to invest in some stocks to help out the older foster kids, who were aging out of the system. Her plan was working. Very well indeed.

Things were easier when she was fifteen, sixteen, seventeen. She'd be somewhere into her third or fourth lap dance with a guy, playing all innocent. He'd have told her enough about himself to be incriminating, and then she'd whisper how old she was. She'd lie about an undercover cop outside, and that she didn't want the customer to get caught. One week Hen conned about eight thousand dollars out of a dozen men in three days. They never even touched her. All they had to do was pay her. It was like taking candy from a baby. Except Hen was the baby. And the candy.

The other dancers marveled at Hen's ability to get a customer to spend. While some dancers made three to four hundred a night, Hen rarely went home with less than a thousand. She was an earner, and the other girls hated her for it. Hen didn't mind. She learned to keep on moving. Even if it meant public transportation.

When Hen turned eighteen four years ago, she swore she'd come back to see the kids as much as possible. But the world was her stage now. As men of power and influence cut larger and larger checks for the orphanage, helping greater and greater numbers of Hen's chicks, she was pulling all the strings.

Only one person had ever understood Hen's true nature. A stranger who in one letter spelled out all that she was. It arrived in the mail one day, all golden like her eyes. Written on the golden parchment was her motto:

I am the one who perches on the precipice of human desire like a peacock. Watch me strut in. I speak to the vibration of insanity that gathers in the culture of lust, desire, and power. My mirror teaches you to stare at yourself. Naked. I am the liberator of truth, truthfully consumed. I ride on honesty's float and I embrace the pageant of each moment. I use facts to feed. That is my parade.

CHAPTER 15

WHEN I WOKE UP THE NEXT MORNING, I FELT MY face sticking onto a piece of cardboard. I'd fallen asleep on the cardboard cover of my notebook, and the ink had leaked out of my pen, creating a giant ink spot on my notebook and face. I could still decipher most of my writing, since the bulk of the blue goo ended up on my right cheek.

On my way into breakfast, DeeLee intercepted me in the hallway, laughing and howling at my blue cheek. "MacBeth? That is not how you attract the boys, honey." She rubbed the spot with her hand. I detected from her reaction it was still there.

"It's ink. Do you have anything that will get it off?" I pleaded.

"Follow me, girl." DeeLee led me down the hall and instructed me to wait outside a door marked AUTHORIZED PERSONNEL ONLY. She returned moments later with a bottle of nail polish remover and a roll of toilet paper. The acetone burned my face, but DeeLee got most of my new birthmark off.

"Now you got a light blue smudge instead of a dark blue one. It's an improvement." She was so thrilled.

"You make it sound like I got a Ferrari instead of a bus pass."

She cracked up again. "Well, it is an improvement. If you are trying to look like a Smurf!" She kept cackling and waddled off to put away the nail polish remover before some suicide risk tried to drink it.

"Thanks, DeeLee. What's a Smurf?"

Her laughter echoed in the hallways as I turned around and headed to the dining room.

After breakfast I found Nessa in the recreation room. She positioned us for the cameras, so my back was to the lens.

"You smell like a nail salon." Nessa unzipped her hoodie and squinched her nose at me.

"You want me facing the back of the room, huh? Feeling paranoid?"

"I don't want your light blue skin to alarm anyone. I'm protecting you. You need some protection." Her neon pink hoodie had little green monkeys all over it. The zipper tab was a bigger green monkey, dangling under her nostrils like a large, animated booger.

"Why are people trying to find you?" she wondered.

"I don't know! If I knew that, do you think I'd be in here? I don't know crap about poop." I was getting a headache from the smell of nail polish remover and started rubbing my temples.

"That's not true." She giggled and snickered at my poop talk. "Tell me everything that has happened so far. Maybe I can hear between the lines."

"Here's what I know, in no particular order. I started seeing pink dots that weren't there; I got a gold envelope addressed to someone named Aleph Beth Ray that said, 'You are more than you think you are'; I got into Columbia early decision; I kissed a guy and burned my mouth; I got Lasik, and instead of correcting my vision it made my eyes and all my senses much, much louder. I found some more gold envelopes that my mother's apparently been keeping in a file. I wrestled an invisible force at the mall, found some mysterious poem that seems to know what I'm going through, and told my mom about the letter to Aleph; she cut off the postmarks on all the letters and turned them in as evidence to Donuts, and now I'm here. That's the long story short, Nessa. I have no idea why people are looking for me, or why any of this is happening. I don't even know who I am anymore."

"Wow." She was very curious suddenly. "You kissed a guy?

Now, that's interesting. What was that like?" She leaned forward onto her elbows, peering out at me from a sea of green monkeys.

"The kiss?" It made me flush to think of it again. If I'd been a normal girl in a normal life, I would've dissected that kiss four million times. But there hadn't been time for that, and I was happy to discuss it in glorious detail. "It was, um, startling at first, and then awesome. Except for the part where his entire life flashed before my eyes. That was a little distracting. And feeling the skin on the roof of my mouth peeling for days afterward. Believe it or not, it was incredibly romantic." I laughed.

"And definitely . . . steamy." Nessa hit the tables with a *ba-dum-bump* for emphasis.

"Now that I think about it, his forehead did say, 'Be careful, the saliva you are about to enjoy is extremely hot,' so there were signs. I mean, I didn't exactly expect the roof of my mouth to get burned. Even Richie had a reaction. Doesn't that prove I didn't make it up?" I was feeling defensive for no particular reason.

"I don't think you're making anything up. Don't be mad at me—I believe you!"

"I know. I'm overexplaining myself because it's all so inexplicable."

"And you're in here? How about this: You're not normal." She paused. "Or you're just an average schizophrenic with paranoid delusions."

"Gee, thanks."

"You're a fool," Nessa teased. "Remember? It was in the cards!"

"I am. I am the Fool. I can't believe my mother gave Donuts the cards. I'm such an idiot for not hiding them better. Did I tell you she cut off the postmarks so I'd really look nuts?" It still infuriated me. Why was she trying to discredit me?

"Only twenty times, fool." She sat back down. "I think you're the Fool who's supposed to become the Magician. You just don't know how to use your magic yet."

"You think the tarot cards are a message or sequence?"

"Duh-efinitely." She raised her fingers to make the air quotation marks, and I grabbed them and shook them like I'd break them off. Nessa started quivering again like she was holding in a big giggle. It annoyed me.

"Can't you hear anything else?" I was sick of overanalyzing. "I'm tired!"

"I'll keep my antenna clean and listen for you." Nessa zipped and unzipped her hoodie and made a sour face. "What about the twins? Isn't there a card with two people on it?"

"The Lovers card? I would love some actually helpful help here, thanks." I wasn't even sure Nessa could help, but I loved the idea. I suddenly thought of something else I'd love, something that would make me feel better. "Do you think I could get my iPod back from DeeLee?" I grinned.

"If not, I can loan you mine," she offered, but I felt bad using hers. Even though technically I'd just be listening, and she had no idea what listening meant in my body these days. "You know what?" she blurted. "There is a guy who is trying to find you."

"Richie? The guy I kissed?" I counter-blurted hopefully.

"I don't know his name, but—his signal is in the ionosphere." She wriggled her fingers and made a jokey *woo-woo* motion with her hands. "He is emitting." Nessa suddenly waved to someone, and when I turned, DeeLee was standing in the doorway. Nessa got up and gave me a little headset motion to her ears, and I prayed she'd be able to get me an iPod. I hoped there was some music in my future.

Nessa was beaming out her eyes. "What?" I demanded. She sat back down and slyly slid something under her hand and pushed it across the table toward me. It was a gold envelope.

"This came for you. DeeLee said to hide it with me after you read it. Otherwise Duncan will know she did it."

We stared at the block lettering. **ALEPH BETH RAY** c/o **ELIZABETH RAY MICHAELS** c/o McCall Psychiatric Institute. It was a recent postmark from New York Ciwy. I covertly opened the stationery under the table, as it was bulkier than usual. I pulled out a gold card but noticed something red attached. Upon inspection the card featured tiny red velvet curtains hanging from the top edge. When I lifted the little pieces of fabric, the following poem was underneath.

DANCE OF THE SEVEN VEILS
Your eyelids are curtains that remove all veils.
Close and open with care, and behold unseen
   trails.

The Seven Rays · 139

Color has meaning, a reflection of health,
Physical poverty, or bodily wealth.
When dark colors forboding do hover with
  stillness,
Make no mistake: This meaning is illness.
With color and sound there is also vibration—
Thinking has frequency, pure and perfect
  correlation.
Between thoughts and reality, alliance is deep.
Think and act well. As you sow, shall you reap.
A word to the wise on the meaning of snakes:
The falsehood of cobra gives not, only takes,
Directed all ways from a source that is known.
Don't fight with the fangs, or all progress is
  thrown.
Beware of all flurries of visual snow:
Harmful thoughts are the substance, the source
  of their flow.
Negativity embodies in snowballs of static;
Toward oneself and toward others it is quite
  acrobatic.
Compassion is best! When viewing others, be
  lenient.
Do not get hypnotized, or life gets inconvenient.
Stay loving, stay kind, and do not intervene.
Unless so invited, stay neutral and clean.
Your eyelids are curtains that remove every veil.

Close and open with care, lest your gift become
    jail.

The blinking! This explained the blinking and the eye-bat switch. But what were trails? This explained a lot for sure. I gulped and regulped each section, desperate for more. I transcribed the poem into my notebook as well. Sound and vibrations—that explained the iPod a little bit, but was it my thoughts accessing their reality? And what about Richie? Were we burned by frequency? Grrrrr. I really hated how vague it was, especially about snakes. Cobras? Directed all ways? What was this? I couldn't help but resent the lack of clarity, and the timing. I wish I'd seen the part about snowballs of static before Bordens. Lame. Now it was telling me not to fight back? *Thanks a lot, anonymous rhyme.* It gave me a lot of information about the stuff I'd been seeing. But I wanted more! More about me, myself, and I. And who exactly that was.

"That's pretty intense," Nessa finally said, finishing reading and breaking the silence.

"I still don't know who I am, Ness."

"Who cares? Join the rest of the planet. Now you're sounding a little too normal." We were interrupted as staff began putting up decorations and a WELCOME sign.

"Visitors Day." Nessa winced. "Makes me want to hide in my room. Like anyone actually wants to see their crazy loved ones."

"By crazy, do you mean us or the visitors?" I wondered.

"The visitors. Duh." Nessa hid the gold envelope in her hoodie and retreated to the safety of her room. I didn't need to hide. There was only one visitor I wanted to see, and I was pretty sure Richie Mac didn't subscribe to the McCall's newsletter.

CHAPTER 16

T WAS ALREADY TURNING OUT TO BE A CLOUDY day. It was sunny outside, but low-hanging static started forming around the floor like a fog machine, rolling around feet like etheric balls and chains. My fellow institutionmates were getting dragged down by the prospect. By eleven a.m., knot-infested ropes were materializing with increasing intensity around each and every person I passed. With each minute closer to twelve o'clock, the visibility of the ropes and double helixes increased, wrapping like mummy gauze around the legs, arms, waists, and necks of everyone in the hospital. It was like watching people become entombed before my very eyes. I couldn't help but wonder: What did the ropes mean, and why did everybody have them?

I scrambled to a mirror to see if suddenly I was covered, but when I looked at my reflection I saw nothing but dirty, greasy, messy hair and an unshowered, particularly uncute and unmade-up me. When I looked deeply into my eyes, I just saw me. I didn't feel crazy. I felt like me. The note—even in all its ambiguity—was helping me.

As the visitors began trickling in—alone, in twos and threes—the pattern became clear. The ropes were doing their dance between people: breathing, helixing, knotting, coiling and recoiling. I eavesdropped where I could. I watched carefully to see how the ropes responded to the exchanges, trying to learn more about why they were there, and see if "The Seeing Key" and "The Dance of the Seven Veils" had more meaning than met the eye.

I heard things like:

"If only you'd take your meds—"

"This is a very expensive vacation. It's costing us a lot of money. Money we don't have."

And then there were the words that didn't say the truth. The "Honey, how *are* you?" that was dripping with fear. The

"We *miss* you!" dripping with need. Insincerity yielded knots. Anger created knots. The air was knitting scarves of knots around the room.

Suddenly a little girl appeared, which was bizarre because I didn't think they allowed kids in here, but she skipped up and hugged a quiet patient known as Stan. She hugged him and hugged him and wouldn't let go, and in a burst I watched as the static evaporated and was replaced with clean, clear space. The little girl gently touched Stan's face, climbing into the lap of the elderly lady she had come with.

"I'm sorry," I heard the old lady tell Stan. "I'm really, really sorry you are going through this." And suddenly their rope became untied. The knots just vanished.

"Thank you. Thank you for saying that." Stan just wept tears of relief. "I'm sorry, too," he said, and another knot vanished.

"When are we going to Six Flags again?" asked the little girl, and they burst out laughing, as if something really funny had happened at Six Flags that only they knew about. This huge sphere like a soap bubble grew around them. It engorged with air, then popped and discharged everything. Everything around them was suddenly gone: the knots, the ropes, the static, the funky-colored dreck. All gone. From two hugs, two I'm-sorrys, a thank you, and a laugh.

"I know you don't want to see me. I know you hate me. But I wanted to make sure you're okay." I knew that voice and whipped around. It was Shirl.

"I'm the opposite of okay, Shirl." Everything came flooding

back. I tried to see if there was any grooze on her, but it all went blurry.

"I apologized to Ryan." She was self-conscious about being in here, and that annoyed me even more.

"To Ryan?" I couldn't help raising my voice. "What about to me?" I curbed my volume just short of yelling.

"I wanted to apologize to you. I'm really, really, really sorry— I just got scared. You'd been acting so weird, Beth. It was really scary. You have no idea what your outburst in front of my locker did. I am dead meat at school. Grenada, Jake, Jenny? They all want to kill me because we're friends. What can I do? What was I supposed to do?"

Even in a hospital, Shirl was still making it about her. I was disgusted.

"Way to make it up to me. Why are you here?"

"How can I make it up to you? You're in here!" Her tone made it sound like she was the victim. I crossed my arms, mainly to keep them from throttling her.

"Go away, Shirl. Just go far, far away."

"I'm so sorry." She was shrinking down, her energy blurring into a ball, but I swore I saw groozy tentacles coming at me from somewhere.

"I'm not sorry. I've put up with all your crap for years, and suddenly things get rough for a couple weeks and you get jealous and bail on me. You're not my friend! You're my worst nightmare!" It was final. There was nothing she could say.

"Don't say that." Her tentacles were reaching out toward

me now, but they were not going to get me. I felt a rush of strength swirl through my brain, waking me up. I felt alive and in control. I wanted to hurt her feelings the way she'd hurt mine.

"You're not my friend. I never want to see you again. Ever. Get out of here." Shirl knew better than to fight me, and I was wondering if it would feel this good to put my mother in her place. It felt good to watch her walk out with her head down, because I was in the right. My resentment felt righteous.

I didn't see it right away, but a python of energy was headed straight toward me, slithering across the floor. Not just any snake, but a twenty-foot-long snake with the diameter of a trash-can lid. It was enormous. I desperately tried to remember the warning in the Seven Veils, but the snake was too big and moving way too fast. I leaped up to evade it, and it pursued me snaking around and through people to get closer. I scurried around, dodging it for a few moments before people started looking at me with concern. The snake rose up to the full height of the ceiling, flaring its hood and hissing at me. As I dove under a nearby table, I realized I couldn't mask my artful dodging any longer. I hissed back, "Leave me alone!" as it began wrapping around my leg. It was Bordens all over again. The serpent was winding around my leg and pulling me out from under the table with seething intensity, corkscrewing its way up to my throat.

"NO!!" I screamed, trying to wrench it off of me. Everyone was looking now, recoiling as the staticky reptile spiraled tighter, choking me. It took all my strength to yank it off my neck, when it bared its fangs and struck me in the center of my forehead, knocking me back to the floor. I collapsed. The taste of metal filled my tongue, and the lone filling in my mouth started vibrating static electricity; it felt like I was chewing aluminum foil. People scrambled to get out of my one-woman snake-fight show, and I would've cared about the fact that they couldn't see this actual beast on top of me, but I was too busy trying to unwrap it from my wrist. I failed, and the violent viper wrested my wrist back at an uncomfortable angle, wrenching my arm behind my back.

Great—now Dolores and some orderlies were coming, and the electromagnetic serpent had me pinned to the ground, spraying my face with a stream of electrical charges that flooded my body with static pinpricks. Two huge orderlies were trying to wrestle me up, but the snake was stronger. My body was now at the center of a tug-of-war, but I could see the tail now . . . made of knots . . . getting clearer and clearer. Someone was at the other end of this rope, and I wanted to know who it was.

"Beth, calm down!" Dolores was freaking out.

"DeeLee, I'm trying!"

"Stop fighting us or we'll have to tranq you!"

Somehow I got up, and I used the serpent's body to pull myself in the direction of its tail. It worked; the snake stopped resisting and let DeeLee and company pull me out the door and down the hall. The tail was darting in and out of my room. I was frantic, I was scared—and so was Dolores.

"Beth, calm down, we'll be in your room in a minute!" They were trying to hang on to me, but I was too fast and broke free and sprinted down the hall. Run-writhing as the tail was wrapping, jerking, and coiling around me. Finally, I got to the door and saw the snake's host. It was a person just as enveloped in knotted snake rope as I was.

"Beth."

I was repelled backward by the discovery, it was so brutal. It felt like an invisible bungee cord was snapping me back and forth over a gorge without moving an inch. I couldn't quite believe my eyes.

"Mom?"

"Beth. You need to calm down." I hadn't seen her since I'd been admitted. The rope between us was vibrating and pulsing. It was knitted with knots. I didn't have much time, so I stepped into my room and pushed a chair under the doorknob to buy some.

"Mom. I need you to tell me something." Knots meant lies, so it was time to unravel them. "Are you really my mother?" The banging on the door started immediately.

She looked surprised but covered it. "Yes." Another knot formed on the rope as she spoke. She was lying.

"Did you give birth to me?"

"Of course! What is this?" Another knot formed, and it engorged with some of the smaller knots into a clot. There was no double helix anywhere to be seen.

"That's not true!" I insisted. The door was rattling, but I

could barely hear it over the blood thumping in my ears.

"This behavior is not going to get you out of here any faster, young lady." It didn't even sound like her; she was so stiff and unnatural.

"Why are you lying to me? Just be honest with me! I need to hear the truth!"

My mother looked terrified and was backing away from me. "Help me!" she yelled out.

"If you don't start telling me the truth, bad things are going to get worse." There were orderlies pounding on the door, but all I cared about was the truth.

"You will not speak to me this way. I am your mother." Another, larger knot clot overtook the others with each syllable. Static was pulsing through the connection like blood. It was a lie.

I closed my eyes, remembering the little hugger girl outside, and stepped toward my mother and put my arms around her.

I pulled apart from her to see if the knots were fading. It was fuzzy and out of focus, but they were releasing. I could feel it.

"Orderly!" she screeched. "She's hurting me!!" And my mother pushed me off of her, and I stood there as my guts lurched. This woman was lying, and the fury I'd been pushing down for weeks volcanoed up inside me. I was about to blow.

"What? What are you talking about? Why are you lying?" I felt the door behind me about to give way. My mother grabbed me and pretended to engage in a struggle. She was staging a fight. I resisted, despite a primal urge to hurt her. Suddenly a force knocked us to the ground. It was Bordens all over again. It held me down, and I spewed out words before it was too late.

"I know about the gold envelopes. Why didn't you give them to me? What do they mean? What is going on, and why are you lying?"

"This is for your protection, Beth," she whispered, but before I could get more, the door burst open.

"Help! She's hurting me" was the coffin nail my mother hammered into me, as four strong hands grabbed my arms and a needle jabbed my back. Searing pain shot heat down my spine. Boom. I went down—and everything went black.

CHAPTER 17

Y THE TIME I WOKE UP, IT WAS DARK. My mouth was drier than a lint ball. My arms and legs were belted to the bed, and I couldn't even reach for water. I squeaked out the word "water" as loudly as I could. Reality came flooding back. My mother had betrayed me. Again. Lied about me. Again. DeeLee entered and quickly undid the restraints and handed me a sippy cup, which I drank in milliseconds.

"You hungry? I saved you some dinner," she whispered.

"Yes. And thirsty. And bathroomy." DeeLee was studying me with a look of concern I'd never seen on her before.

"That was bad news, MacBeth," she added.

"I wasn't trying to hurt my mom, DeeLee. I wasn't. She made that up." It was the truth.

"I'll wait for you outside, then, but hurry." I raced to my toilet and peed for an eternity. I washed my hands and knocked on my door so DeeLee could let me out.

"Follow me. And don't say a word."

As we walked silently down the hall, I noticed that she was becoming increasingly sweaty. The armpits on her scrubs had huge circles of perspiration on them.

"I don't know why I'm doing this. I could get—don't tell anyone, Beth." DeeLee was nervous.

"DeeLee. I know what happened yesterday was bad. But if giving me dinner will get you in trouble, let's not do it. I'll be okay."

"I'm taking you down a hall where the surveillance camera is broken, okay? Please remember: This didn't happen."

I was hungry, but her nerves were freaking me out. DeeLee stopped in front of a door and unlocked it.

"I have to lock it behind you, so knock two times when you're done." The beads of sweat on her faint mustache were noticeable.

"Thanks. This is so cool of you. Did Nessa ask you to do this?" She didn't answer, but opened the door and let me walk in. I heard the lock click, followed by the sound of her footsteps.

"Hey, Beth." When I turned around, there was someone I'd never expected to see. And someone I'd never wanted to see without my makeup on. Maybe I was hallucinating?

"Richie? Are you really standing there?"

"I know, it's weird, right?" He was holding a stack of something, and it occurred to me he'd been dispensed to bring me homework.

"How are you, Beth? Are you . . ." His eyes were taking me in. His jeans hung below the waistband of the top of his briefs. He ran his hands nervously through his hair and still looked like a rock star.

"Am I crazy? Was that what you were about to say?"

"No, no—I really don't think that." Richie was uncomfortable. "I've been so worried about you. I wanted to see you, but I didn't know where you were. . . ."

We stood there looking at each other for a long moment. I couldn't for the life of me see any energy around him. He looked gorgeous. I registered somewhere south of disgusting.

"Is that work I've missed from class?" Anything to distract from my creepy hair.

"No, Beth. No. It's not from class."

"Oh. Is it for me?"

"Beth. I know things lately. I know things I shouldn't know. I know what people are going to say, I know what's going on in their lives, I know why people act certain ways—" It was rushing out of him.

"Me too!"

"I know."

"How do you know?"

"Because I think you gave this to me. I wasn't sure at first. But then . . ." He trailed off and took a deep breath. The silence forced me to recognize how disgusting I felt, complete with BO and bad breath. I smelled myself and took a step back and grabbed a seat out of nose-shot.

"I started having these dreams." His voice was shaking. "Bizarre dreams. I dreamed that my mother yelled at you and stuff. On a bus." This stopped me in my already paralyzed tracks. Was Car Crash Lady Richie's mother? Had I been carrying around her prescription? McAllister wasn't the name on the bottle.

As if answering my thoughts, Richie said, "My mother has a different last name than me—it's Kimball."

I froze. Alice Kimball. "Was . . . is your mother, by any chance, uh . . ." I wasn't sure which direction to take this.

"An alcoholic?" He nodded emphatically. "Yeah. My mom doesn't just drink. She drinks to win." Slowly something dawned on him. "Wait. Did my mom actually spit on you? On a bus?" Holy mother of us all, he did know things.

"Before I answer that, do you know if your mother was involved in some bad car crash?"

Richie did a spin and doubled over before popping back up again. "My mom was in a crash that killed her entire family.

She was the only one who survived." He was as blown away by this revelation as I was by the confirmation.

"Wow. Richie. I met your mom. Alice, right?"

"Um. Uh, so she did hock a huge loogie on you?" He was horrified and mortified.

"Pretty much, yeah." My answer flinched him to the core. "But it was a charming loogie."

"Wait—did she drop her bottle of pills?" he blurted.

"Yes!" This was exhilarating. Maybe I wasn't insane! Maybe Richie Mac and I were insane together!

"Okay, so listen to this. I started dreaming a phone number." Richie was all business, more emphatic than usual, and it was beyond hot.

"A number you knew?"

"That's just it. It wasn't a number I knew. It was out of state. I'd never seen that area code before."

I couldn't read Richie. Nothing was coming off of him that could tell me where this was going, and I was at a loss. No dots, no ropes, and no braids. And definitely no grooze.

"Richie. I can't read your mind." He moved toward me, reaching out for my hand.

"I called the number. It was an office in New York City. An office called 7RI. Looking for you."

My brain warped. I had kissed Richie Mac and knew the impossible was afoot, but now he was dreaming my life and dreaming phone numbers that led to offices that had sent packages to me? Offices where people were—

"What? Wait, wait." I took a deep breath. "Are you sure it's me?"

"Oh, I'm sure." Richie opened his stack and began laying stuff on the table. Pictures. Pictures that contained images of me at every age. Telephoto pictures of me from when I was a baby until recently. There were security camera stills of my episode at Bordens. There were even security cam images of me at McCall's. A freeze ran up my spine and caught in my throat like a sudden dry heave. Someone had been watching me? My whole life? This wasn't flattering. It was super upsetting.

"They didn't ask me how I knew you; they just asked if I would deliver a package to you directly. I told them I had no idea where you were, but they knew. They knew exactly where you were and asked me to come here and give you this package. Sorry, I opened it. I had to make sure it wasn't going to hurt you."

I studied the pictures, nauseated that someone had been photographing my every move. There were dates on all the photos, and all of them were ink-stamped with ABR and T7R. It was so creepy, this sense of being stared at. And having been oblivious to all of it, completely unaware that any of it was going on.

"They insisted I give you this as well. They said you've been looking for it?" Richie placed a gold-leaf envelope on top of the photos. There was that block lettering again. It read **ALEPH BETH RAY**.

"Why this name? Did they tell you anything about why they keep using this name?"

Richie shook his head. This was overwhelming. For both of us. Sweat was pooling in the creases of my knees.

"I've been going nuts," he said. "I was going insane not knowing where you were." No one had ever wanted to see me like that. My brain flashed on our kiss, and I thought I would pass out from all of it.

I extended my arm to take the envelope and got a whiff of my dog-butt armpit. There was that same wax seal. I carefully peeled it off, waiting for him to respond while clutching my elbows to my sides, praying my eau de BO would stay put.

"Seeing you was all I cared about," Richie whispered. "For real."

Richie glanced at me before staring at the floor. "Please don't think badly of me for not finding you sooner. I feel terrible that you've been in here alone."

"Feel free to join me," I joked, pulling the contents out of the envelope, unfolding a piece of paper with an embossed seal on the corner. It was a birth certificate. I was scared to read it, and I handed it to Richie.

"Could you read this for me?"

"It says, 'Certificate of Live Birth, State of New York. Aleph Beth Ray, November 3rd, 1991, 1:07 a.m.'"

"What's that supposed to mean?" I yelped. "Is that supposed to be me? What the hell is this supposed to mean? Did they tell you that?" I was freaking out. My heart raced; my head clogged with the sound of pounding as my throat closed up.

Richie was concerned. "Please don't be upset. It would kill me to think that I upset you—"

"No! I don't know. Look at where I am! I don't know anything anymore. I don't know what's real and what's fake and what I'm seeing and what I'm imagining and it's all a little intense." I started hyperventilating my halitosis all over the place. I really didn't want to cry in front of Richie Mac. He tried to hand me the birth certificate, as if that would help, when another piece of paper fluttered to the floor. More annoying school-teachery block lettering for both of us to see: **YOU ARE MORE THAN YOU THINK YOU ARE.**

"NO KIDDING!!" I yelled to the floor, in the direction of the piece of paper. I wanted to scream. Which explained the screaming.

I must've lost my balance, because Richie grabbed my elbow and sat me in a chair. As his skin touched mine, a huge jolt of electricity sparked between his hand and my arm, throwing us both back a few feet.

"Ow!" I reeled and squealed.

"What the—?" He rubbed his hand.

Without speaking, he reached to pull me up off the ground. As we raised our hands toward each other, a small current of electricity traveled between our outstretched fingers. We raised alternating fingers, watching the current change position. Richie held his hand near mine, bringing his face to my fingers. He kissed my hand from a distance, letting the current connect with his lips. It was hypnotic.

Suddenly the current flared onto his left cheek, and Richie grabbed his face.

"What happened? Are you okay?"

"I think it zapped a metal filling." He smiled, confused. "This is nuts. Nuts."

"What are we supposed to do? What am I supposed to do with this stuff? What did they tell you?" I was winding myself up as I spoke. I impulsively checked my pulse to confirm that it was racing.

"Nothing. FedEx delivered this packet this morning. My instructions were to get this to you within twenty-four hours."

"But why send it to you? Why not send it here—" Of course they'd never give it to me at McCall's. My heart was pounding in my brain, clogging my ability to think think think.

"Can you take the packet for me? I can hide the birth certificate, but they'll take the other stuff." He seemed to understand, but there was a knock at the door and the sound of the lock turning. It was DeeLee. "Time's up, guys."

He quickly collected the pile. "This isn't where you belong. I'm going to figure out a way to get you out of here." He shot me a longing look, and I didn't want him to leave.

The electricity between us was real. I wanted to kiss him again. And again and again. He smiled bashfully as if he knew exactly what I was thinking.

"I will see you soon, Beth; I promise" were his last words as he touched his lips with two of his fingers and sent me an air kiss. I remelted.

After a minute DeeLee came back to collect me. She wiped her brow and took a deep breath, assaulting me with three words that would haunt me for the rest of my life:

"Girl, you staaaaaank."

Back in my room post grub and scrub, I spent hours wondering about the electrical current between me and Richie Mac. Was I contagious? Was there something going on between us that was like a virus? Would it get better and go away or get worse and kill us both? What would happen if we kissed again? Would we be electrocuted? Could I be zapped into oblivion? Fried like an egg? Or stir-fried into a vegetable? I wasn't just freaked. I was superfreaked. Richie had gone from potential hot piece of ass to assassin in one fell swoon. And I wasn't over the swoon or him. I wanted him more than ever.

Despite my swoon fever, a big part of me wanted to find out what would happen. Find out lots of things. Like why was my life this interesting to complete strangers?

Was I Aleph Beth or wasn't I? Was I adopted, or stolen, or what? And if I wasn't who I thought I was, why did anyone care? It was so twisted it made me itch and twitch to think about it. Didn't my mom love me at all after seventeen years of playing my mother on TV? I was tired of all the questions. I frigging wanted answers. And that meant getting the eff out of here.

The next morning Nessa was listening to an escape plan involving my new birth certificate, when she interrupted me.

"Broadcast the plan to Richie. If you're that connected,

you can probably tell him telepathically." Nessa looked at me a long time, attempting to communicate telepathically with her thoughts.

"Stop that." It was stupid. "I can hear you; you don't need to flood my brain with images of Richie. I get it." She pulled down her hoodie zipper, stuck her tongue out at me, and rezipped.

"Then don't look at me like I'm wrong. Try it. What's the worst that can happen?"

"I think I'm already living that scenario."

"Then picture something different. Tell Richie exactly what you want and what you need. Maybe he'll even give you a ride to the airport. Or more." Nessa did a little booty-shimmy-shake in her seat and said, "Maybe he'll even check your oil, Olive."

"Shut up. No way."

"Um. I think we're already beyond no way."

"Way way. If we already have some kind of accidental feel-see connection—with what he saw between me and his mom and his dreaming phone numbers—I guess I could experiment with sending him thoughts. I'm—it's scary. I'm scared."

"What else you got to lose? Feel the fear and do it anyways." Nessa got really still as TJ, the male nurse, walked over with meds and gave us each a little cup.

"Who you talking to?" TJ winked at me. I looked at him, and looked at Nessa, who was nonplussed.

"Nessa?" I answered.

"That's funny." TJ laughed as I looked at Nessa, who said nothing.

"Why is that so funny?" I asked.

Mr. Nurse just shook his head and widened his eyes, leaning down and whispering so Nessa couldn't hear. "I didn't know you loved the sound of your own voice so much, Beth." He offered an odd smile and walked away.

I looked at Nessa. "Weird jobs attract weirdos." I shrugged.

The next two days were full of planning and brainstorming with Nessa about all the stuff I'd need for NYC. Airfare, cab fare, a hotel. In between making practical plans, I experimented with mentally telegraphing to Richie Mac. "Richie Mac. Pick me up. Bring me to the airport. Fall in love with me and help me through this. Please, thank you." Saying please and thank you made it feel less manipulative. I felt kind of lame doing the whole thing, but it was an exciting experiment. What if he showed up? It gave me a whole new level to look forward to. I didn't believe it would work, so I got really lost for hours, dreaming of the things I wanted from Richie Mac: flowers, long kisses, an incredible episode involving losing my real virginity (versus my iPod-ginity, which was long gone), vacations in exotic places, adventures that would take us around the world! I went for it. My wishiest fantasies covered the gamut from basic to heroic. Romance by the pyramids! Sex on safari! Massages in the Maldives! Surfing in Sydney (I didn't surf, but I wanted to)! Running with the bulls in Spain (which sounded more scary than fun, but I was running out of original fantasies)! Saving starving children in Malawi while stopping disease. I wished like it was an all-you-can-eat wish-it bar. I pictured our wedding (huge, two hundred guests), beautiful bouncing babies (two), one big happy family with homes and havens around the globe and the kind of everlasting, fiery love that people dream about. If I was going to wish, I decided to wish big. So, I wished gargantuan. I gargantu-wished.

Meanwhile I maintained my schedule at McCall's, but Dr. Donuts was on me like white on rice. He was clearly in contact with the mother, so my escape plan remained in a cone of silence. I played the part of totally compliant teen, and he was so very pleased with my progress.

"Thanks for all your help, Dr. Duncan."

"Are you enjoying spending time with Nessa?" It was the nicest tone he'd ever taken with me.

"Very much so. She's a very cool person."

"You seem to talk a lot. What do you talk about?"

"I don't know. Girl stuff. Nothing major."

"And how does that work?" Donuts was scribbling on his notepad, which didn't necessarily mean I'd said something smart.

"What do you mean?" Why was he getting so preschool on me? It was unnerving.

"When you talk about girl stuff, does Nessa participate?" Donuts grabbed a tissue and blew his nose.

"Yes!" I was getting irritated, but tried not to show it.

"How?" Was he serious?

"By opening her mouth and forming words." It was sarcastic, but I couldn't help myself. I tried to calm down.

"No, Beth. Nessa isn't doing that."

I was really losing it now. Was this a test? I needed to be cool and collected. I forced myself to go to a happy place, picturing sand castles on a sunny beach. Cliché, I know, but it released all the tension that was building up from Donuts baiting me. No wonder people felt crazy in here.

"Nessa isn't doing that," he continued in that kindergarten teacher voice, "because she hasn't spoken for over ten years. Nessa is a mute, Beth. She can't speak."

His energy was clear. No static, no garbage, no knots. Doctor Donuts definitely was not lying or screwing with me.

"Because she is a patient, I can't go into detail. But she has something called selective mutism. It is often a response to severe trauma. It can present as a form of post-traumatic stress disorder." He kept speaking about the disorder as if it were the most routine condition in the world. "Nessa hasn't spoken in over a decade."

I tried to stay calm. I tried to review all of my conversations with Nessa in chronological order and determine whether she didn't speak, or if she just kept her hoodies covering her mouth, or if she just didn't talk in front of others. Her mouth was always covered. I guess I had no idea. Was I hearing her in my head? All my confidence went out the door, but I decided to fake it.

"I know," I lied. "I pretty much do all the talking. She doesn't seem to mind, and I guess I really like the company." The doctor scratched his ankle and uncrossed his legs, all relaxed. I tried to cover my anxiety. I had no idea if I'd been conversatin' with a telepathic mute or not, but I needed him to believe I was fine.

Seeing the thoughts, hopes, dreams, and fears of people can be scary. Everyone carries this thick prism of gunk that they see the world through. Each person has layers of stuff, making it hard to see anyone clearly. So until someone invents soul glasses that will remove all distortions from their perceptions? Worrying about what people think? Is a complete waste of time. But then and there I prayed to control his thoughts, transmitting the all-important message *Beth is healthy.* It seemed to work, and I left his office sensing that he was writing nice things about me on that pad of his.

When I saw Nessa an hour later, I was frantic.

"Happy day before your birthday," she said, mouth covered. "He's coming tonight!" She reached in her pocket for something.

"Nessa. Would you take off your hoodie? Please?"

Nessa peered out at me and nodded her head and unzipped her jacket. It was the first time I'd seen her hair flow freely during my entire stay.

She looked at me with so much emotion in her eyes I softened. I couldn't be mad at her.

"Have you been 'speaking' telepathically to me this entire time?" Nessa's eyes widened, her chin bobbing and nodding slightly.

"Most people need notes, like Dolores. I 'head talk' to lots of people." Her eyes filled up with tears; then she smiled and put her hand on my shoulder. "But you're the only one who has ever listened, Beth. You." She sounded happy. Without ever moving her lips.

"If I asked what happened to you, would you tell me? Could you tell me why?" I grabbed her hands and held them tightly. I was touching her with every intention of feelseeing her movies, and it wasn't working. Oddly enough, Nessa laughed.

"I really don't want to talk about it." And then Nessa burst out laughing. Not audibly, but this silent, open-mouthed guffaw, with no sound coming out. She wasn't going to tell me or let me see, and I had to be okay with that. For now.

Her eyes were filling with tears. "I know you have to leave, but I don't want you to go." Nessa embraced me tightly. "I am going to miss you so, so much. I wish everyone wore soul glasses like you, Beth."

Soul glasses. Nessa pulled those words right out of my head! The ability to feelsee all the layers of a person: the good, the bad, the ugly.

"You have to leave tonight, Beth. Midnight. I'm going to help you. You have to get to New York." Nessa was insistent. My armpits started drenching themselves, and I felt a little nauseous.

"It's okay to be scared, and it's okay to fail. But you have to try. Not trying isn't an option." Nessa was squeezing courage into me. I was suddenly so angry she was in here. And angry that I was in here too.

I was determined to unearth the truth, despite this demoralizing chapter and the lying pseudoparent who helped write it. Nessa pressed an envelope into my palm, touching her forehead against my forehead. Then she pulled something out from under her hoodie.

It was a wad of cash and "The Dance of the Seven Veils," the poem Nessa had held on to for me.

"Thank you for seeing both sides of me," she telegraphed. "The one who speaks and the one who doesn't have the words. When you finally find out who you are, come back and tell me sometime. I'll be here if you need me." My throat clogged shut with a hard lump.

"I promise I'll do everything I can to get you out of here." I clutched her, unsure when I'd see her again.

"Same." She smiled knowingly. "Your answers are in New York. Come back and feelsee me sometime, Olive. Okay?" Nessa wiped a tear off her face and pulled her hood back up into position, blowing me a kiss. She did it all without saying a word.

CHAPTER 18

At 12:01 a.m. on November 3rd, my real birthday, I was ready for action. I was released from my room for a shower but headed to the night desk instead. With two grand from Nessa hidden in my waistband, I presented two items to the attending night nurse: my real birth certificate and the name and phone number of an attorney

Nessa had found in the yellow pages. She studied the name. "Aleph Beth? This is a different name, hon."

"That's my real name," I said with as much authority as I could muster. "Check it out if you like." I was bluffing, but I needed the time. As she called the attending physician to approve my release, I thought of all the birthday cakes and presents and parties my fake mom had showered me with over the years. Hosed me with was more like it. I gnashed my jaw from the injustice raging inside me and refused to cry. There wasn't time. I was alone, and no one was going to hold my hand and explain it all to me. That particular gift certificate had expired.

"We can't release you until tomorrow morning. Go back to your room," the attending nurse said quietly. Grooze was stretching tentacles into yoga poses around her.

"I am eighteen. I am of legal age, and if you don't let me out, my attorney and the police department will be here to make sure you follow the law." I was winging it, but she was listening. "You are holding me against my will. I am old enough to sign myself out, and you know it."

"A birth certificate is not a photo ID. If it all checks, you'll be out tomorrow." Her grooze calmed down. It wasn't interested in me, thank goodness, because I had bigger fish to fry. Tomorrow meant Donuts and my mother. Tomorrow wouldn't work. "I need my backpack. My photo ID is in there." I knew it wouldn't match, but I had to try. My adrenaline leaped an inner high jump as I held my ground and raised my voice. "And I'd like to call my attorney. I am not kidding around." She backed up, intimidated. I wasn't sure if she was about to signal security or get my stuff for me.

I was fifty yards from an emergency exit. Out of the corner of my eye I saw Nessa hiding behind the janitorial cart, as we'd planned.

"Hang on, I'm the only one on duty. I'll have to have someone get your belongings out of the locker. Why don't you sign yourself out, while we're waiting?" Big knots formed on ropes between us as she retrieved a document. She was lying, covering her hand with the clipboard as she pressed a red button marked SECURITY. *Damn it.*

I stayed calm and signaled Nessa. Who promptly yanked down the fire alarm. A hellfire of blaring horns and emergency lights reverberated throughout the facility, sending the nurse into a panic. Within seconds the halls filled with any patients who weren't in locked rooms. The night nurse fled her desk to help the staff corral the patients, pointing at me. I hauled ass toward the emergency exit. Without looking back.

The volume of the fire alarms easily covered the shriek of the emergency exit siren. Outside, the cold air hit me like a bitch slap. I ducked behind a tree, letting the adrenaline rush me toward the street. Which direction would get me toward Chicago? I'd planned on jogging to a gas station, using my cash from Nessa, and calling a cab. I watched the exit door, knowing I had just moments before someone would race out to chase me.

And then? I saw something that sent my brains splattering everywhere. As the alarms rang and the sounds of approaching fire trucks filled the air, a guy was leaning against an old car across the street, looking at me. A wave of disbelief passed through me as the guy waved. It was the one. The only. Richie Mac.

A psychiatric aide burst out the door as I ran to his El Camino. I jumped in and ducked down without speaking as he sped away from McCall's. We passed two police cruisers and a fire engine. "He's screaming for help," Richie said. "I'm pretty sure he saw you get in the car." He peeled the car onto a side street, getting me the hell away from the drama.

Sirens followed us in the distance. Richie turned off his lights and drove like a pro down several streets. He pulled into an empty driveway with an open gate. Parking the car and closing the gate behind us, we hid and waited as two police cars flew right past.

"I heard you needed a ride. I didn't know it was going to be a getaway." He looked at me, half smiling, half confused. All cute.

Once I caught my breath, I was panicking for a different reason. There was a very good chance that Richie Mac had heard every single one of my crazy-ass, romance-novel thoughts. That Richie had received unlimited access to my daydreaming and wishing festival. I was mortified.

"Who told you I needed a ride?" Maybe it was a coincidence. *Please, let it be a coincidence!*

"Uh, I'm pretty sure it was, uh, you?" He pointed to the center of his forehead and then pointed to mine, making a back and forth motion with his index finger. "Or should I say your wireless carrier? Beth T&T?"

Up till now, everything that had happened I could cover up. No one knew *exactly* what was going on, but now? I was exposed. Completely naked. And nauseous. Never in my wildest dreams had I seen my day of dreaming turning into this. I stammered, feeling a burp form in my belly. I was suddenly having indigestion, not from breaking out of a psychiatric hospital with cops and fire trucks in my wake, but from my wish buffet. I thought I might throw up, but what would I throw up? Images from all of my girly-ass fantasies? Would little holograms of mini-me and mini-Richie fly out of my mouth? Would mini-we start cavorting around on the sidewalk like a bad telenovela? My ears got hot hot hot with self-consciousness. I wasn't horrified; I was horri-*fried*.

I must've looked woozy, because suddenly Richie nudged my side. "Beth?" he said in a soft voice, grabbing my elbow. "It's okay." I looked into his eyes, my heart pounding in my tonsils and my nose. Thank God I'd showered.

He opened a window and let in some fresh air.

"You look pale. Maybe you should eat something. I know you can't eat meat." My nausea was fading, and I was suddenly overcome with the smell of . . . the smell of Mexican food? "I got some bean and cheese burritos. I don't know why I picked them, but I haven't known why about anything in a while."

I wanted to eat them, but I couldn't. It was the first time, the very first time in weeks? months? maybe my whole entire life— that I didn't feel alone. And that feeling was so good, so strong, so substantial that it made me realize how lonely I'd been feeling. A sense of relief and sadness splashed me into my own personal water park. The feelings pushed me hard down the slide, into the giant pool of relief. I didn't know what to do. And Richie knew it.

"It's gonna be okay." He was watching me closely.

"I'm not crazy?"

"Maybe. Then again, maybe I'm crazy too." Why was he smiling? "But I don't think so. I think 'special' is probably more like it."

I let out this huge sigh so big it was like a tremor. Richie Mac grabbed my hand, electricity shocking us. Instead he traced my wrist really lightly and looked into my eyes.

"This has been really scary lonely," he said.

"I know," I said. It was the truth, and it felt so good to be seen. So really, really seen that I didn't want to stop looking into his eyes.

"We have to go, Beth." Sirens in the distance were getting louder again.

Headlights came around the corner as I instinctively ducked down. After the car passed, Richie opened the gate, turned on the car, and pulled out. He placed a reassuringly kind, gentle hand on my head that made my hair get all staticky. I welled up.

"Let it out. If you need to cry, you can cry while I drive, okay?" He got it. The tears started flowing and the snot started streaming. Everything that hadn't felt safe to express poured out of me. I laid my head on his front seat and released a geyser of snot and sadness. I cried until the tears lulled me into a heavy, drugless sleep.

5 | THE HIEROPHANT | ו

*V*A-VA JOHNSON HAD BEEN MAKING UGLY PRETTY SINCE SHE was old enough to hold a lipstick. She learned to make her freckles disappear by age eight, and after experimenting with colored contact lenses to conceal her topaz irises, she'd taken to wearing sunglasses and head wraps to stop the inevitable gawks at her exotic palette. Golden curls framing yolky golden eyes in a caramel package? It was insane. And then sprinkle in bronze freckles? It was too much to take. Va-Va had grown up with looks that sent men and women into paroxysms of worship or jealousy. People unwrapped her like an unexpected gift every day of her life. So Va-Va simply stopped giving it, displaying it, and sharing it. "You practically a Muslim, girlene!" Daddy Benji would shriek at her. "Take off the burqa!" he screamed on her twenty-first birthday. "You givin' me the creeps with your bag lady outfits!" She never told anyone she would've put her name under wraps if she could have—it would have hurt her dads too much, and Va-Va didn't believe in pain. There was enough of that in the world.

"Va-Va! Get your butt over here and do my makeup! I am later than Santa Claus at Easter, baby!" Papa Frank was on the phone and late for a gig, and the only thing that made him madder than being late was when Va couldn't do his makeup. "Baby doll getting too big for Daddy, honey. I barely see her anymore. Serves me right for raising the greatest hairstylist and makeup artist in the ATL. She don't have time for drag queens now that the prom queens done found her candy ass." Frank smacked Va-Va on the tushie as she fixed his wig and applied his Liza Minnelli makeup in record time. Just as she'd been doing since she was, like, four. "Am I getting too old to do Liza, baby? Do I need to work on Carol Channing?"

Va-Va laughed. "I'm late to meet a client. Have a good show." She kissed his black wig good-bye, remembering the cardinal rule: Never tell a drag queen the truth.

Post-traumatic makeup and wig application was equal

parts psychology and artistry. If someone had been hiding for years because of a scar or a disfiguring something-or-other, they needed a lot more than makeup to help get them out of the house. And whatever that was? Va was full of it. Nobody knew why Va-Va worked with some people and not others. Money couldn't get you an appointment, and a referral didn't always work. Only Va knew why she worked the way she did. Va-Va and whoever had started sending her those gold envelopes by the time she was old enough to read.

But Va-Va worked constantly. When Va-Va mixed foundation on a piece of glass for a client, it was like alchemy. Whenever she poured it into the chamber of her airbrush and shook it miracles came out. Scars disappeared.

"I'm not using primer," Va-Va cooed to Loco, the acne-riddled young man who was a regular client, "because the Accutane is giving you the face dandruff, and I don't want to dry you out even more."

He nodded gratefully. "The Aquaphor is really working. Thank you for that."

His eyes welled up, and she shushed him and turned on some music. "You are gonna rock that prom, baby. Rock it." She gently dabbed the corner of his eyes before any tears could fall. "You handsome, baby. You got so much handsome they should call you hand-more." He laughed as Va-Va sprayed a finishing mist over his perfectly painted, pockmark-scar-free face. He admired his newly clear complexion as Va-Va packed up her stuff. Behind her back he clumsily pulled some crumpled bills out of his pocket and tried to sneak them into her makeup case.

"You better not be spending any corsage money on me, Loco. Put that away right now." Loco froze and knew it was useless. "Don't make me scrape everything off you! Get out and rock the night. If shorty still lovin' on you next week, you bring her by my Smashbox counter and I'll trick her out with some samples, got it?" He kissed her on the cheek before dashing out of her work space.

Even completely covered up, Va-Va was—as her two dads would say—"Not just gorgeous—drop-dead gor-justice!" She loved them so much for adopting her. She'd never had the heart to tell them how badly she'd been beaten up because of her "faggot fathers." Her shrouded look helped Va dodge ignorance and hatred, two bullets her talent couldn't always protect her from.

When Va-Va had turned eighteen she'd received her favorite gold card. She carried it everywhere. Someone had written to her soul in perfect lettering:

I am the one who paints beauty over nothingness. I am the one who sees truth where there is death and numbness. I animate the dead. I pull, I pluck, and I beat things into a rebirth of color and life. I kiss the pale death that life glazes over innocence and reanimate the corpse through light. I am the veil of beauty. Once I am lifted, truth is never the same.

Va-Va sensed an approaching change like a tide, getting closer and closer. The sands of her life were about to shift right beneath her feet. And she couldn't wait.

CHAPTER 20

A BIRD CAWED, AND I AWOKE TO THE FEELING OF sunlight on my right cheek. My left cheek was glued to some flaky, crusty stuff. I slowly pried my face up as drool poured out of my mouth. Then I remembered where I was. It was morning, and I was alone in the front seat of the car. I sat up and looked around. We were at some gas station, and

I could see the pump in the car and Richie in the mini-mart. In the rearview mirror I discovered an enormous strawberry of wrinkles, car-upholstery-seam impressions, dried tears, and crusty booger rivers covering my face. I was thirsty and starving, and I desperately had to pee.

"Is anyone chasing us?" I creaked with a morning frog in my throat as Richie got back to the car.

"Not yet. You need the bathroom? I brought you a change of clothes." He read my mind.

The restroom was clean (thank God!), and I had never been so grateful to pee in my entire life. It was a religious experience! I had no idea what time it was or where this place was, and I was too happy to care. I was free! At least for now. I washed my hands, face, and armpits in the sink and looked at my reflection. Other than the fact that it looked like I had blush and weird imprints on only one side of my face, I was okay. I pulled on the T-shirt and hoodie Richie gave me, and I appeared not happy, but maybe peaceful. I couldn't think about the future, and in truth I didn't want to. I just wanted to keep feeling okay for as long as I could and get to New York City.

When I got outside, Richie had coffees, waters, and food for us. "I decided to keep driving. I figured it might be safer than the airport. In case there is an APB out on you."

I nodded as I shoved food in my face. I tried to eat delicately, but my hunger made that impossible. I would've consumed everything through every orifice of my body if possible; I was that starved. I must've eaten fast, because when I looked up, Richie was staring at me like I was on fire.

"I'm a little hungry." I was getting no feelsees from the food, thank goodness. I could eat in peace.

"You? Hungry? You don't say?"

"And I have this slight headache." I really did.

"It's a dehydration headache. Crying can dehydrate you. Take it from me." He said it really quietly, and it made me regret any mean or judgmental thought I'd ever had about him. I was fully teetering on this tightrope between feeling completely comfortable and totally awkward. And we hadn't even touched on the soul glasses or what was happening to us. Which was kind of completely thrilling.

"Another thing that can dehydrate you? Extreme loss of nasal mucus. A highly underrated fluid." He started wiping something off his right leg while looking at me, and I realized his jeans were covered in what I was pretty sure was dried snot.

"Don't worry," he said with a smile. "Better for the environment this way. Less snot rags for the landfill." And then he laughed.

"What?" Mortification swept through me.

"Your head slid near my leg while you were crying, I guess. My thigh was soaking wet for hours. I didn't know jeans could get that wet. I guess all that snot kept us from getting electrocuted, or something."

"Shut up!" I said while playfully hitting him, which literally created little sparks of electricity. We got back in the car, where he pulled a map out of his back pocket and we started driving again.

"I called my brother." He scratched his neck, and I could see stubble growing in. "He's going to call if we need a heads-up. Otherwise, if anyone asks? He doesn't know anything." I remembered Bordens and wondered if Ryan had told the story to Richie.

"You know, my best friend is obsessed with your brother." I needed to float it out there.

"Oh, no—I hope she didn't—" He shook his head, horrified.

"Participate in his attempt to break the world record in deflowering young women everywhere? She tried."

"Condom on her locker?" He winced.

"Yes, actually. But I'm pretty sure she put it there."

"What? Why would anyone do that?"

"Because they wanted attention and were obsessed with your brother."

"And wanted to look like a slut? He never sleeps with girls more than once." I didn't think that was true for Jenny Yedgar, but I didn't say anything. If he could read that thought, he'd have to ask me.

"I think she was jealous, kind of maybe." I wasn't sure I wanted to go down this road, but there I went.

"Really? Of what?"

"Of the fact that I kissed you. Since you're related to Ryan, that makes it complicated for her."

"Excuse me. But I believe I kissed you," he corrected me. "Now that I know you better, I would've done that differently." His lips were pursed, and he raised his eyebrow knowingly. The air was flirty, filled with the fact that we hadn't kissed again.

"Instead of pretending it was my birthday?"

"No, I still would've done that. That was a great line."

"That was a terrible line, dude," I blurted, and he laughed when I said it.

"It worked on you!"

He was enjoying this. He turned to me with a sly smile and said, "You got inside me when we kissed, Beth. And you made me feel—it was really . . ." He got self-conscious and trailed off and sipped his coffee. I willed myself to breathe in the moment. I could smell his skin and wanted to brush against him, but I pretended to be watching the road ahead of us.

"Okay. I have directions to New York," he said, changing the subject. "But I'm kinda tired."

"Yeah?" I wasn't sure what he wanted me to do.

"Um, would you mind driving for a bit so I can get some sleep? The coffee isn't working." He stifled a yawn.

"Oh, yes, of course. Sorry."

"Are you sure?" He was trying to be a gentleman and not ask for help.

We switched positions, and I got behind the wheel. We drove out of God-only-knows what town as Richie Mac slept and snored. For miles I drove with my hand near his head. I'd secretly static his soft hair with our electricity whenever I could.

We'd been driving for a few hours, avoiding highways. It was taking longer, but we finally found a roadside diner on Route 30 somewhere outside Lima, Ohio. During lunch Richie finally decided to embarrass me.

"Surfing in Sydney, huh? Massages in the Maldives?"

"Oh, no."

"I saw a lot, Beth. It definitely wasn't coming from my internal cineplex."

"Oh, God." I buried my head in my arms. It was too humiliating for words.

"That your El Camino?" our waitress asked as she poured more coffee. Richie nodded. I kicked him under the table for being so stupid. "The cook wants to know what year it is. He fixes up cars and stuff."

"I think it's an '81," Richie mumbled, looking at me helplessly. Our waitress didn't bat an eyelash and headed back to the kitchen.

"Congratulations on making it easier for authorities to identify us, dude."

"Congratulations on getting into Columbia, by the way." He was trying to cover his gaffe.

I whispered, "I guess those plans are kind of on hold. Indefinitely."

"We should probably talk about what you wanna do when we get to New York. I say we go straight to 7RI—"

I noticed a state trooper pull into the parking lot. I was suddenly cold-sweatsville.

"Don't panic," Richie said in between bites of eggs, "but have you noticed that other car out there?" It stood out because the motor was running, yet there wasn't a driver.

"What? No." My head spun nervously toward the parking lot.

"Illinois plates." He discreetly picked some food out of his teeth. "Between the state trooper and that car, I think it's time to bail." He slid some money onto the table. "Go to the restroom and wait for my cue."

I quickly slipped toward the exit and into the pink-tiled bathroom. I washed my face and hands and tried combing my hair out with my fingers. I used the facilities and washed my hands again. What was taking so long? There was a small window, and I stood on the radiator and peered out into the backyard of the building. An ugly green station wagon pulled up, and Richie jumped out to help me. "Let's go, go, go—" I heaved myself up and out the small window, practically pulling my pants off in the process.

"Ouch!" We jolted each other as Richie caught me. I ducked into the filthy car.

"The cook gave me a shortcut in exchange for the El Camino."

"If by shortcut you mean piece of crap car, nice job!" I teased, secretly thrilled by our maneuvers.

"We gotta keep driving. Fast as we can."

Between me hoping that I looked good in profile and cautiously wondering if Richie Mac and I were ever going to make out again, he interrupted my thoughts.

"You look great. You always look beautiful, by the way. Don't worry." Busted! It was sweet enough, but I prayed his all-access pass to my inside scoop stopped somewhere. Then, I realized I'd drunk too much OJ.

"You have to pee again, huh?" He sighed.

Dammit! It was easy to forget he could read my mind when he was so thoughtful and gorgeous. This led to other inconvenient thoughts, like, *Must stop wondering about kissing in front of Richie.*

"It doesn't matter if you're thinking about me or the can when you're next to me or if you are far away, remember?" Richie did a "ha-haaaaah" chuckle that was pretty smug.

"Could you not call it 'pee'? Or 'the can'? Could you say 'restroom' or 'powder room'?"

"But that's not what you think. I'm just repeating what you think—don't get all fancy with me."

This was really irritating. What was he thinking? How come I wasn't picking up on that? I felt like he was actually blocking my thoughts. Like maybe he knew something I didn't? But beyond that? I was receiving no signal on Radio Richie.

"So if you pick up on my thoughts, how come I'm not picking up on yours?"

"Good question. But we have more urgent problems than that right now. Like a *restroom*. And fuel. Just in case the word 'gas' offends you." Richie rolled his eyes and pulled off at the next exit before I peed myself.

"See? You thought the word pee again!"

"Get out of my head!" I wanted to kill him.

"A minute ago you wanted my tongue in your mouth, and now you want to kill me? Make up your mind, woman."

It was the first time anyone had called me "woman." And I kinda liked it.

"There's a first time for everything, Beth." And Richie smiled at me so hard I thought my cheeks would burn, inflate, and explode with all of it.

I had to pee so badly I didn't even care about the car following us or Richie reading my mind, listening to things I really didn't want him listening to. We pulled in to a gas station and I leaped out of the car in a scramble toward the facilities.

"I will wait for you outside the restroom."

"No!!" He was testing me.

"I can't leave you in there alone."

"Come on!!" This was really undignified.

"Beth. It's not safe. Deal with it."

He wasn't budging, so I figured I'd have to run water.

"You can run water if you don't want me to hear anything."

"Oh, God." I felt so naked.

"It's not like you're naked."

"Stop reading my mind!"

"Now you know how other people feel!"

As he escorted me to the dingy restroom, I had an idea.

"Why don't you try sending me some thoughts for a change? Then I'll know you are not pee-vesdropping." I slammed the door and turned the faucet on full blast. I was busy making a toilet-paper seat cover, but that didn't stop him from yelling over the faucet noise.

"I have to go next. You're going to have to stand facing

away from me while I go 'cause I'm not letting you out of here alone."

Oh, brother. I had to do more than pee. There was no way I was letting him in this bathroom when I was done.

"I'm coming in. Open up!" he yelled.

"You are NOT coming in here next!" I yelled.

"I'll hold my nose." He laughed.

"It's not *that* bad." This wasn't happening.

"Oh, it's happening! I'm coming in there."

"Then get me some matches. The door is locked. I'll be fine." Humiliation, thy name is Beth.

"Come on, Beth." He was totally messing with me.

"Hold it or find another bathroom." He was silent. "And get me some matches or I won't come out of here." I wanted to die.

I was trying to wave the smell away when I realized something was wrong. Again. I waited for Richie a minute and then two and then three, and I started to get nervous. *If anyone is listening,* I said to myself, *keep Richie safe and help me.*

I peeked outside. Our car was there. I headed out and Richie appeared, waving me urgently toward the car.

"Let's go. Don't argue."

"Where'd you go?" He was wiping something black off his hands.

"Get in the car!"

"No. That really scared me! Where'd you go?"

"Get in the car, Beth!"

I got in, but I was annoyed and told him with my thoughts to back off.

"I'm trying to help you," he answered.

"I know! Stop telling me what we need!"

"Beth. Shit. Some cars with Illinois plates are pulling in." I blinked into my sight, but it was of no use. I couldn't see a thing.

Richie peeled us out of the gas station, and the nondescript car with Illinois plates was right behind us. Moving fast. Alongside two other sedans with Illinois plates.

"Who are they?" I looked and tried to get some kind of reading on the cars, but I couldn't. All I could see was the obvious: There were three cars tailing us. Fast. I cranked my neck and watched them following us, looking for a color, a rope, a dot—anything!—to tell me who they were and what they wanted. I turned around.

"Your mom probably hired someone—or it's unmarked cop cars."

"Or it's our friends in New York?" I slumped down in the front seat, focusing on the cars and wishing they'd go away.

"Hang on." Richie swerved as one car pulled up alongside us and sped in front. "Another guy's behind us, and the third is trying to pull into the passing lane."

"What now?" I asked Richie. "Should we pull over? Talk to them?"

"We're the only four cars on this road. It doesn't feel safe." We were on a four-lane blacktop with a dividing patch. Richie's car was going seventy miles per hour, and the only escape was across the divider strip going the other direction.

"You think I can make it?" he asked, reading my mind.

"Should we pretend to pull over and gun it?"

"Or we could just gun it—" And with that, Richie made a hard left into the divider. The green wagon lifted in the air as we hit uneven turf and then jackknifed into a U-turn into the opposite lane. My body slid into him, and the electricity began jolting us. The force of the turn wouldn't let me pull away. Our hair and bodies were sizzling with electrical current.

"Go, go, go, go, go!" I yelled, watching the three cars skid and slide into chaos across the divider. As we raced in the opposite direction, transformer sparks began cascading down on either side of us. The power lines turned into giant sparklers, raining fire behind us.

"Whoa," Richie and I said simultaneously. In the distance I could see all three cars fishtailing out of control, careening dangerously close to each other and dodging the fire showers. The second I pulled away from Richie, the power lines stopped their pyrotechnics.

Our pursuers far behind, we increased our lead, racing off onto side roads as quickly as we could. We sped north, both of us silent from the chase and our impromptu firecracker. I broke the silence. "I wonder what would happen if we did that in water." I laughed.

Richie was all business and changed the subject. "Now they know what this car looks like, we should probably hide out. If we can find a motel with parking off the street, we'll hide there until dark." We headed northeast about thirty minutes until we found exactly what we were looking for.

The Laugh Inn was a perfect dump of a motel, with units and parking away from the street. Richie parked in back and then walked up front to pay with Nessa's cash. I hid under his coat in the car, nervously wondering what would happen once we were in the motel room. I didn't know anything except that we'd continue our magical mystery tour under the cloak of night.

The place seemed deserted as we snuck into room eleven. "I know you'd rather have two rooms in case nature calls, but I can't let you be by yourself. And the manager thinks I'm here alone."

Maybe his telepathic powers weren't working after all, I thought. There was no idea more appealing to me than being alone in a room with Richie Mac! As we got our key and snuck into our room, he smiled. I cursed myself for having romantic thoughts in front of him.

"Or maybe you should just be honest about your intentions." Richie smirked at me in the hottest way possible.

"I have no intentions," I lied as we settled into the clean room.

"Okay, then. Be honest about your feelings."

"I have no feelings." We looked at each other in silence for a good long minute before bursting out laughing. I was really stupid when I liked someone. But at least I was funny. After the laughter died down, there we were, looking at each other.

"Thank you for helping me." I meant it.

"Don't thank me. We don't really know who these 7RI people are, but . . . as far as intentions go, I think their intentions are good."

"What makes you say that? They could be the guys following us for all we know."

"I don't know. Maybe I don't know what 7RI's intentions are, and I'm hoping they're good so I don't have to be more freaked out than I already am."

"Okay, so who cares what their intentions are? What are your intentions?" If he could read my thoughts, I might as well just speak them.

"To get you to New York. Maybe find out why this is happening to you and me, or if it's permanent." I hadn't considered the permanence and didn't want to. "And make sure you are safe."

"That's it?" I moved closer to him. The electricity started charging like it had in the car, and my hair became staticky. We stood there, our strands of hair reaching out and entwining with each other. The pull of the static from his head to mine was so strong it was tugging my long strands at the roots.

"Beth—" His breathing got heavier. I caught our reflection in the mirror; we looked like we were trapped in a plasma orb. "There's nothing I want more than to touch you again, but I don't think this is a good idea."

"Why not?" I knew the answer, but wanted him to say it.

"Because electricity is literally zapping between us when our heads get too close?"

"Really?" I smiled, feeling so pulled into this current that I couldn't pull back. "I hadn't noticed." I got closer, and our hair was entangling in a wild dance of static mambo. I put my face as close to his as I could stand. My skin was burning from the heat of proximity.

"Don't you feel that?" I asked. My heart was pounding.

"Yes." Richie closed his eyes.

"Doesn't it feel nice?"

"Un"—he took a breath—"be"—another breath—"lievable." He was gently tipping his body toward mine.

"I think we're supposed to try—" I let my lips graze his lips. A violent crack ripped through us. The jolt threw me five feet backward into the air onto the bed and catapulted Richie into the television in the corner, knocking him onto the floor.

"Beth! Are you okay?" He winced, not okay in the least.

"Wow" was all I could muster.

"I don't think I'm ready for that."

"Yeah. Me neither." We were now terrified of each other all over again. And all I wanted was a hug.

"I know what you mean," he said.

"About wanting a hug?"

"Yeah. This has been kinda lonely, huh?"

I nodded, frustrated. We looked at each other across the room, dazed by what had just happened. We wanted to kiss each other.

"Why didn't that happen in the car? When my head was draining the entire contents of my sinuses onto your lap?" I half smiled from across the room.

"Either the moisture killed it, or maybe because that wasn't, you know, uh, 'charged'?"

"Speak for yourself," I joked to cut the tension, "but when I'm in the mood, I have found the snot faucet can really seal the deal. Most guys dig it."

"Yeah, snot glue is a real deal-sealer." He was rubbing his scalp, and I noticed that mine was still a little sensitive from the electrical tugging.

"I know it's random, but do you know what they call the layer of your scalp near the hair root?" It was stupid how much I knew about hair. But when you're a nerd who loves her hair as much as I did, hair-formation was a necessity.

"I don't know. But I have a feeling you do." He laughed.

"Would you believe it's called the horny layer?"

"No, it's not! You are making that up!"

"I swear. Isn't that funny?" I was scratching my scalp for emphasis. "My horny layer hurts!" We started laughing so hard I almost forgot where we were.

"Does the electricity happen if we touch feet?" he wondered aloud.

We crossed the room and pointed our toes at each other. It generated an electric microcurrent. Richie started looking for something, as if he had an idea.

"Have you listened to music much since this started happening to you?" My cheeks got pinker than bubble gum.

"Yes." I wondered if he'd had iPod-gasms, too.

"Can you see, I mean feel . . . people . . . doing things?"

"Uh-huh." I nodded, and really dragged out the word.

"Pretty rad, right?" He shook his head like it was the greatest thing ever. I was self-conscious, but I could not argue.

"I can't believe that's happening to you, too."

"That I can deal with. I have an idea." Richie got up and fished around in his bag for something. "Now—don't be mad, but I have this thing called a headphone doubler. So two people can listen at once?"

"So you can seduce girls to your favorite playlist?" I joked. Richie put this two-headed cable into his iPod and connected two sets of earphones. I started to take my shoes off.

"Better leave your sneakers on in case we get shocked again. And keep one hand in your pocket."

"Why?"

"It'll prevent any shock from making a path—"

"Oh, right. Respect all voltages," I said in a deep voice.

"What's that?"

"This saying from an old science class. 'Remember, kids, it's not the voltage but the current that kills. Respect all voltages.'"

He went somewhere with his eyes and I was trying to block all thoughts of his mouth from my brain. I wanted to feel his pillowy, kissable lips again and smell his yumminess.

"Yeah. I remember my dad was planning on cutting this scary power wire outside our house. He had my mother stand there with a wooden plank, and he said, 'If I get shocked, just knock me over with the two-by-four.' I was terrified."

"That he'd get shocked?"

"No. That my mom wouldn't hit him if he did get shocked."
He snorted. "She hated him."

"What happened?"

"My dad cut the wire. Nothing happened. And she hit him anyway. Knocked him out cold." He shook his head as a slow, stunned giggle eked out. Then Richie Mac started snorting so hard, tears were streaming down his face, and it made me laugh too.

I tried to talk in between gasps for air. "What did you do?"

"I started crying." This made him snort even harder. "My mom is not the most reliable lady." We laughed until it trailed off into sighs.

"At least you know who your mom is." It felt strange to say it. The truth brought us right back to earth. My desire for him was scratching at my insides, scrambling to get out.

"Here. Put these on. We'll lie head to feet. Keep one foot on the floor, maybe . . ." He placed the iPod between us, and I put my head on a pillow.

"What are you going to play?"

"Something good. I think you'll like it."

"Wait." I got really nervous and self-conscious about what we were about to do.

"What? Are you okay? I'm sorry—I didn't even ask you if you wanted to—" Richie suddenly felt bad, I could tell.

"No, it's just—I wish it were with you."

"You are with me. If it's too weird, we don't have—"

"No. Let's."

I laid my head back on the pillow and took a deep breath, barely able to contain my excitement. I had no idea what song he was going to play, and this added to my shiver fest.

"You're wondering what song I'm going to play, right?"

I smiled. "This is not fair."

"Would it make you feel better if I told you that . . . after we kissed, and stuff started happening? This song popped in my head. I'd never heard it before. So, the first time I listened to this song, I thought of you."

I actually blushed.

"I want to hear it. Don't tell me any more."

And Richie carefully handed me the headphones, placing the iPod between us. He bent his leg at the knee (so I wouldn't smell his feet?), kept one foot on the floor, and lay back. There we were, head to toes on a bed in the middle of nowhere. I couldn't help myself and sat up. I was scared of doing something stupid. Or wrong.

"What if it's weird?"

He propped himself up on an elbow, worried. "We don't have to—" He was concerned.

"No, I just—I mean, this might—"

"Get embarrassing?" His smile put me at ease. I nodded. "It won't. I mean, maybe it will. But that's part of the fun. So, is it okay if I embarrass myself in front of you?" He was being sweeter than I'd ever seen him. I nodded again, smiling.

"Is it okay if I embarrass myself in front of you?" I wanted to double-check. I mean, this was sex without the sex, pretty much. "I guess you don't have to wear a condom." I laughed nervously. "I mean, this is probably the safest sex there is." *Oh, Beth, shut up!* I thought.

"How about this? If it's too much or too weird, just pull the earphones out and I'll do the same. Okay?" He waited for me to nod. "You're safe, Beth."

I believed him. I flopped back down onto the pillow and waited for Richie Mack to press play. I felt his leg pressing against my leg, and I closed my eyes, exploding with nervous excitement. And then a guitar played. The opening guitar from my favorite song in the universe. He knew. Richie Mac knew my favorite song without me saying a word. Tears welled up in my eyes that he was playing my number one personal anthem, and something like a roller coaster drop whooped into my throat from the sheer joy of it.

Foreign breath was compressing me now, a heavily charged panting coursing through my body as if someone were breathing me. I felt a tongue in my ear, and the light wetness contracted every tiny muscle at the base of every tiny hair on my body, showering me in goose bumps, tightening my stomach in the most delicious blur. I saw Richie's body move out of the corner of my eye. His bent leg was moving slightly.

The song soared and my arms flew over my head, and light fingers were brushing themselves against my skin—soft mouth, lips, and tongue kissing me deeply but feather-light. My body groaned, and my foot flexed as newness coursed through me. I gasped as my body lifted slightly off the bed, my legs entwined, something beautiful engulfing my entire being.

That's when I felt a tap on my leg sinking me back down onto the bed. It was Richie, propped up, looking at me, motioning me to prop myself up as this wave peaked. Staring into each other's eyes and breathing in sync was too much. I closed my lids, and he tapped me again. I opened them and we were locked in a gaze, eyes wide open, visible waves of electricity coursing between our pupils. I was all dizzy with the music and the headphones and his eyes and then, and then, and then—it elevated us. Our bodies surged with a huge transference of electricity, lifting us off the bed and levitating us over the mattress in suspended orgasmination. All the while looking into each other's eyes. Pupils, rods and cones, and infinity sparking lights into my heart, my spine, my cells. We were floating and generating current, pulsing and convulsing in our own electrical storm. His head jerked back and I saw him scream. Mine yanked back too, constricting every fiber in me, and I screamed as more intensity released. We both fell back onto the bed, off the magic carpet. Collapsing as Justin Timberlake finished singing. . . .

"I'm love stoned and I could swear that she knows. I think that she knows. She knows, she knows."

I watched Richie shake off the last moments of colossal buzz. Letting him pull the thoughts right out of my head.

"You wanna go again?"

I think my smile said it all. And when we finally collapsed hard into the deep of sleep many hours later, I had the sweetest rest of my life.

6 THE LOVERS

*Z*ARA O'CONNOR HAD ALWAYS FELT LIKE SHE WAS missing something, for every second of her nineteen years. She felt like she had been part of a pod and then that pod disappeared. It was like there was a time before she even understood time, and that was where she had remembered feeling safe and sound and connected.

Connected to something or someone, and her life was this constant struggle to reconnect. To reconnect to something she didn't even distinctly remember. Zara felt like she was walking around with this giant power cord and plug that needed to find its proper socket before she could do anything with her life. Zara's lack of socket made her feel completely lost, completely disconnected from everything around her. Or maybe that was just because she was the only ruby-eyed, dark-skinned girl with superwhite parents living in South Bend, Indiana.

Z's cornrows, piercings, and dark kohl eyeliner couldn't conceal her purply-pink eyes. Or the fact that she was flat-out smokin'. All the ugly in Indiana couldn't hide it. Her mom used to lie and tell her she was *not* adopted. That she was rescued. But Zara knew something got left behind. Something she had dreams and nightmares about with alarming regularity. Sometimes her dreams didn't even feel like her dreams; they felt like someone else's. Even the music she heard in her head sounded like somebody else was writing it. Sending it to her, zipping it through her. Becoming a DJ was the only thing that made the noise go away. If she couldn't connect, she could get lost. Mixing beats and mash-ups had become an obsession to the point of distraction. It felt like if she followed it long enough, it would lead her where she was going, but she didn't know where or why. Or, more importantly, when.

Zara's fave spot, My Big Twelve Inch, was a former record store that had morphed into a DJ hangout. The store still sold twelve-inches and turntables, since any DJ with any pride had to know how to needle drop. Z could juggle a beat or cut and scratch, but these days laptops had replaced turntables, and her mixing board was really the keyboard on a MacBook Pro. Trading and sharing MP3s was much easier than converting vinyl to digital. But Zara didn't care about easier, and she'd been slowly, painstakingly converting as much vinyl as her hard drives would hold. DJs worshipped her for it. Which was why people always shared their good stuff with Zara. She held some serious keys to an analog/digital kingdom, but she didn't post her mother lode on LimeWire or Napster. If you wanted Zara's stuff? You'd have to barter with her. If she didn't trust you? It didn't matter how good the trade was. You wouldn't get a byte.

Zara was converting "Say I'm Your Number One"—an old twelve-inch by a one-hit wonder named Princess—when it arrived. Inside the package was audio gold: an underground mix CD from a Detroit DJ who'd bartered with Z for her infamous Bad Brains bootlegs. Lovingly referred to as the Triple Bs, these were the sort of one-of-a-kind treasure Z had painstakingly converted from cassette. The TBs didn't come cheap. Zara had heard about a female MC in Flint who spat some genius rhymes. She told the guy that if he wanted the Triple Bs, he'd have to find the rhymesmith and deliver the goods first. The note inside said, *Is this her???? Crah-zay-zay!*

Zara put the CD in her laptop and downloaded it. The first track was a girl spitting syllabic over the Swiss Beatz sample from "Bring 'Em Out" by TI. It didn't sound human at first, just this lunatic combination of melody and beatbox. There was no way to describe what Zara heard on that mix, because it was indescribable. No one could understand the MC's rhymes; they were rhythmic nonsense. But Z finally felt plugged. She listened from inside the pocket of the rhyme and heard ideas and words where others heard an MC spitting incomprehensible strings of verbal double Dutch. Zara understood it was a language, and she started translating every syllable into English like a hip-hop scholar.

"What a waste of time," her mother said, catching Z listening to the same fragment over and over. But Z knew different. Z heard lyrics that sounded like prophecies about legends about miracles. Z also knew she had heard the only thing in her life that sounded like her future.

A few days later, a single state north of Zara in Detroit, Michigan, a similar argument was taking place. "Did I black out?" was the question Innee always asked after battling. "I guess I repeat the same rhyme to the same beat, but I can't remember it when I'm done or before I start. It's the weirdest thing—I think I'm blacking out or something—I just don't remember. Until I hear it back. Then I remember it perfectly. So I listen and I try to keep writing it in a journal to keep it all straight in my mind. Nobody understands my rhymes anyway. No big."

Innee's name, legend had it, came from the belly button of the same name. No one knew exactly where she'd gotten her amethyst eyes, and Innee knew better than to believe that purple eyes were "common in Lebanon." The only two things she knew about her life before adoption: It started far away in Lebanon, and there was a lot she didn't know.

For months Innee had been making a demo with Detroit producers Phatty and Phreaque. The producing duo were trying to understand how the young MC worked. It was difficult to replicate her sound take after take. The room was beyond tense.

"If you change the music, the rhyme will change is all. I've recorded myself enough to know this. If you change the music, the rhyme will change." Innee was insistent.

"How can you call what you do a rhyme? It don't even mean anything. Time is money." Phatty was being a jerk, and he failed to understand her style.

"Call it whatever you wanna call it, Phatty. I don't care. I hear music. I flow. It's a story in its own language. Whatever." Innee had a confidence beyond her years, and it both impressed and galled people.

"You tryin' to tell me you sayin' somethin'? That same gibberish over and over? Sounds like you just makin' it up as you go along." Phreaque didn't like her, and it showed.

Innee really didn't need this. Recording was not a big deal to her, and the idea of being famous wasn't at the top of her list. She couldn't explain what she did or how she did it. She just did it.

"Don't you want a career?" Even the engineer was annoying her.

"I don't care if I do a single or a whole record. You wanna work with me? Do the track and I'll do my thing. You don't wanna work with me? Somebody else will come along." Innee just stood there, not caring, looking down at the bling of a big-shot producer like it was a turd. "Love me or leave me, baby. But I ain't laying down shit without a contract. And that's the truth whether you believe my rhymes are goofy or Gucci."

"It's a demo deal—" Phatty was notorious for ripping kids off, and Innee wasn't having it.

"Is the 'demo' for 'demo-ralize'? Because you're not gonna demoralize me by making me beg for this. Love me or leave me. Love will get you everything. Anything else is for chumps—" Innee was interrupted by the abused assistant they called Shiny.

"There's a call for you," Shiny chirped meekly.

"We are doing business. Take a number," Phreaque barked.

"You are doing business. I make love. Not war." Innee stood up and walked toward Shiny, grabbed the cell phone right out of her hand, and walked out of the room. "You looking for me?"

"Is this MC Tongue?" It was the eeriest thing—the voice on the other end of the phone sounded familiar.

Innee softened. "Who you looking for?"

"MC Tongue? 'Cause you rap in tongues?"

"Who wants to know?"

"DJ Z. I want to meet you. I'm in Detroit." And suddenly Innee had an urge to hug this person. She had to meet this girl, like, immediately. And she didn't know why. "Meet me at Street Corner Music. Thirteen Mile and Southfield."

"When?"

"Now." Innee hung up, set the phone down, and left without even saying good-bye.

Half an hour later Zara was poring over the huge vinyl collection when she smelled something like warm chocolate velvet pouring over her body. Not real hot fudge, but, like, emotional chocolate. She would describe the feeling for the rest of her life as her velvet chocolate moment. Something so warm, smooth, and delicious—like a blanket of hot fudge—poured over her entire being the second she heard the little bell on the door ring. Looking up was like being pulled into the embrace of someone you loved and lost so long ago you almost forgot they existed. Zara and Innee felt each other at the exact same moment, because they weren't looking at each other. They were looking at themselves.

"Holy fishes! Yo, you twins or something?" some hesher in the store yelled out.

Innee and Zara couldn't respond. They stood there seeing, feeling, smiling, and crying. Knowing that the holes that made the pain finally had the plug. Through the joyful tears Zara reached into her pocket, handing Innee the message in a gold envelope that her heart had memorized long ago:

I am the one who mirrors you back to you. I can shine or
I can shatter, piercing all illusion with my edges. I teach
the black and the white, the dark and the light. As above,
so below. As within, so without. Look at me. And see all
you believe.

CHAPTER 22

I DON'T KNOW WHAT TIME IT WAS WHEN RICHIE started gently saying my name. "Beth? We have to leave soon, much as I hate to. I ordered some food." He was smiling, and as I stretched like a cat to wake up, I realized that I was mush, my body flooded with dopamine and oxytocin from our adventures in mutual autoeroticism.

There was a knock on the motel door and the smell of fresh, hot pizza. I turned to catch Richie paying a delivery guy, and I realized that the pizza that triggered my first feelsee felt like ages ago. Richie opened the box, and the smell was delicious. I laughed.

"I'm not getting anything off of this pizza!" I grabbed a piece and shoveled it into my mouth without incident. "No feelings from the dairy cows, the wheat harvest, the yeasty doughy journey, or the lives of every employee who had anything to do with this magnificent creation!" It was heaven. I was eating faster than I could manage, and I leaped toward the sodas Richie had ordered, sipping frantically so I could swallow. "It's a birthday miracle!"

Richie was chewing, silently studying me with a shine on his face. "Did you just dream about dogs chasing you?"

It was true. My heart leaped. "Yes!" Then dropped. "You can see my dreams, too? Why can't I see yours? This is so unfair!" I wanted a two-way street! What happened to the two-way street of our first kiss? I wanted that insanity again.

"I don't usually have dreams," he answered without really addressing my question. "I sleep pretty hard, as you've probably noticed with my snoring." A piece of cheese dangled from the corner of his mouth, and it amazed me how sweet it was. Why were the things that grossed us out with some people adorable with others?

"I know what you mean," Richie added, clearly eavesdropping on my thoughts. I dragged myself up and splashed water on my face and looked in the mirror. I looked good! My skin was glowing and my eyes were sparkling, and despite the fatigue my body felt fantastic. Clearly the benefits of love had not been understated. I heard him laugh.

"Love is not overrated, huh?"

"Stop me-eavesdropping." I was smiling as I said it.

"I can't help it! It's all coming from you. Like, you have this noise and I'm automatically getting the echo." He seemed as confounded as I was. "I don't think it works both ways, to tell you the truth."

"Well, that's annoying, unfair, and a whole list of bad words. It should work both ways!"

"You can sleep some more in the car, but we really have to get going. We lost a lot of time. It'll be light soon."

"Can I at least shower?"

"There's no time—I don't know where they are. You can sleep some more in the car."

We hustled out of there, and when we'd been driving about twenty minutes, I realized I couldn't sleep. The electrical charge between us was too much for me to rest. My entire face was still buzzing. I started massaging my face to see if it was actually vibrating or just felt that way. Suddenly Richie blurted, "Alright, alright, alright!" hitting his ears.

"Do you feel that too?" I couldn't get it to stop.

"Uh—I'm not sure. You mean the chronic face buzzing?" Richie made a buzzing sound.

"Body buzzing too."

"Yeah. I hope we didn't overdo it. There are some unknowns at work."

He was right. "I guess that means you don't normally levitate when you make out. Or have electricity shooting out of your eyes?" He laughed as if I should know better, so I covered. "Are you having any visions since we've been driving together?"

"Other than hearing your thoughts? All of your thoughts? No." I wondered if my visions were going away before I'd fully understood them.

"Beth, I really don't think it's going away."

"You don't?" I just wanted to know who I was. "Was I born with this? Or did I catch it like a virus and give it to you? Maybe it disappears like a flu?"

"No. I think we're buffering it somehow."

"Does it get buffered from—" I couldn't bring myself to say it: I was wondering if it had to do with attraction.

"I think it's more than just attraction." He smiled.

"Again with the answering my thoughts."

"You think physical attraction is muting your visions?"

"I don't know." I really didn't.

"Are you saying that you are attracted to me?" Richie was pretending not to know the answer to that, which was incredibly cute.

"I don't know—I mean, I don't get the sense that you're attracted to me," I teased. "So that couldn't be it."

"You don't think I'm attracted to you?" He sounded shocked. "I've been drooling all over you since the minute I met you."

"But you're a player. You kinda drool over everyone."

"Not true. Drooling and playing are two different things. And with you? I should wear a bib." I got all shy, but I knew he knew that I felt the exact same way.

CHAPTER 23

E GOT QUIET AS THE SUNLIGHT BEGAN PEEKING OVER the eastern horizon, illuminating the empty interstate in front of us. We rode quietly for a moment, relishing the warmth of the sun as it lit everything up. I was enjoying watching the light shimmering off of a distant stream of water when I noticed something under the windshield wiper. There, pressed against the glass of Richie's car, was an envelope. A gold envelope.

"What's that? Pull over." I pointed to it just to make sure it was there.

"Looks like a gold envelope to me." Richie pulled over and plucked it off the glass.

"Maybe it fell out of my bag?" I wondered aloud, knowing it wasn't true.

Richie handed me the envelope, which was addressed to Aleph Beth Ray. It was a little damp. And unopened.

"They found us at the motel?"

"They certainly found the car."

I couldn't get my brain around it. I ripped it open, scared to see what was inside. It turned out my fearsees were right. The block lettering read:

GET TO NEW YORK, OR YOUR
MOTHER WILL DIE.

My heart stopped. It had been okay when they were messing with me, but now they were threatening my mom? As angry as I was about her, I knew they probably weren't joking around. Richie silently started the car and kept driving east.

"Give me your cell phone. I have to call my mother." Richie produced it without hesitation. I dialed the house. No answer. I dialed her cell phone—no answer. I didn't leave messages. I didn't know what to do or say. These dueling swords were fencing inside me: One side wanted to stab her, while the other needed to fight off the enemy and make sure she was okay.

"I'm sure she's fine" was all Richie could muster.

"No, you're not sure. And she's not picking up."

"There's probably some explanation. They didn't say she was dead; the note says 'or your mother will die,' right? So she can't be dead yet."

None of it made either of us feel better. There was nothing to say, but I couldn't help myself. "So. This is Ohio?"

After several silent hours, dozens of unsuccessful attempts to reach my mom, and a couple gas station stops in Ohio and Western Pennsylvania, Richie pulled off the road and into a strip mall in the middle of nowhere.

"What are you doing? We have to keep going." I'd felt so tense since reading the envelope. I was getting a headache.

"There's a Kinkos!" I had no idea why we were stopping, but I was way too tired and anxious to argue. "We need to stretch and you need to lighten up. There's not much we can do from here." It was true. Richie produced two old baseball hats from the backseat and handed one to me. "Incognito, anyone?"

As we entered, I pulled my baseball hat down over my eyes.

"Hat off," he said, and I obeyed. "Say cheese!" He quickly took the photo with his cell and commandeered a computer in the public computer area. Two employees were frowning over a video security camera hanging out of the wall, clearly in a disagreement.

The mulleted employee was holding a fistful of wires. "The satellite radio is messing with the video, I swear—"

"Don't you mean *you* were messing with the video? You broke the cameras. I just made manager, dude." The new manager looked like he was barely twelve, and he was unsuccessfully Spray 'n Washing a giant ink stain on his pants. The stain was winning.

"You wanted satellite radio, dude! You were all, like, they never watch security, let's pipe in some music—"

"Do not blame me for your stupidity—"

"I'll fix it, I'll fix it. Just chill." The sound of a digital meltdown was quietly playing in the store: Satellite radio whizzed through stations randomly.

"Sorry about that," Kid Ink Stain yelled to us. "We are trying to fix it."

"No worries." I waved, and Richie shot me a look. I smiled at our great timing and watched as he got all serious on a computer. He was so beautiful it made my heart hurt. Even with a hat pulled down and a scowl on his face, I wanted to make out with him. My body floated over as I remembered our levitation, and I thanked heaven. If things had to suck, sucking with Richie was an excellent consolation prize.

I stood behind him at the monitor and watched, riveted as he plugged the words "fake IDs" into the Google search. A wide assortment of sites appeared, and Richie knew exactly which one he wanted. Downloading a fake ID form in seconds flat, he pasted the digital photo of me into the appropriate slot and asked, "What's your name, little girl?" And smiled a killer beamer that'd make BMW proud.

I laughed for the first time in hours. "Hmmm. I guess Elizabeth is out of the question."

"She was an overrated queen." He smirked, trying to cheer me up. Where was this coming from? He knew more than I'd given him credit for. "I know. You think I'm kind of a dumbass." He smiled again, slaying me.

"No—I never said that."

"You didn't have to. Remember?" He pointed to my head, then to his, to emphasize this inescapable, increasingly annoying truth.

"Remember what? How can I remember anything when you're so dreamy?" I said in my best dumb girl voice. "I'm just surprised is all."

"Girls aren't the only ones who play dumb, you know. Name?"

"Are you making one for yourself?"

"Already got one."

"What's your name on it?"

"Adam. Adam Lavelle."

"Then that makes it simple."

Reading my mind, he rolled his eyes. "No way, Beth! That is corny!"

"Too bad, Adam. That's the name I want. I'll take Lavelle as my last name, too. If ya don't mind."

He shook his head as he typed my new name into the form without hesitation. He typed three little letters that cracked me up: E. V. E.

"Adam and Eve? If Kinkos is the Garden of Eden, I'm seriously bummed."

"Don't be getting ideas about nudity, apples, or snakes and stuff." Richie laughed. "Now go set up a dummy e-mail account in your new name. I gotta print and laminate the crap out of those." He winked. Fifteen minutes, eighteen dollars, and one new identity later, I marveled at what a good criminal Richie was.

"I'm not a criminal," he said to my thought. "I'm just creative."

"I'M SO SCREWED!" The new manager was still freaking out.

"I got it, I got it—" Mullet was attempting to soothe him. "Satellite radio coming online momentito, check it out—"

As I settled in behind a monitor to start an e-mail account with my new identity, Latin horns started blaring over the in-store speakers.

"What is this?" screamed the Stain.

"Mambo!" Richie and I called out. Simultaneously. We looked at each other.

"How'd you know that?" I wondered aloud. "Wait. How'd I know that?" I asked Richie. He shrugged as the music changed stations to a different kind of Latin groove.

"Rumba?" Richie and I said at the same time. Richie got up and swirled his hips, looking down at them in wonder. I followed suit, wondering if my body knew how to rumba suddenly.

Another station piped on, and Richie and I were pulled toward each other across the computer aisle.

"Salsa?" we asked simultaneously, as our feet started moving involuntarily into what I guessed was salsa footwork. Richie twirled me with ease, laughing at the motions we were doing.

"Have you ever salsa'd before?" I asked him as my feet did their thing.

"Never," Richie declared, twirling me into a back-and-forth, side-to-side pattern.

"You guys are pretty good," offered the Stain, when the music changed into that big band sound my grandmother loved.

"Swing?" we said together, and Richie spun me into a hold and flipped me upside down. Our bodies instinctively performed steps we didn't know existed. We waved our arms and shook our hips to the music in the empty Kinkos.

The Mullet fiddled with a remote control, triggering a thumping seventies disco beat. Richie entwined me in his arms with a squeeze. We looked into each other's eyes and announced our next dance: "Do the hustle!" We laughed.

"What's the hustle?" asked the manager, still scrubbing at his ruined khakis.

"We have no idea!" Richie blurted. "I mean, our parents taught us?" he added quickly, covering our spontaneous dance skills with a lie. A country and western station clicked on, and Richie and I began whirling each other into some kind of line-dancey two-step.

"I love Travis Tritt," the Mullet offered to no one in particular, and I couldn't believe I was dancing like a pro with a fellow amateur.

"Why is this happening?" Richie marveled.

"I have no idea," I said, which was true. It was such a high; I didn't want it to stop.

"I don't want it to stop either." Richie spun me like cotton candy and embraced me in both arms. We started to kiss, but the electricity shocked us back to reality, forcing us to separate.

"Was there a power surge?" the Stain asked Mullet, commenting on the flickering light we must have generated with our mouths.

"We should finish up here," Richie said sadly as we returned to our respective monitors to get our stuff done.

Richie made hotel reservations in Philly with our new identities, emptying the online cache afterward so no one could trace our steps.

"Being on the lam is fun," I whispered as we wrapped up, impressed with his abilities. All of them. God, I had no game at all.

"Being on the lam with me is fun," he corrected. "Don't get it twisted, Aleph." I was mush again, and then I suddenly remembered what I'd been trying to forget: My pseudomother's life was in danger and I was a dancing fool! A dancing fool who was both distracted and attracted. I felt incredibly guilty all of a sudden and needed space. A small jolt passed through me as Richie tried to put his arm around my back as we paid, and I pulled away.

"You don't have to pretend you don't like me, dude," he said. "That stuff is for phonies who need games because they don't have it going on. Are you okay? Are you worried about your mom? Because you know I can relate to that, alright?" I hadn't meant to pull away.

"Yes, I'm worried. But please stop reading me." I didn't want to get all depressed and heavy. "From now on my thoughts are like the bathroom: No pee-vesdropping and no me-eavesdropping!"

Once in the car we peeled onto the freeway again. I almost choked when I saw my fake birth date on my new fake ID. "Thirty? You think I look thirty???"

"You gotta be at least that old to dance that well!" he snorted. "You're an old soul, Beth. Consider it a compliment. Don't sweat it. I dig older women. For reals." He winked at me, and I thought my heart would explode from the crushing. "Don't explode on me, Eve. Eden needs us, remember? Get some sleep."

"On one condition. Don't be a fly on my dream wall, Adam!" As I tried to get comfy for some sleep, I couldn't help but notice the intense twinging sensation on the right side of my abdomen. Terrible feeling with a great word: mittelschmerz. I was ovulating, or at least my doctor told me that was what was happening when I had that now familiar sensation. It buzzed and fussed uncomfortably until I put my head down on the seat next to Richie's leg. My hair was zapping against his thigh from the charge of it all.

When I woke up, it was almost daylight. "I think someone is following us. I'm gonna hide the car in a lot near the Philly train station. We'll cab it to the hotel and get some rest. I think we should just take the train into New York after we're cleaned up. The car is too risky, you know?"

"Thank you." I didn't want our time alone to end.

"For what?" He smiled like he had no idea how grateful I was. I looked at him. "Like, for everything. Duh."

"You're the one who told me to stop reading your mind. I am officially psychically deaf. If you wanna say something, say it out loud. Preferably in court. With a stenographer and digital recorder present." I thanked him with my mind and my heart. And Richie Mac just grabbed my hand and held it. Electricity and all.

"Uh-oh," Richie said suddenly. I didn't like the sound of it. "I'm pretty sure we got two cars following us now." I turned and looked. Illinois plates were practically waving from the front grill.

"How far are we from the hotel?" My stomach lurched.

"I don't want to lead them there. I want to drop you before I drop the car and see if I can lose them on foot. Thirtieth Street Station will be filled with people—we should be able to lose them in there."

I wondered how he knew so much about Philadelphia, and he pulled the question out of my head. "My grandma lives here. Take all your money in case we get separated." He was seriously stressing, so I did as he told me. "Go into the station. If I don't find you in five minutes, get a cab to the Rittenhouse Hotel on Rittenhouse Square and check in. Any taxi driver will know it."

Thirtieth Street Station loomed ahead, and Richie drove

through a red light and got some distance between us and the car behind us. He turned a corner, yelling, "Now! Just walk normally. Don't draw attention, and pull your hoodie up—"

I slipped out of the car with my bag and headed toward the side entrance. Richie sped off long before any traffic passed, and I felt pretty slick as I entered the train station.

It didn't take long for that feeling to pass as a tidal wave of static began to fill the terminal. I let out a big exhale, put my head down, and kept moving forward, not engaging any of the energy moving around me. As I headed out to find a cab, I saw a woman who looked like my mother dragging her daughter across the terminal. There were static chains between and around the pair, and I wondered why we chain ourselves to people we supposedly love. Like a bell cutting through noise, my thoughts answered my question: *Fear. Fear enslaves.*

I was sitting there watching people when Richie finally found me.

"What are you doing?" he asked, freaked out. He was looking around at the ceilings; there were video cameras mounted everywhere. "We gotta get outta here." He was nervous. "Go to the hotel, I'm going to pick up some things. Keep your head down, Beth. Think."

"Relax, dude. I'm eighteen. I'm not breaking any laws." I was kind of annoyed with his tone. "What stuff do you have to pick up, anyway? What things? Where are you going?"

Richie mumbled something about cell phone chargers and took off. One second he didn't want me alone, and now he was practically jettisoning me in a strange city. I couldn't read his thoughts, so I decided to follow orders and head outside to catch a cab.

As the taxi drove me through the streets of Philadelphia, the visions were back, and a million thoughts raced through my mind: Was my mother okay? Was 7RI out to hurt me or help me? I wasn't overwhelmed anymore. I was determined. I was tired of feeling like everybody else knew something I didn't.

I wanted to make sure Richie was okay. Then I laughed at myself for thinking like a girlfriend with a guy I'd only actually, physically, kissed once.

THE LINE

RICHIE HAD BEEN TRYING TO SLEEP FOR A while. The lady's voice had been in his head on a continuous loop, telling him what to do. Over and over again. Without ceasing. It was driving him crazy.

"Drop her in Philadelphia at the Rittenhouse Hotel. Meet

me at Longwood Gardens. Longwood Gardens. Longwood Gardens," like a chant in his head.

"Alright, alright, alright!" he'd screamed in the car, grabbing his head to make it stop. It seemed to shut the voice up for a while. He was relieved Beth thought he was talking about something else.

When Richie finally arrived at Longwood Gardens, he felt nauseous. He stooped over a water fountain and downed a liter in seconds. He stifled a burp.

"Hello, Richie McAllister." A little lady in a brown outfit and black orthopedic shoes was smiling at him from a nearby bench.

"Your voice isn't as irritating in person," Richie joked.

"Sorry about being so repetitive," she apologized. "I brought you a sandwich." She motioned to the seat next to her, holding two brown paper bags on her lap. "You must be very hungry."

Richie thanked her and started wolfing down the food as soon as his butt hit the seat. He ate half a sub in two bites. She extended a red plaid thermos.

"Would you like some coffee?" Richie was too busy chewing to form words, so he nodded.

"I'm Mary," she whispered, pouring the steaming liquid into the little red cup attached to the thermos. The coffee was already light with cream, and it smelled delicious.

"Thank you for meeting me here." She giggled. "I am sorry to have irked you with my directions and such." Richie was nervous suddenly. What if she'd put something in the coffee?

"There's nothing in the coffee, I assure you." She grabbed his cup and took a sip as proof. "See?"

Now Richie knew how Beth felt. Knowing someone could read your mind wasn't comforting. He shook off a cold sweat and rubbed his clammy hands from the eeriness.

"Am I in trouble?" Richie asked. "Are you going to hurt me or Beth, or something?" He rubbed his temples and fought back tears. "Your voice in my head isn't very nice," he said, his throat cracking with a healthy dose of fear. "I mean, your tone is nice, I guess, but it's making me really upset. Really, really upset." He let out some coughs to loosen the tightness in his chest. "I'm listening to you. I'm doing what you tell me to do. But I—I'd like to know—" He just wanted some answers.

"I'd bet you'd like to know when it's going to stop?"

Richie nodded. The idea of the voice stopping overwhelmed him. He'd been driving for days with incessant instruction in his ears, and it felt like a verbal fire alarm going off in his head every five minutes. If he wasn't hearing Beth's thoughts, he'd been receiving Margo's nagging instructions. It made him want to jump and scream and shake it off, but he couldn't. He couldn't control the constant itching in his brain. Itching that he could not scratch.

"I know this hasn't been easy on you, but we appreciate your help. We really do." Mary was opening an envelope crammed with bills. Richie could see they were hundred-dollar bills. Lots of them.

"What is going on? Can you tell me? Am I going to die? I

feel like I'm going off the deep end here, you know? I mean"—
Richie buried his face in his hands, all previously withheld
anxiety pouring out of him—"is Beth going to be alright? Is
she—are we—going to be okay? The electricity? Did we do
something wrong?"

"I will answer your questions. Take a deep breath, Richie.
It's going to be alright."

Richie took as much air into his lungs as he could, trying
not to lose it. The stress of the trip, his feelings for Beth, the
instructions in his head, all of it had taken a toll. He quivered
as he exhaled, his body shivering from nervous exhaustion.
"Why did the kiss burn my mouth? Why did all the skin peel
off my body? Am I sick?"

"The shock is there for your protection." Mary felt bad for
the young man; he was trying so hard to be brave. "It's like a
fence. Or a force field."

"The jolt of electricity is to protect us?" His tone was sarcastic. "It freaking terrified us."

"I understand. Think of it this way, Richie: When you are
scared of something, it has power over you. In this case, that
something is an energy. An energy so big it isn't *like* playing
with fire; it *is* playing with fire. Misuse it, or act from fear, and
you will get burned. Badly."

"Will that happen every time we kiss? Is it a curse or something?" He hoped not.

Mary had to be honest. "For the men who truly love Beth,
the spark will mutate into a magnificent light . . . and there will

be nothing to fear." Nostalgia got the better of her, and Mary teared up a bit. "But true love is a rare thing." She quickly dotted her eyes with a small handkerchief and cleared her throat.

"Beth is very special. As you know." Mary had a soothing quality to her, as if she knew exactly what he needed. Her voice was nice, familiar. "The moment Beth's heart opens to lust or love, there is a powerful biochemical change in her body." Mary looked into Richie's eyes to make sure he was listening, willfully slowing down his breathing with the pace of her speech and her piercing stare. "There, encoded in Beth's very DNA, almost like a virus, is the capacity to share her power, her supernatural gifts, with her suitors. With the *right* suitors. For the purposes of procreation."

The word "procreation" jolted Richie's butt off the bench. Making babies? Kids? Having kids was not something he was ready to do, and his entire body recoiled.

"The Seventh Ray must be kept from sharing the Line until the right time." Mary's words whipped him off balance.

"The line? What line? What's the line?"

"Her genetic line. Her bloodline. Beth's destiny is to continue the Line, following strict rules designed to protect her, to protect her partners, and to protect her progeny."

"Partners? Plural?" This didn't sit right with Richie at all, and his stomach turned. He fidgeted childishly as if he hated the idea of Beth kissing anyone else.

"Plural, yes. Partners. It's not for the queasy." She put her hand on his knee.

"Beth must bear seven children in sequence. With seven

different fathers. As quickly as is humanly possible. Her predecessor took too long, and that will necessarily impact Beth." Mary sighed.

Richie retied his shoes and stood up, straightening his shoulders and staring down at this irritating woman who was clearly insane. She may have gotten into his head, but he had to protect Beth.

"You can't 'protect' Beth," she cooed. "This is her destiny, Richard. This is beyond you." Mary hated this part of being the Keeper. The supernatural never went over well, but it was part of her job.

"That's crazy." His voice was steel. "You are crazy. You can't tell her what to do. It's her body and her life."

"I won't have to tell her what to do, I assure you. Her body will do that whether we want her to or not." Mary was trying not to laugh. Richie started pacing, deeply troubled by this woman and the insane nonsense she was spewing.

"I'm sorry to laugh." She exhaled. "I could show you things to prove I'm not crazy, young man. But there isn't time. The Seventh Ray is a time bomb, and given the troubles of puberty and adolescence, she is a time bomb that could explode at any moment. It appears that you were the match, my dear."

"What about what Beth wants? She just got into college, and I'm pretty sure she wants to go. Have you seen her grades? She's, like, Einstein brilliant. She won't want this. Who would want this? It can't be true."

Mary softened at Richie's protective nature. "I assure you she has free will. The Choice is to be made consciously, not frivolously." Mary wanted to hug him, and she recalled the pet name Richie's poor mother used. She summoned it easily. "Richie? I'm not joking, my darling one. Or should I say, 'darlin'un'?" He flinched as Mary said the words his mom had called him since he was a baby.

"What am I supposed to do?" Richie wilted back onto the bench. "I'm not ready to have a kid."

"Of course you're not ready. You're not supposed to be ready."

"I want the voice in my head to stop! Your voice. Beth's thoughts . . ." He scratched his scalp as if his fingernails might do the trick.

"I understand. I can help you with that." Mary placed her hands on the top of her thighs and rubbed them back and forth as if warming them.

"Can't we—I just want to spend time with Beth without voices in my head, finish school, have fun—get to know her without this insanity going on." Richie went to mush thinking about her. "I've never felt anyone the way I feel Beth. It's in my core."

"Well, it's wonderful to feel that. And it's nice to want things with her. But that's not possible. None of that is possible." Mary had to nip this in the bud.

"But I'm doing what you ask. . . ." Richie was bombarded with dread.

"It doesn't matter. You must never see her again."

"What? That's not going to happen. I have to see her again. She means the—" He stopped himself.

"She means the world to you, I know," Mary finished his thought. "You can say good-bye, but I'm afraid you must never see her again."

Richie sprang out of his seat and flung around. He threw the remaining coffee out of the cup and wanted to punch a wall. Mary instructed him to calm down without saying a word.

"If you have sex with her"—she stood up and grabbed the cup and screwed it back onto the thermos—"I assure you her DNA can rip through any latex condom or birth control method you may try." Richie got red with embarrassment at discussing birth control with a woman old enough to be his grandmother.

"This is really unbelievable. How can you be so technical about this? Why should I believe this?"

"I'm sorry. This is fact. I am trying to help you. Beth has shared her power with you—accidentally, like a flu—and it will be with you until you procreate with her. It will get stronger and stronger until you have sex, at which point the power will leave your body completely, and she will move on, have the child, and select another mate. Until she has biologically satisfied her destiny, she has zero control over this. None. But you do." Mary hated doing this. The look on his face broke her heart, but it had to be done.

Richie stood up and took an uneven breath. "Alright. But answer something. What if I stay with her?" It took all the strength he had, but he had to ask.

Mary was visibly shaken by this question. "I can't recommend it."

Richie sat down again and gently grabbed Mary by the shoulders. "What will happen if I stay with her and we just love each other?"

"It is not an option. You will find each other quite irresistible, I assure you. Your desire for each other will increase until fertilization is achieved. If you continue having sex with her after conceiving a child? You will die." Mary let the words land, silently waiting until he understood. His hands dropped from her shoulders.

"Failure to abstain has killed many men, all the men who have tried it. Human DNA cannot handle repeated acts of conception with the Seventh Ray."

"I'll die? Are you kidding me?" Richie started laughing. "You are telling me if I have sex with her more than once, I will die?"

"Not right there, not on the spot, no. But over several lunar cycles, yes. And much, much sooner than you would have, had you not bred with the Seventh Ray." Mary stood up and began pacing slowly in front of Richie with great deliberation.

"If you continue to engage romantically with Beth, you will die. If you break it off with her and never see her again, the symptoms you are experiencing will diminish rapidly over the next lunar cycle. Your body will return to normal, and all biochemical and physiological traces of your interactions will leave your system." Mary reached into her satchel, handing him a new cell phone and the envelope of cash.

"There isn't any time, darling one. Please give this cell phone to her, and then disappear. I suggest you figure out a way to say good-bye and do it as quickly as possible. We thank you for your help. We value your life. We hope you do too."

And with that, Mary walked away, leaving Richie alone on a bench with a red plaid thermos. He yanked at his hair as if he could pull this new information out through his scalp. An invisible tourniquet knotted his stomach and cut off all air. His heart sputtered around a thought he didn't want to have. For the first time in his life Richie wondered if this is what love felt like.

CHAPTER 25

ARRIVED AT THE RITTENHOUSE HOTEL EXHAUSTED and excited. "Room for Eve Lavelle?" The man at the reception desk looked at my fake ID and handed me my key without blinking.

"The bellman will show you to your room, Mrs. Lavelle."

I smiled. It was a lie that I wanted to be true. I couldn't wait to see New York with Richie and unravel this confusion once and for all, but that would have to wait one more night. One more night on the lam together. I still wanted to kiss him and all the stuff that kissing led to. I wasn't even scared. I was ready. Pyrotechnics and all.

The bellman led me into my room, but I couldn't enjoy it. The hotel phone was staring at me like a challenge, taunting me, saying, *Make sure she's okay, make sure she's okay, phone home, track her down, double-check* . . . and on and on until I finally did something stupid. I picked up the phone and called home.

"Hello?" My mother picked up on the first ring, and relief shot through me like gunfire. I realized I hadn't thought this through. I'd planned on hanging up, but I didn't do that.

"Are you okay? Is everything okay?"

"Despite the fact that you ran out of psychiatric care and left the state without talking to me? No, Elizabeth, everything is not fine." She was seething, and my relief boomeranged into scorn. I was talking to the person who had betrayed me at McCall's, and not the woman I'd grown up with.

"I wanted you to know that I am okay. And I wanted to make sure that you're safe."

"Safe? You want to make sure *I'm* safe? I finally break you free of those loonies and you decide to run back to them?" Loonies? What was she talking about? She responded before I could ask.

"Did you see the cards they sent you, Beth? Those aren't the kinds of things you send small children! I swore on my life that

I would do everything in my power to protect you from those people, and—" She was losing it, babbling a mile a minute.

"Slow down. Why didn't you just tell me? Why all the secrecy?" My voice was cold. My heart was shutting down.

"I'm your mother. I may not have given birth to you, but I created you—I made you who you are. I shouldn't need to defend my actions." There was a hysteria in her voice that was disturbing.

"So, I was adopted, right?"

"You were *rescued*. I have been *protecting* you your entire life. I vowed never to let them hurt you. Never in my wildest— how dare you betray me like this! How dare you?!"

"How dare I? How dare *you*? Did you steal me from a maternity ward or something? I don't understand—this makes you sound sketchy!" I was furious. She'd withheld information from me. "I deserve to know the truth, Mom! Adopted? Not adopted? Rescued? Fostered? When someone you love asks for the truth, you tell them the truth! There's nothing that can't be forgiven, but hurting someone with lies? What is that about?"

There was silence for quite some time before she spoke again.

"Since you don't know what you are dealing with, I am going to give you the benefit of the doubt. You can come home and we can pretend this never happened." My head shook, and my eyes rolled involuntarily.

"Or you can continue this insanity, and you may never come home." She had to be kidding, but her tone was no joke.

"Listen to me: If I come home? If I don't go to New York? You could die." I had to tell her that. I owed her that. Even if this was insane.

She sounded like a crazed robot. "No, this isn't about me." My mother wasn't intimidated by the disclosure. "Come home or don't come home. Ever."

"You're making me choose?"

"I don't see it that way." Her voice cracked with sadness. My heart sank.

"I'm sorry you are in so much pain, but Mom—"

"DON'T CALL ME THAT! IF YOU GO TO NEW YORK YOU MAY NEVER CALL ME THAT EVER AGAIN, DO YOU HEAR ME?" I had heard my mother lose her shit, but this felt like a portapotty knocking over, spilling everywhere. It was foul.

"You don't mean that!" I couldn't match her aggression, and I didn't have the energy to try.

"You will be dead to me. I will box up your room and burn your belongings. I will destroy every trace of you, Elizabeth. That's how serious this is."

"Destroy every trace of me?" I repeated. Okay, now she was the crazy one. She wasn't right, she wasn't making sense, and I wanted to cry and talk her down, but there is something that happens when someone says they want to destroy you. This little part of me, a part that maybe I didn't even know was there, grew four million times larger in an instant. And it roared for the first time in my entire life.

"You will not destroy me. I'm sorry you want me to choose between my past and my future, to choose between living and lying. But if you aren't going to answer my questions or help me get answers to my questions, I have to find them myself." I slammed down the phone and hung up on the woman who'd raised me. The room vibrated with my anger, which was flying off me like shattering glass. I stood up as it got stronger, but it pinned me down. I screamed through it to stand up, and I saw my reflection in the hotel mirror: My rage was my own worst enemy.

As I took a hot shower and cried and scrubbed the disturbing vibes off me, I knew I'd find her when this was all over. More importantly, I knew that even though she was upset, she was alive. She was safe for now. If I got to New York, as the last gold letter promised, she wasn't going to die. For now. That wasn't enough for me, but it had to be. I dried off and passed out. Hard.

It was almost six hours later when a knock at the door woke me up. Room service delivered a bag of brand-new, clean clothes and some bean and cheese burritos. I dove into the burritos like a banshee. I worried about where Richie was, but I figured if he was smart enough to buy me a fresh outfit, he was probably alright. Something inside the burrito bag started vibrating. Inside the bag was a cell phone.

"Hello?"

"Hello, Eve. It's me, Adam." Richie sounded funny. "I wanted to get you a massage, but not until we're in Malaysia, right?" He was forcing himself to sound chipper.

"You mean the Maldives?"

"Yes, massages in the Maldives. How could I forget that?" He sounded really tense. Not scared, but stressed. Driving a girl cross-country while dodging troopers and unmarked cars with Illinois plates might do that to a guy.

But I needed to know, so I said it: "What's wrong?"

"Nothing." He was so lying. "I'm just checking in with my parents and doing some stuff so nobody gets suspicious. I called your mother's office—they said she's out sick."

"I know. I talked to her."

"You did? Is she okay?"

"Yes. And no. I mean, she's safe, but I'm dead to her." There was a silence. I could tell he didn't know what to say.

"Well, I got you the prepaid phone. I'm the only one who has the number, and I bought one to use when I call you, so—"

"Your voice sounds weird. What's wrong? Tell me."

"Beth. Everything is fine. Your mom is safe; you're safe; I'm safe. I'm just really tired, I guess. I'm going to go see my grand-mother for a bit. I'll be back at the hotel in a while."

"But—," I blurted right before he hung up.

"Gotta run. Get some rest." And he was gone.

CHAPTER 26

I'D BEEN PACING THE ROOM FOR TWO HOURS. Richie never returned, never showed up. I'd moved beyond worried into the village of freaking out. It had been hours and I had no idea where he was. I was scared. My calls to his cell phone went straight to voice mail. I tried to stay calm when a distinctly non-golden envelope slid under the door. I ripped it open: *Had to deal with some stuff. Get on the 6 a.m. train to NYC. Meet me in front of the lions, NY Public Library, 5th Ave at 42nd Street. 9 a.m. Don't worry. Richie.*

Don't worry? For days he'd been paranoid about leaving me alone, and now he was abandoning me? How the hell did he have so much confidence in my safety, suddenly? *Whatever, dude.* There wasn't time to be annoyed. The sooner I got to New York, the sooner I'd have answers. I put on my big-girl pants, checked Eve Lavelle out of the Rittenhouse, and got Beth Michaels on the next train to New York, New York. I kept my head down on the ride and wrote down as much as I could remember about what had been happening. It kept me focused and kept me from seeing things I might not want to see.

When I got off the seven a.m. commuter train at Penn Station, the blast of New York exploded into my range of vision like a nuclear mushroom cloud. The feeding frenzy of energy was everywhere, and on everyone. Grooze bisected by shards of incandescent light filigreed the air like lace-o'-lanterns. Shapes of light punctured the static field in a beautiful battle royale.

I used the GPS on my phone and rushed to our meeting spot at the New York Public Library. I didn't even care that I was a sweaty pig. As soon as I got within twenty feet of the world-famous lions, all visions stopped. There he was. I raced up to him like a kid, throwing my arms around him and getting shocked. "Ow. Let's walk around and see amazing things today. Can we?" I wanted to hug him, and I wanted to resolve our electrical problem as soon as possible. Kissing and more needed to happen soon. Or I would really go insane.

"I wish I could hang with you all day." His smile tilted. Richie didn't have a tilted smile, and the effect was nerve-racking.

"Are you my remote control? You just turn the TV off and I can't see, or what?" I held up an imaginary channel changer and clicked in his direction.

"I wish. I wish a lot of things." The tilt disappeared. There was no smile on Richie's face.

"Like what?" I laughed at his serious look. "We're in New York City! We're going to have a day together! We gotta stand in the middle of Times Square and bask in all the neon!"

"I have to leave, Beth." My ears got hot and my spine went cold. My entire body got confused. Richie was holding his breath. "My mother is very ill. I need to get back to New Glen."

"What's wrong? I'm so sorry. What happened? Is it serious?" Richie reddened. His face contorted like he was choking on a bone.

In the silence before he responded, my brain started swimming with electricity. I could actually feel neurons popping through my brain's hemispheres, waking me up and adrenalyzing my heart and lungs. I felt supersized; everything felt supersized. It was the feeling I had had in Bordens, in McCall's, and it was coursing through my veins. Richie Mac was lying.

"What's wrong with her?" I held down the gush that wanted to cover him. I was livid.

"She overdosed." A knot materialized out of thin air. The grooze was back, forming a barrier between the two of us. My brain was crackling like fast-burning tobacco. My face must've changed, because he said, "Wait. Don't get mad at me. This isn't my fault—I'm not against you. I understand you." He was pleading with me, all pretense leaving him for one moment.

"If you want to leave, just leave. But don't lie about it." The grooze wall between us was getting thicker and thicker. I felt this urge to jolt through it with electricity, just for revenge. "Or is it that maybe you've been lying this whole time?" I asked.

This made him mad. Grooze braids returned, knotting toward me. He couldn't even look at me. I was livid. "If you pretended to like me, maybe you could cash in? Is that it? You were acting the entire time?"

"I wasn't pretending. If you wanna call me a liar, call me a liar, Beth. If you wanna reduce everything we've been through into some lie, go ahead. Don't hold back." He was nodding, getting angrier now, tapping his hand on his leg as if he wished there were a gun there. The braid started wrapping him up, mummying around him like a sarcophagus. Did he feel trapped? I didn't care.

"Yes, Richie," I said, asking for it, "I called you a liar."

"I don't need this." He looked devastated and got quiet. "I'm done with this, Beth." Rage pounded my head into mush. I wanted to scream. Instead, a giant bolt of lightning swiped at him from somewhere behind my head, knocking him to the ground. Thunder cracked. Passersby ducked from the noise, looking up at the sky before nervously continuing on their way.

"You didn't have to do that," he said, slowly getting up but scared.

"I didn't know I could do that." It was a gorgeous day, but dark clouds were gathering directly above us. I didn't even care. I wanted an answer. "I just don't understand why. I'm tired of people lying to me!" Balls of static made tidal waves over his head, crashing down around him.

"You know why! All of this is scary! I don't want anything to do with this anymore. I don't want anything to do with you anymore. You are dangerous!"

The words landed. Another thunderhead formed above us as my stomach lurched. I wanted to scream, when another crack of lightning exploded from behind my head, knocking Richie down and scorching his jacket. He stood up dismissively, patting down the smoking fabric with his hand. People were running for cover as if it were about to rain. As if it were Mother Nature, when it was actually my nature. My shoulders were shaking uncontrollably.

"You know what, Beth? This is good-bye. You don't have to make this hard." Richie was as close to crying as I'd ever seen him. It hurt me so bad I didn't care.

"You want my permission?" My voice was shrill, holding back tears. "No. I'm not okay with you leaving. Because this kills me. This really kills me." I could barely speak. Thunder rumbled somewhere in the distance.

"You'll live." It was icy.

"How much did they pay you?" It had to be about money. That was the only explanation.

"They offered me twenty grand. But I wouldn't take it. Because it wasn't enough." He spat the words at me. "Have you thought about me? About what this has put me through? Or am I too stupid to matter?" I was ashamed to admit it, but I really hadn't thought about him. Not for one second had I considered all of this, really considered it from his perspective. Suddenly, it started to drizzle.

"You haven't given one thought to me or what this would do to me, I know. Well, you ruined my life. We kissed, I fell for you, and it wrecked my life." Grooze was pouring out of him now, coming toward me in torrents. "My life was pretty bad already, so imagine how unbearable you'd have to be to make it worse." Static knots tied between us faster than I could count. He turned and started walking away from me. The drizzle became a torrential downpour.

"Wait! Don't leave me here alone. I'm scared. Please don't walk away now." A rope was coming at me full speed from his solar plexus.

"I never want to see you again." The rope made a noose and wrapped around my neck, knotting tighter and tighter as he walked away. "Believe it."

His words razored my throat, and all my blood rushed

somewhere, everywhere but through my body. As the rain pummeled us, I saw something getting pulled out of my body. It was a throbbing blob of red that looked an awful lot like an animated heart. My heart. It was spurting blood and dangling on a long piece of barbed wire, dragging on the ground behind Richie Mac as he walked away. Forever.

CHAPTER 27

I DON'T KNOW HOW LONG I WANDERED THE
streets of New York City, soaking wet, confused
and disoriented. I didn't know who I was or
why I was here, and I had little interest in finding out. A gray
sedan tailed me as I zombied around the city. I didn't even care.
At one point the driver got out and handed me a gold enve-

lope. I looked at the driver, took the envelope, dropped it on the ground, and kept walking. I found the nearest subway and rode it back and forth for hours. I was numb, and I hated the world. All at once.

I was tired of running, tired of seeing, worrying, and wondering what this was all about. All I cared about was Richie. My heart hurt, my stomach hurt, and I felt as if every ganglion, every nerve ending, was extracting itself from every one of his, cell by lonely cell. I swear it felt like our torsos had been connected—like conjoined twins—and suddenly, brutally severed. Without anesthetic.

I noticed the visions were back and stronger than ever. But I felt like a chain saw had cut right through me and I was bleeding everywhere. There I was, meandering the streets and stepping into the shelter of a stoop or leaning on a mailbox, a parking meter, a stairwell, a wall, or whatever, to bawl. It was uncontrollable. The betrayal and abandonment would dry-heave through me. Big messy sobs of a kind of pain I had never felt. I was deeply vulnerable and raw, not entirely out of place amongst the walking wounded of the Big Apple.

Nobody stopped to ask me if I was okay, and I wanted to talk to someone, anyone, but I had no one. Not my mom, not Shirl, and not Richie. All I wanted was Richie.

I was sitting crying on some stoop downtown when a sweet little nun asked if I'd like to come in, sit down inside, and have some water? I lost it. Her kindness made me cry harder, so I just nodded as she led me into a building and into a large meeting room filled with folding chairs. She offered a chair in the back row and brought me a box of tissues and a glass of water. "You are welcome to stay as long as you need to. It's an open meeting, so I'm sure it's quite alright if you stay." I looked at her, and tears were streaming down my cheeks, snot running down my lips. I blew my nose, and it reminded me of the snot on Richie's pants and I lost it all over again. "Is there anyone I can call for you?" There was nobody to call. I was alone.

That truth and her charity sent me over the edge. "Is there a bathroom?" I choked through tears.

She took me to the restroom and I made one of my toilet-paper seat covers and just sat on the toilet, put my head down, and cried for what seemed like hours. I exhausted myself and just slid down onto the floor and slept. I didn't care about the toilet near my head, or the germs of New York City frolicking on the floor. I didn't care about anything. When I opened my eyes, there was a set of black orthopedic shoes outside the stall. I opened the door, and there stood the little old nun in a matching brown top and skirt.

"Hi." She had a nice voice. "I didn't want to wake you"—she smiled—"but I did want to check on you."

"I'm dead." I really was.

"Yes. You have to die sometimes so the real you can be born." What was she talking about? "Follow me, please. You need to eat something." She helped me up and led me out the restroom door. I followed her down a hall to a small room with a table, some chairs, and a coffeemaker. She poured two cups and offered me cream and sugar.

"Humans form so much crust. Butterflies do this best. They become milk in the cocoon. The caterpillar simply liquefies before changing into butterfly form. Total liquid, can you imagine? Then it morphs into itself, and the wings have to strain against the protective membrane before it can fly. If you poke open a cocoon before the wings are strong, the butterfly will not survive. But this is instinctual, not painful. Very few humans accept the milk or the strain. Humans choose pain to remember who they are. You are no exception."

Was I hallucinating or just exhausted? This lady was trippy, but her coffee was good.

"I'm sorry, but why do you care?"

"I'm a nun. I've devoted my life to caring." She was hunting for something in the cupboards; then she found a box and began fiddling with it. "Forgive me. I'm Sister Mary." She extended her hand to shake mine. "Nice to meet you, Aleph Beth." How did she know that? "Do you know what your name means?" She pronounced Aleph like "olive" and Beth like "bait."

"Aleph Beth means one, two. A, B? Pee, poo? I'm really feeling the poo part of the name right now." I was starving, and Mary put the open box of cookies in front of me, grunting at my dumb joke.

"In the Torah and other sacred Hebraic and Aramaic texts, the Aleph Beth is the creative force of all that is. You need A to get to B. You can't have one without the other—"

"I wasn't raised Jewish, by the way," I interrupted her. "I don't speak Hebrew or anything. For the record."

She waved away my statement like dust and continued, "As the alphabet is to words, the Aleph Beth is to life. If a person were named Aleph Beth, they would be able to create life. Lots and lots of life. The Aleph Beth can create life with their thoughts. If your thoughts are bad, your life is bad. Good thoughts? Good life! If you were the Aleph Beth, your life would reflect what you believe."

"That's quite a superpower."

"Everyone has it, actually. Yours is on steroids." She smirked at her own joke.

"Oh, really?"

"It's a blessing or a curse. Most people think seeing is believing." Mary's giggles started again. "Quite the opposite! You see what you believe!" I was too tired to argue, and I needed to get to 7RI and face the music.

"Look: You don't know me, and you don't know what's been going on for me. But trust me: I didn't ask for this. And I know you probably won't believe me, but I see things around complete strangers, okay? I don't have 'beliefs' about complete strangers, so how do you explain that?" Mary smiled patiently, but it felt condescending.

"That is the gift of Sight, Aleph. You also see . . . what they believe." It rang true, but I didn't want to talk about it anymore.

"I should go."

"Where? You have nowhere to go. Do you?"

"No, I don't." *You old bag* is what I wanted to say but didn't. "What do you want from me? I'm a nobody. I'm an eighteen-year-old with no home, no mom, no dad, no friends, no boyfriend, no money, no prospects, and no future. I am nothing."

Mary smiled at me as if this were an inside joke. "Let me guess," I asked her. "You're from 7RI, aren't you?"

"Excellent. Please stand up, Beth." Mary was almost giddy. Since I had no will to sit anymore, I wobbled up.

"Would you like a glimpse of yourself? If you are willing?"

"Whatever." I was exhausted and didn't have the energy to resist her.

"Close your eyes and then look in the mirror, if you will. We can't always see ourselves clearly." I felt her tiny hand on the small of my back. "This should help." It felt like she released a bounce of energy through her palm that pulsed through my entire body.

I opened my eyes, turned to the mirror behind the sink, and gasped. I was covered in grooze. Liquid grooze beaded and flowed around my edges in torrents. Little figures frolicked inside of it, transmitting images from every unpleasant scenario in my entire life: every time my mother lied to me, Shirl lying to me about Ryan, Richie lying to me at the library. Every awkward ouch—big and little—was playing out inside the moving field around me.

"That is your pain, yes?"

It was my pain. All of it. The shape-shifting mercury suckled my edges. There was no place on my body where tiny nightmares were not vampiring me. Mary pointed to a space:

the separation between myself and the cresting tide of grooze.

"The pain is not you. Do you see?"

I nodded.

"But do you understand?" The nun seemed doubtful.

"It is on me and it's around me, but it's not me?"

"It's not a question."

"The pain is around me. The pain is not me. I am not my pain."

"Very good." Mary looked into my eyes and whispered, "I think you dropped these." I glanced down to see she was holding my gold envelopes with the corners cut off: the cards that Donuts had confiscated! For the hundredth time in less than a month, my mind was smithereens.

"Are you ready for your tests, Aleph Beth?" Mary asked. "There's not much time. There is still a life at stake, you know."

"The woman who raised me hates me, but is okay as far as I know. Is that what you mean?" Mary shook her head no.

"What tests? Whose life?" This was infuriating.

"Someone very important. And yours, of course. Are you ready?"

"Wait, wait, wait. 'Someone important' and my life is at stake? What are the tests? Will they kill me? Do I have a choice?" I had a feeling I didn't, but I had to ask.

"I can't tell you what the tests are, or who is counting on you. But yes, you do have a choice."

"Do I have to kill people, or anything?"

"No." Mary giggled to herself. It irritated me.

"Haven't I been tested enough? Why me?"

"Because you are more than you think you are."

"Will the tests tell me who I am?" I got excited for a second. "So. I'm not crazy?" I offered aloud, just to be sure.

"You're many things. All sane. You live without illusion or delusion, that's all. It is the world that's gone crazy, my dear." Mary spoke with conviction. "If you choose to do these tests, you will know exactly who you are. I promise." I believed her. "But there's not much time—"

"Okay, then. I'm ready."

"Remove the cards from the envelopes, Beth."

I slid the seven tarot cards onto the table and looked at her. "Why are they called tarot cards?" I asked.

"People have had to hide their beliefs or face persecution. Historically, these were like stained glass windows, telling stories to the faithful in a time before literacy and public education, when you could get killed for believing." She continued, "They are a code. For Torah. Hear what happens when you switch the *a* and the *o*?" Tarot. Torah. I was intrigued.

"Now put them in order, please." I did as I was told, following the numbers on the top of each card. Fool, Magician, High Priestess, Empress, Emperor, Hierophant, Lovers. Simple.

"Very good. Now. Which one are you?" she asked. I pushed the Fool card toward her.

"Excellent," she bubbled. *That was easy,* I thought.

"Now. Which one are you becoming?" Mary's voice was sweet one second and scary the next. It was intimidating.

I remembered what Nessa had said and slid the Magician card next to the Fool.

"What does the Magician have there in the image?"

I looked at the picture and recited what I saw. "The Magician has four items. Some kind of baton in his right hand, then a cup, a disk, and a sword in front of him on a table?"

"Yes. And what are they?" I was confused. Hadn't I just told her? "I don't know. Tools?" I guessed. Mary stood up.

"Time to test your tools, Aleph Beth. Follow me. Take the cards." I followed her. If all the tests were this easy, I was going to breeze through it.

Mary walked me down the hall and stopped at some stairs. "Sit down here." I plopped on the steps and looked at her impatiently. "Watch that door." She indicated a set of double doors about a hundred yards away at the end of the long hallway. "Tell me when you see something, and describe exactly what you see," Mary insisted.

"With my eyes, or with the visions?"

"I'm not interested in what anyone can see; I'm interested in what you see." Mary checked her watch. I hadn't ever described the visions to anyone as they were happening. This was going to be interesting.

A few moments later people streamed out through the double doors. It was an informal gathering of parents, and everyone seemed to know each other. "It looks like a school meeting? Babies and small children hanging onto their parents?

The kids are all being carried." They were on shoulders, hanging on legs, scooped safely into arms.

"Look again, Beth." She was tapping her foot slightly.

I blinked into my sight carefully. What emerged made me do a double take, as I saw not one but three children suckling off each parent's neck. Odder still were the coddling motions they made, rubbing the heads, arms, or chests of their carriers.

"They're not children. They're like . . . like suckling energy parasites or something. Nursing off their hosts?"

"Exactly. Why?" Mary asked.

"I'm not sure."

"You need to find out why."

"How?" *The hell am I gonna do that,* I added to myself.

"Have you tried talking to them?" she purred. I rolled my eyes at her.

"I didn't know I could talk to them." She gave me a *silly goose* look.

"Can I get closer?"

"Probably a good idea, dear. Or should I say, 'duh'?" Mary checked her watch again, shooing me off to chat with the grooze.

I moved toward the milling crowd. I asked a young "mom" what they were doing. "It's an SLA meeting," she answered, and I asked her what that was. "Oh, Sex and Love Anonymous? It's like AA but for sex and love addicts." *Those must be interesting meetings,* I thought, and smiled. There was a particularly gremlinesque munchkin feeding off her as she spoke. It looked at me with hungry eyes, foaming at the mouth. We locked our gazes. I beamed a question to the munchkin without speaking: "What do they need you for exactly?"

"They need us and we need them. It's the perfect crime." I was so relieved it spoke English.

"I can speak whatever language you got," it gurgled at me, energy grooze dripping off its little fangs.

"Why do you need each other?"

The nursing munchkin laughed. "To forget!"

"Forget what?"

"Well . . . if you pick at a scab long enough, it'll never heal! We're the scabs! We keep them distracted so they never have to change."

"Don't they want to change?"

"Hehehehehehehehehehe. No. They want to focus on their pain, silly! They want to live there, over and over again. We help them! We can't attach to the ones who want to change!"

"How are you helping? I don't get it. It looks like you are draining them."

"Of course we drain them! They don't want real energy! They want an excuse. They want to stay numb. We keep them safe and numb. The devil you know is better than the devil you don't, right?"

I watched the crowd. Most of them nursing wounds, feeding their little groozelins. I sighed.

"Don't act like you've never needed an excuse! We let them off the hook! We are their magic bullet!" I didn't totally get it, and the munchkin seemed to read my mind. "If you feel dead, you never have to live! If you never have to live, you never have to fail. Ever heard of a security blanket? That's me, me, me, me, me, me!"

The feeding frenzy between the wounds and their wounded got louder and louder. I must've been staring, because a tattooed hipster eagerly jumped into view out of nowhere. "Is this your first meeting?" he asked as his vampire baby clung to his earlobe, smacking its chops, slurping the magma out of the hipster's soul. "No," I answered, "I'm just looking for someone." I quickly retreated to Mary's side, completely creeped out.

"And . . . ?" Mary raised her eyebrows, waiting for my report.

"The parasites are keeping them stuck?"

"Good. What are they?"

"Scary." Mary narrowed her eyes like I was being ridiculous.

"What else? What are they?"

"This is going to sound stupid, but I'm guessing they are personal demons?" Mary patted me on the back with a congratulatory slap.

"Eureka! Yes! For a smarty, you're awfully slow. Follow me. Hurry!"

Once outside, Mary ushered me to a bench in a nearby park. "Tell me what you see."

"Okay. There's a woman walking with a severe stoop." She was trudging along the street with her head down, with severe osteoporosis. "It looks heavy, maybe three feet by three feet square."

"Keep going. Elaborate."

"I see a woman carrying a box. Is it some baggage? Psychic baggage. It's weighing her down."

"Why?" Mary asked.

"Why are you carrying that baggage?" I whispered softly, and like a jack-in-the-box the top opened, revealing a monkey. The monkey began shouting in the stooped woman's ear, "You don't matter! You don't matter, stupid! Get going, stupid! You're so stooped, stoop-id!" The monkey's body was filled with a jumble of scrambled pictures I couldn't discern.

"What are the pictures?" I asked the popping primate.

The monkey looked at me and said, "Don't give me that look. She won't look at me! She packed me away, and she can unpack me at any moment, but she won't! So don't give me that look! I'm no monkey on her back; I'm everything she pretends didn't happen! Her father never hit her! Her husband never loved her! Her mother never died! The tears she never cried! She'd rather lug me around, get it? Get it? What you don't acknowledge can't hurt you, right? Right? Right? This is free will at work, baby!"

I turned to Mary. "Did you see that?"

"I did. Did you? What's the difference between that and what you saw ten minutes ago?"

"What's the difference? One is baggage. The other is a demon. One isn't unpacked? The other is. Baggage is stuff they ignore; the demons are wounds they know about or focus on?" She nodded, but I'd seen other things I didn't understand. "But what about those tentacles? And strings that suck light?"

"Hang on. Why do you think those demons inside were babies?"

It was clear that most people were so hypnotized by their wounds, so engrossed in their pain, that to get rid of it would be like ripping a baby out of their arms. "People nurse their pain puppets because they're attached to them? Maybe they keep them company?"

"Fair enough, my dear. Everything you are seeing is a reminder that this world is merely a reflection of another reality. Now, look to your right, please."

As I watched New Yorkers filtering by, every limp, every tick, every physical hump, lump, and bump seemed to have an energy performing live for a captive audience of one. Each sideshow told a different version of the same story: a tale about how that person was thinking or feeling, or what they were denying or focusing on. There was this turbulence on every person, crystallizing their life force into an electromagnetic puppet show.

"Who is pulling the strings?" she asked.

"If the grooze monkey was right, if the person has forgotten who they are, the puppets become the puppeteers. They are controlling the show." Mary clapped enthusiastically. Suddenly, a young woman pushing a stroller walked through their midst. She had a clean cord of light extending from the top of her head, glowing up into the sky. No grooze or energy mosquitoes; she carried a wave of calm with her, washing over distress like a tide. She was neutralizing energy demons in her wake.

"What did she do?" Mary pressed me.

"She's peaceful."

"And?"

"It cleared something?" I watched. Her presence was so calming it made people's puppeteers disappear. They walked straighter, calmer, and more happily than a moment before. And after a few steps they remembered their shows. Reruns to remind them of who they thought they were.

"How does she do that? I can't ask a cord, can I?"

"Did you study kilowatts in school?" I nodded. As degrees were to temperature, watts were to power. Units of power.

"If you shined a sixty-watt bulb in the dark, could you see it?" Mary asked.

"Yes."

"If you shined a huge kilowatt bulb in the same room, could you still see the sixty-watt bulb?" Probably not, I thought, and she answered for me. "Some people carry more kilowatts. Just as people are susceptible to negative energies, they are influenced by positive energies as well. Megawatts are bigger than microwatts."

"So the brighter light outshines the smaller darks?"

She stood up and clapped. "Bravo, my dear."

"So, I'm not schizophrenic?" I wondered aloud.

"Ah. I'll show you, and you tell me." Mary led me to a far corner of the park.

A homeless man was standing and performing in front of a painted brick wall. The sun hit him, casting a shadow behind him. He moved. The shadow would move on a delay. I squinted, and I noticed he had not one shadow, but several: a marching army man, a snake, a bouncing ball, a lobster (!?!), an alligator, and other shapes I couldn't really identify. All moving independently. I squinted even harder and saw the explanation: His puppeteers were casting their own shadows! He had a dozen of them, each performing a different show, competing for his body. The man would jerk in and out of each movement, marching like a soldier then clapping his arms like alligator jaws, jumping up and down like a ball before hissing and jabbing his arm like a snake. I crossed the street to give him a dollar and move closer to the action. What looked schizophrenic changed shape before my eyes. He was the perfect puppet, responding in real time to the tugs of his various puppeteers. I put a dollar into his empty hat on the ground, and he looked into my eyes.

"You see?" he asked.

"I see," I told him. "What's your name?"

"Sergeant Corporal Leonard Chomp-Chomp Pythonacious!"

"You got a lot going on, Sergeant."

He laughed. "There is a lot going on! People say I'm a lunatic, but I say I'm connected! I am wireless! A one-man wireless, cellular band! Dialing the infinite, baby. I ain't crazy; I just gotta stay connected!"

His puppeteers seemed to shake their heads at me from the wall. The alligator said, "No. He's wrong. He plugged into a station, alright. Ours."

Almost involuntarily Sergeant started shaking his head and

marching again. "Negatory, negatory, negatory, sir. Yes, sir!"

"That makes sense, Sergeant," I whispered. "That makes sense."

And he looked at me, ceasing all dancing and motion for one moment, and smiled. "What can I do for you, little lady?"

"Tell my friend Nessa that I send her my love, sir."

"Will do, will do! Sending Nessa top secret information, stat! Ten-four!"

"Thank you, Sergeant." I waved good-bye and resumed my irregularly scheduled program with Mary.

"Enough of the sideshows, my dear. You passed the first two of six tests. You have twenty-four hours to complete all six tests, or someone will die."

"You said I wouldn't have to kill anyone!"

"Not directly you won't, but there are always consequences." Mary pointed to a gray sedan waiting across the street.

"Go to Inkstop Tattoo on Thirteenth Street and Avenue A for further instructions. You might want to read this on your way. Consider it a hard-won gift." Mary handed me another gold envelope and walked away without saying good-bye.

"Am I going to see you again?" I asked. She turned around and shrugged. "At this point, that is entirely up to you." She winked at me before waddling away.

I got in the back of the sedan and was tired as soon as my ass hit the seat. It was past lunch, and I decided to inaugurate my journey the only way a beat-down gal could. "Driver. Take me to a coffee place. And a place with food. Please!" He pulled over. I got a quadruple black eye and grabbed a bean and cheese burrito for good luck en route. I didn't need to get my motor running; I needed to get it sprinting. I ripped open the gold envelope Mary had given me to read:

THE GREAT WORK

When you see dots, then your journey begins.

Harness your thoughts, or the dots become pins.

These dots will take shape into pictures with time,

their messages clear, their meaning sublime.

On every person there lives a mighty great cord,

a higher connection, a sacred light sword

that separates all that is true from the dark,

that connects everyone to the source of their spark.

The primary cord is quite sacred and true,

but there are others less clean, filled with

    sewage and goo.

When connection is jammed, cut off, or just lost,

then darkness attaches, at quite a great cost.

Dark matter is fluid and takes many shapes—

learn to decipher what gives and what takes.

Baggage that's psychic is real to each man.

Some lug it around for a whole lifespan.

Personal demons attach to their host.

Take care to learn which ones harm the most.

Beware the stories the lower self does tell

to oneself, to the world; it can rot like a smell.

Energy vampires can take many forms.

In flesh and in spirit, they drain and deform.

Study the parastraws, tentaclaws, too—

they suction the light off of me, off of you.

Your spark burns so bright they are

    drawn to the glare.

The darkness wants light, so proceed

    with great care!

They'll gather like moths when your energy leaks

and peck at your source with invisible beaks.

With free-floating bugs please use caution! Beware!

The darkness will cluster round ray light so rare.

Guard yourself from their parasites' extension cords.

Be hypnotized by neither their dances nor swords.

As I digested the poem, I had only one smartass thought. *Now she tells me?* I had to laugh at the "gift" of Mary's revelations. I really could've used this particular gold envelope a while ago, but maybe I was supposed to figure it out the hard way. The Great Work rhyme made perfect sense. But the joke of Mary's timing? Was on me.

CHAPTER 28

THE TIMING OF MY CAFFEINE SHAKES WAS ANOTHER story. Giant java jitters were in full effect by the time I opened the doors at Inkstop.

"Beth?" asked a Mohawked manwich at the front desk.

"That's me. I'm here for instructions."

He laughed. "Follow me." I tailed him through the graphics-heavy parlor and down the hall to a small, private room in back. "You are in for a treat," he said as he walked me there.

"That's editorializing," I suggested, knowing there was no way in hell I was going through with this.

"Oh. You a tenderfoot? A virgin?" I assumed he was asking if I had a tattoo.

"Tenderfoot? Does that have something to do with one's ability to handle pain?" I really didn't want any tattoos. I liked my skin. I didn't want anything on it. Anywhere.

Mohawk smiled. "Don't worry. Her needle is very kind. But . . . you think you'll need a pussyball?" I did not like the sound of that, especially combined with the virgin comment, and my face must've said so.

"It's a tennis ball. To squeeze. Or bite. For the pain?" He was taking pity on me, and it felt lame.

"I'm just here for instructions," I said. "I'm in kind of a hurry."

"Right." He opened the door to the private room and waved me inside. "She'll be with you in a moment."

I stepped into the dark room and wondered what was about to go down. It looked like I'd be getting a tattoo. Ugh. Or a piercing? Eek. I looked at the tools lined up like weapons. Latex gloves. Rubbing alcohol. Giant piercing awls. A shiny gun with multiple needles coming out of the head. What was I doing?

Someone could easily torture or poison me with any of the devices on the rack. Cold sweat went through my shirt, and I was reminded of my failure to buy deodorant. I stank.

I took a deep breath and decided I'd go with it. I wanted to record this chapter. I'd been through hell already and wanted a memento to remember that I survived. And besides, I was sure there weren't many 4.1 GPA blond nerds who'd inked themselves up.

The door opened, and an exotic punk princess with bumper bangs, dreadlocks, and violently azure eyes walked in. Her long dreads were pulled back into a high ponytail and her skin was almost translucent.

"Do you have something for me?" she asked.

I had no idea what she was talking about, so I handed her the gold envelope with the Inkstop address on it. She looked at it and shook her head.

"Nope. Something else." Her eyes were staring deep into me, and it was intimidating. I remembered the seven tarot cards Mary had given back to me, and I handed her the entire stack.

"Pick one," she insisted, and I realized there was probably a right and wrong answer. I studied the cards, remembering the Hebrew letters for Aleph and Beth were one, two, pee, poo on the first two cards. I took a guess and handed her the third card: High Priestess. She took it and smiled, and I unheld my breath.

"Good job. Take off your shirt, Beth," she said sweetly, and to my surprise pulled two tiny mutts out of her bag. That couldn't be sanitary, I thought.

"What's your name?" No response; Dreads didn't say her name. "And you are?" Still nothing.

"I rescued these pups. You mind if they hang out with us?" She set them into a cozy box lined with blankets.

"That's fine."

"They weren't weaned properly, but they're doing real good now. Aren'tcha, fellas?" She put down a bowl for them and they drank it up, making lapping noises.

"If you won't tell me your name, should we talk about my tattoo, then?" I wondered, all sincere.

She looked at me and shook her head emphatically while pressing a pedal on the floor that adjusted the height of the table. "I can't tell you anything. I'm sorry. Take your shirt and bra off and lie facedown on the table."

"I don't have any say in what goes on my body?"

"No way." She sighed. "It's been chosen for you."

I looked at Dreads with dread in my eyes.

"I didn't make the rules," she offered sympathetically.

"There are rules? More rules? For what? From who?"

"Facedown on the table, please. There's not much time."

I self-consciously obeyed as Dreads flipped a switch. The room turned into a black-light den, illuminating all this previously invisible calligraphy on the walls. "You can read it later. Facedown, please."

"Do I get any numbing cream or anything? I'm really exhausted. And I really wasn't planning on getting a tattoo today. Or ever." I was starting to lose it and change my mind. This was a mistake! "Let alone permanent markings on my one and only body that I have absolutely no say in. I could get up, put my shirt on, and walk out the door, couldn't I?" I pushed myself up and looked at Dreads in her goggles; I was about to leave. Dreads leaned over and pulled off the goggles. "It's a faith walk, Beth. I know you don't know me, and you don't have to trust me. But I'm not asking you to leap." She put her hand on my arm. "I'm going to build you a bridge."

"A bridge to what?"

"How about something small? Like your destiny."

"Yeah, what is my destiny, by the way?"

She touched a piece of hair that was matted to my face and tucked it behind my ear.

"Please listen to your heart with this. You'll be glad you did."

I felt a brisk breeze on my back as the smell of rubbing alcohol hit my nose, then a cold, wet chill as Dreads began rubbing it everywhere. I tried to think of something funny to say to cut the tension and blurted, "Don't shoot!" Silence. "Tattoo gun? Get it?"

Dreads stared at me without blinking for what felt like five minutes. And I immediately wanted to kill myself for being so lame.

"We call them tattoo machines actually. There are some scratchers who use the term gun, but most real tattoo artists don't." *Duly noted,* I thought, and prayed I hadn't offended the woman whose hands I was entrusting with my flesh.

Dreads sprayed something and then began to trace a pattern from my shoulders to my sacrum. It tickled and prickled my entire back. Whatever she was doing? It was going to be large. And—I surmised—quite painful. "You want to listen to some music? It can be a distraction. Although some people enjoy the intensity of the sensation."

I was screwed. "How long is this going to take?" I wondered aloud. Scared.

"That depends"—she giggled—"on how squicked you get."

"Squicked?" Saying the word freaked me out.

"Yes, squicked." Her inflection did nothing to clarify. I didn't know what it was. But whatever it was, it didn't sound good. She finally took pity on me.

"People say it about piercings, but it happens when I work with newbies. It's squirm factor, basically. The more you squirm, the longer it'll take." I had never regretted caffeine intake more in my life. I was jittering just lying there. "I'm going to be using an Aluminum Orion on you. It's like an ink-generating Mercedes that will be executing one thousand stabs per minute. I'm known for work that doesn't bleed, but I suggest you become a corpse."

Play dead while amped on espresso, no problem. "What is the design of the tattoo exactly?" I wondered aloud. Again.

"I'm sorry. That is a secret, so I can't tell you that. But I can tell you this: It's not my goal to hurt you. Quite the opposite."

Dreads handed me a long straw attached to a water pouch. "I'm going to put this under the face cradle. Sipping it will calm you. Let me know when you're ready."

I looked up at her without hesitation. "I'm ready. I wanna do this." I laid my face in the cradle and let the pain begin. After a moment I felt it sting. Hot scratches. Searing, vertical scratches etching into my back. If this was a test of pain, I failed. I felt every inky jab. But the pain focused me. It was as if the needle were a sewing machine, stitching together every single part of me. For three hours I experienced all of my weaknesses—my fears, my insecurities, my doubts, and my resentments. I watched as every single piece of psychic baggage I'd seen, every personal demon I'd faced, every bit of grooze, and each pain puppet I'd witnessed hanging on anyone all knitted together into a powerful quilt. My strengths were there too—my compassion, my kindness, my sense of fairness, and, well, anything I'd ever liked about myself. I felt it all weaving together. Stab by holey stab.

When it was finally over, it felt like she'd needled every square millimeter of my back. It felt huge. I winced as I adjusted my position, and I realized the design might be really ugly. Or really stupid. I had no idea. I didn't even care. As she frosted me like a cupcake, spreading thick goo over my back and covering the freshly raw skin with cling film and medical tape, I felt different. I had no desire to see the tattoo anymore. I tucked my bra into my pocket and put on my shirt.

"You won't be able to see it until you receive further instruction. It'll be covered in the Bepanthen cream and the dressing until then. I seriously recommend you not deviate from plan. Okay?" I nodded as she handed me a tube of what looked like diaper-rash cream, and I realized that I did have a choice. I'd used free will and elected to get the tattoo. And if I hated it? I could elect to get it removed.

Dreads gave me some almonds to munch on, and I staggered out of Inkstop Tattoo onto Avenue A with no idea where I was going. It was a brisk day, and the energy of folks wanting to get out of the cold was palpable. All I could feel was heat on my back, and the slicky slime of cream and cling wrap under my clothing. I was actually sweating, and I realized I felt alive. Not scared, not freaked out, but alive. Awake.

"Beth!" I heard my name, and it was Mr. Mohawk, jogging up behind me. "You forgot this." He smiled, handing me a large gold envelope.

CHAPTER 29

*T*HE ENVELOPE HAD THIS ADDRESS: 414 EAST 14TH Street. That was it. I handed it to the driver. I didn't have time to waste.

We quickly arrived at 414 East 14th Street, which turned out to be a church. Immaculate Conception Church. I went up to the huge double doors. They were locked. I looked around for a clue as to what to do. I was stumped.

I stood there for a few minutes, knocking on the door, trying to look for an alternate entrance or see if another gold envelope was waiting for me somewhere. Nope. A gray sedan pulled up in front of the church. The window rolled down halfway. A stunning woman with long jet-black hair and big sunglasses peered out from behind the tinted glass. Serious bling dangled from her ears, and her wrist bore stacks of charm bracelets. They were gorgeous. In honor of her hair, I decided to call her Jet.

"Hi, Jet!" No response.

She held out her hand. I realized I had to give her one of the cards, and I scrambled for the next one in the stack: the Empress. Jet took it, nodded, and smiled.

"Call Shirl" were Jet's first two words to me. I would've wondered how she knew Shirl, but given the lifetime of photos 7RI had of me, it was safe to assume they knew everything about me. Still, I had to be sure.

"Shirl? The Shirl?"

"Yes." Was Jet's third.

"Did I do something wrong?"

"Not yet." And with that fourth and fifth word Jet rolled up the window, then rolled it back down—"The name is Dolly"— before zipping it up again.

I held the phone and hesitated. Why did I have to call Shirl? I couldn't for the life of me see how that would be a test. A few moments later the sedan window hummed down.

"Call Shirl. Now."

I was frustrated. "Can I get a hint?"

"No. It's a test."

I tried to blink into my sight and see if there were clues around Dolly. I thought of my mother, and I remembered her threat about my stuff. All my stuff. Maybe I could ask Shirl for help. I dialed the number.

"Hello?" Shirl had that tone when you don't recognize a number but pick up anyway.

"Shirl. It's Beth."

"OHMIGOD. Are you okay? Where are you? Are you at McCall's?" Shirl's voice was pitched so high and loud I had to pull the phone away from my ear as she babbled a mile a minute.

"Shirl, Shirl. Stop. I need your help—and don't ask questions."

"Why not?"

"Shirl. You kind of owe me?"

"I know, I know, I know. I'm sorry. I'm so glad you're okay. Of course! Anything!"

"Okay. So, my mom is threatening to burn all my stuff. Go to my house. Go and get as much as you can out of my room? I'm kind of indisposed."

"Holy crap, what, what, what? Oh, no, okay, okay, I get it. I'm leaving now—I'll call you when I'm there."

Dolly rolled down the window and looked at me. She folded her arms on the ledge, and I stared at her beautiful jewelry. She had the most gorgeous gems I'd ever seen, dripping on her arms. I felt like I was going into a trance looking at her.

"Before Shirl calls you back, I've been instructed to ask you to tell me what happened." What was she talking about? Huh?

"What happened when?" I suddenly felt really ugly. She was beyond gorgeous.

"Tell me what happened with your stuff."

"I don't know." I shrugged. It felt like she was looking down at me even though she was seated.

"You know."

"No, I don't."

"Fine. I'll sit here." She sighed. "And I'll pretend you don't have the capacity to discern what happened to your stuff."

"I do?"

"Really?" Her voice was the kind of condescending that makes you feel naked and stupid. "Are you being serious, Aleph Beth?"

"Fine. Wanna tell me how I can do that?"

"No. You are supposed to tell me what happened."

"I assure you I can't."

"Come here." I could've sworn I heard her add "you twit" onto the end of it. In her mind.

"I'm not a twit," I added, just in case.

"Nice work!" She motioned me to come closer. She casually unfolded her hand, dangling it out the window. She waited there with her hand extended, looking at me expectantly.

"What?" I didn't get it. She began shaking her head as if I'd tracked dog poop on her new white carpet.

"If you were to accidentally brush up against me? Might you get a clue, clueless one? If that was your intention?" Dolly was over me.

"Sorry. I guess you've done this before?" I asked her hesitantly, and she shook her head and looked at me as if I were wearing a clown costume at a funeral.

"This isn't my first time at the rodeo, Beth." Dolly opened her beautiful palm and looked the other way, giving me permission to touch her hand.

As I touched her, Dolly broadcast the following instructions to me. Loud and clear, like a megaphone in my ear: "Picture your mom. Picture your stuff. It's the same as holding it. For you. Now do it." And then she pulled her hand in and smiled, broadcasting without saying, "You twit." I'd picked up more than that from our touch. I felt that Dolly had shoplifted every single one of the items she was wearing.

"You're quite the kleptomaniac, aren't you?"

Glancing at her diamond-encrusted Rolex, she said, "You have sixty seconds, starting thirty seconds ago," before zipping up the window of the car.

I could see what happened to people and things by picturing them? How was I supposed to know that? I couldn't even calculate how the hell that worked, but I gave it a shot. I tried to picture the first thing that came to mind: my blue teddy bear.

Suddenly, the car's black windows filled with little boxes of moving images, like an in-store display of TV monitors. Quick cuts were flashing on the screens: I saw my clothes being pulled out of my closet. Images of my bedroom dresser being emptied. Flashes of my bed being stripped of sheets, my walls becoming bare. I could see my books and all my belongings being carried out of my room. I saw a heap in the backyard. All my stuff piled up: on the ground, on the grill, everywhere. My mother soaking it with lighter fluid. Dumping cans of lighter fluid on all my stuff, tossing a match onto the pile. Everything going up in flames. Images of a fire filled every screen. I watched as my blue teddy bear flew into the flames. My throat closed, choking off all air. My life was burning before my very eyes. My cheeks got hot and wet. I knew it was true. I knew that every last shred of my stuff was gone.

The window rolled down. Dolly stared at me expectantly.

"My mother burned all my stuff." Dolly nodded, as if she already knew this was true, and handed me a gold envelope. The car window rolled up and she drove away.

I stood there, unable to feel my feet. What time was it? Where was I? The phone rang. It was Shirl. She was crying.

"I'm sorry, Beth." She sounded hysterical, and coughed. "Your bedroom is empty, your closets, your walls, your drawers—everything is gone. I got here too late!"

"I know—"

"There's a terrible smell"—her coughing was bad—"and some kind of burned mess in the backyard. It looks like she torched everything. Oh, man, this is—" She wheezed. "I'm so sorry."

I was dizzy and felt like I might throw up. "I gotta go, Shirl—" Even though I had no idea where.

"Call me later. I'm so, so sorry."

And then it dawned on me. "It's okay. It's just stuff."

"What?" Shirl was way more upset than I was.

"It's just stuff. It doesn't matter."

"Really? But you love your stuff. You name it." She coughed some more. "Well, then I might have some good news."

"Yeah?"

"I still have Betty."

I had to laugh. Of course she still had my favorite bag.

"I'm sorry I didn't give it back to you. And I'm sorry about what I did to you, all the lying and stuff. Uch, this has been the worst time in my life. I can't believe how crappy I was. I suck. I'm so sorry, B. Do you forgive me?" Words were rushing out of her like wildfire.

"I forgive you, Shirl."

"Really, for real? Ah, shoot, your mom is coming. Gotta run. Call me later!"

I clicked off the phone, knowing every piece of my old life was in that charred pile in the backyard. The thing was, it wasn't my life anymore. Everything was different.

CHAPTER 30

OPENED THE NEXT GOLD ENVELOPE AND LOOKED around for my ride. I felt the cream and cellophane slide against my back, amazed that my fresh tattoo didn't hurt. Amazed that I had a tattoo at all. The gray sedan was nowhere to be seen, so I hailed a cab to my next test: 123 East 15th Street. The address belonged to the Christ

Lutheran Church. As I stepped out of the cab, a young woman wearing a wildly colorful ensemble waved. She was something to behold. Her hair fell past her shoulders and was dyed magenta. Magenta, but featuring equally spaced, horizontal, jet-black stripes. Her punk rugby-shirt tresses were topped with a dapper animal-print fedora. Her fashion plumage was very peacock. Peacockian.

She made a dramatic show of extending her palm, face up. I handed her the next card: the Emperor.

"That'll work," the rooster purred, pocketing the card. "Beth?" She sported the most exquisitely painted-on makeup I'd ever seen: luminous foundation, a fuchsia glossed mouth, deep magenta eyeliner, and the slightest hint of blush. Her extreme eyelashes batted like mini feather-fans, and I realized I'd been staring. With my mouth open.

"Beth? Are you okay?" I nodded. "Then please follow me."

Even in her expensive and ornately festooned platform ankle boots, she walked quickly; I could barely keep stride with Lady Peacock. Each step was fast and purposeful. Everything about her was intentional, from the precise blunt cut at the bottom of her hair to the immaculate tailoring of her topcoat to the almost aerodynamic positioning of her shoulder bag. She was the most specific human being I'd ever encountered. I was riveted. I didn't even bother asking her name or what we'd be doing. I intentionally brushed up against her. There were images of an orphanage and huge amounts of money being given to that facility. Before I could continue, she stopped in her tracks. "Please don't do that, Beth.

I'm serious." She was very clear and matter of fact. "We're here."

The entrance was painted like a trompe l'oeil. So, the door? Had been painted to look like a window.

I laughed. "You make a better door than a window." And Peacock nodded. "I mean, this one really does, right?" I looked at the red neon name above the door: THE EMPEROR. Of course! Peacock opened the door with the window painted on it, and I followed her into a red-lacquered hallway. At the far end a hefty Hawaiian man with a sumo-size belly sat on a stool one-tenth his size. He nodded to Peacock, pulling back the burgundy velvet curtains that led into a club. Little booths lined the walls, as bartenders and various staff busily cleaned the horseshoe-shaped bar. And poles. Poles?

"Are those—"

"Stripper poles?" Peacock laughed. "Yes, but I like to call them dancer pillars. Much more polite, don't you think?" She flicked off her coat with such speed and grace I almost missed the intricate embroidery on the lining. I focused on the floral handiwork inside the coat because I couldn't think. I was too terrified that my next test involved said pillars. Cancel that. I wasn't terrified; I was petrified. Frozen solid.

"Let me remind you, Beth, that someone's life is at stake. I would hope that, you know, that reality would make any anxiety you might be having feel, I don't know, kind of petty. Wouldn't you say?" I didn't feel petty. I felt sweaty.

"As you can see, the Emperor serves alcohol, making this a topless club. Not totally nude, lucky for you." I had never felt less lucky in my entire life. "Your test requires you to do a set—that's one to three songs—and strip until you make a minimum of one hundred dollars." I thought I would vomit. "You will put all of your tips in the donation box at Christ Lutheran Church when you are done."

I stuttered, "But I can't dance! I'm a terrible dancer, actually."

"That's not true," she said. I remembered Kinkos with Richie and was glad he wasn't here to see this. "Are you sure your issue isn't about being judgmental? A fear of being judged?"

"Being naked in front of strangers isn't high on my list, no." I tried to smile.

"But forcing people to be naked against their will? That's okay?"

"No! I never said that. What's that supposed to mean?"

"Hmm. What you did at your high school, to those kids? You didn't mind stripping them down to their secrets without their consent, did you?" Oh, man. I felt dread in my belly. Was this karma? Was this payback for unleashing the truth back at New Glen?

"It wasn't your truth to unleash," Peacock answered my thought. "That's why it was a violation. Abuses of power are serious violations. Time to pay your fine, little lady." I had no response. If this was karmic retribution, all the arguing in the world wouldn't help me. Peacock looked at me blankly. "I have a pair of practice shoes for you. It'll give you a chance to get comfortable on the horseshoe." She pointed to a U-shaped stage. "The club opens for happy hour in about forty minutes. Follow me."

Peacock led me into the dancers' dressing room, where a few girls were getting ready in front of lockers and mirrors. Nobody said hello, and a chilly resentment filled the air. My guide unlocked a locker and removed a costume: a schoolgirl outfit and a pair of Lucite platforms with a transparent six-inch heel.

"I'd tell you to move slowly, but there's not that much time. Go get 'em!" Peacock was enjoying this.

I grabbed the shoes and scurried back into the main room and seriously considered vacating the premises. *Get over yourself,* I thought. *No one cares. It's just a body.* I still had my street clothes on and was concerned about the cling-film situation on my back. Not to mention my potentially disappointing, surgically unaltered breasts. But the staff ignored me as I hopped up on a horseshoe and took the Lucites for a spin. They were shockingly stable. I lost my balance a couple times but recovered quickly. A busboy looked up at me with pity in his eyes. "It's for charity," I whispered on behalf of my pride. "This is for charity, Beth. This is to save a life." A voice suddenly boomed over the speakers, "What music do you want? Do you have a stripper name, Beth?" Oh, great, they knew my name. Wonderful. "And please don't say the name of your first pet and the first street you lived on," he added, referring to the porno name game everyone played in high school.

I felt like a deer in headlights and went with it. "Is Bambi taken?"

The DJ sighed. "We have two other Bambis, but they aren't dancing tonight. Music?"

I shrugged, but then I remembered Kinkos and my iPod. Yes! What if I could channel something besides sex? Without Richie? I racked my brain for a performer who could really shake it, and "Beyoncé!" popped out of my mouth before I could even think about it. I paced back and forth a few more times as "Single Ladies" started pumping through the sound system. I closed my eyes, breathing into the music, saying, "Dance, please; dance, please," when my butt started booty-quaking involuntarily, my body launching into steps I'd only seen in music videos. I crawled on my knees a bit and rocked the 'dancer pillar' like a jungle gym. When the music stopped, so did I. "That'll work," said the DJ, and I looked down, squinting into the lights, and noticed the pity-eyed busboy with his jaw on the ground. "Was that okay?" I asked him. He nodded and gave me a stunned thumbs-up.

Backstage, Peacock helped me remove the cling film from my back. "Some tattoo," she commented, and I informed her I wasn't allowed to see it. "None of us were." She wiped off the cream and handed me a new thong, still in its packaging.

"None of you? None of you were what?" I wondered aloud, wrapping my shirt around my waist before swapping my grandma panties for the equivalent of dental floss.

Peacock caught herself, drastically changing her tone. "Comfortable on stage at first."

"Speak for yourself," piped in a random dancer who introduced herself as Aries. "I was practically born with a pole in my mouth." I looked at Aries and could've sworn she winked at me.

"A lot of the dancers prefer women," Peacock whispered. "Don't worry about it." Peacock quickly helped me into the rest of my skimpy schoolgirl outfit, complete with a very short mini-kilt and breakaway top. "Put that long blond hair in pigtails and let's go," she ordered. I was not about to disobey.

As I waited backstage to go on, I peeked out and surveyed the room. About twenty men were scattered around the club. I did the math in my head and prayed for big tips. I would've prayed for big tits, but it was a little late for that.

And then it slammed me: I was about to take my clothes off in front of complete strangers. For money. It was ridiculous. Demeaning. Humiliating. I'd be naked in front of strangers, against my will. I had stripped Jake, Grenada, and Jenny down without their consent too. Whether they were jerks or not jerks didn't matter. Whether I thought I'd been saving Shirl or not didn't matter. It was wrong. I was wrong. Yes, dancing naked was fine for Aries, Grenada, Peacock, or lots of perfectly willing girls who had zero problem with it. But every part of me was stopped by the truth: It wasn't me. At all. Supernatural Beyoncé ability or no Beyoncé ability.

The previous dancer finished, scooping bills off the stage before jiggling by me. "Ladies and gentlemen, please give a warm welcome to . . . BAMBI!"

In that moment I knew without a shadow of a doubt exactly who I was. And I knew that I couldn't go through with it.

"Put your hands together for . . . BAMBI!"

I was motionless. Peacock popped her head behind the curtain. "Beth? Come on! You're on!"

I took a deep breath and looked the dazzling lady right in the eye. "I can't do it, whatever your name is. It's not for me." She made a face.

"Wait one second," she said, and disappeared as another dancer rushed past to take my place onstage. I cringed at what might happen because I wouldn't obey the gold letters or pass tests that someone else had written for me. I prayed that no ill would befall another person because I couldn't go through with it.

Moments later Peacock reappeared. I couldn't read her. She motioned to follow her back to the dressing room, and she silently watched me as I changed back into my clothes. Finally, she shook her head. "You're making a big mistake. Are you sure you won't go through with it?"

"Maybe it is a mistake, but it's my mistake. And if someone's life is really at stake, it's not because I wouldn't take my clothes off and dance for a bunch of men." Peacock let a big grin cross her face and pulled something out of her bag. It was the greatest thing I'd ever seen. It was another gold envelope.

"Congratulations, kid. You passed." My heart leaped for reasons I didn't fully understand, but I think it had something to do with truth and being true. To myself.

CHAPTER 31

PRACTICALLY SKIPPED MY WAY TO THE NEXT destination, 209 East 16th Street. The gold envelope had an address and nothing else. I was so high from the adrenaline of my experience at the Emperor club that food had become irrelevant. I looked for the address and found a beautiful old church called St.

Ann's Church for the Deaf. I looked around for clues, paying attention to everything. I was watching a few people using sign language as they walked in and out of St. Ann's. I didn't "speak" American Sign Language, and I was silently wondering if this was part of my test. My questions were answered when a strange beauty in a reddish-orange dress approached me and extended her palm. I was one step ahead of her and placed the card called Hierophant into her hand. "Well done, Beth." I nodded. She blinked her golden eyes and craned her neck to the right. "Follow me," she said. The thing was, she said all of it without saying a word. *Just like Nessa,* I thought with a smile.

I studied her as we walked. Sun-kissed tiers of curls haloed her long neck, grazing the straps of an ornately embroidered backpack yoked around her mocha shoulders. She had that ridiculously gorgeous, deep golden coloring that people spray-tan themselves silly trying to replicate. Her amber eyes were extraordinary, and passersby did constant double takes in her direction. She took it in stride, nodding graciously if someone smiled or stared too long. I couldn't help myself, and I timed a step so I could brush my leg against hers. Images of drag queens flashed through my mind's eye, when she interrupted my peeping with, "Not without my permission you won't." I immediately felt guilty and blurted, "Sorry."

"Here," she said without saying, opening the door to a building with trefoils on the front of it. It was a heavy old door, and she opened it with a push. Inside, Goldy led me into a modern, gray cement room. Two young girls in party dresses sat in chairs, giggling. The twelve-year-olds were normal in every way except for one: They were completely bald. Their mothers hovered nearby, reviewing wig options with a smocked man who was also bald. Dozens of rows of canvas and Styrofoam wig heads on shelves lined the walls. Heads and wigs everywhere. Alongside partial heads were metal wig stands and bases with suction cups on the bottom. Mannequin heads wearing wig caps and cotton wig liners were interspersed with more foam heads. Large hooks and nails covered any remaining space, dangling wigs of every style, length, and color. Hairpieces and extensions hung from spare wall space. The room was an ode to hair, both real and fake.

"Are these all yours? Do you make these?" I asked quietly, not wanting to disturb the clients.

Goldy finally spoke. Even her voice was golden. "People from all over the world donate and sell their hair. The longer and the more unprocessed, the better." Goldy helped the bald stylist outfit the young ladies with fabulous hair. Their smiles were ecstatic, and their mothers held back tears. Goldy took a Polaroid of each girl and tacked it on a wall of photos. "You're on the Wall of Fame now!" she cooed as the stylist led them out.

"Where are the donations from?" I wondered aloud. A row of nails held yards of braids and ponytails waiting to be converted into wigs.

"The darker hair is from Indians and Asians—India and

China are big resources for us. We can't take bleached hair, so the naturally lighter colors are very desirable. And more expensive, obviously."

I examined the price tags on various items. They ranged from a few hundred to thousands of dollars—four thousand for a natural blond wig more than twenty inches long. There was wavy hair and straight hair, curly and coarse, medium and fine.

"Have a look around; I'll be right back." Goldy exited a door and popped her head back in. "Listen carefully." And then she was gone.

When I closed my eyes, dazzling streams of energy, astounding fields of color and texture, poured out of each natural wig and braid. As I toured the space, I traveled the world, seeing the lives of all the people who'd grown their hair and sold it. The family of twelve girls in Mongolia who supported their family by growing their tresses, cutting them off, and getting paid handsomely for it. The Chinese women who cried after chopping their long braids at the scalp, sorely needing to feed their families. There was a tribe of Native American men who each wept after shearing thick, twenty- and thirty-inch tails from their skulls. The group of moms in Finland who'd saved the long-ago cut braids of little ones, clearing out their closets to help those in need. I grazed my hands along the aisles of hair, feeling the lives of every person it had belonged to. I squinted my eyes and saw the ropes of energy emanating from each sample. Forcing myself to hone in on it, seeing the gradations of intensity and quality of each sample. This hair was not dead. Every strand was an antenna that was dialed into a channel far, far away.

I squinted deeper into the Sight. Shadows flickered out of the corner of my eye. It looked like hair in one part of the room was moving, casting shadows on the walls. The hair didn't move at all, but the shadows did. The energy of the hair was revealing itself in fantastic projections. What about the new owners and wearers of the wigs? Could they feel anything? Could they sense the lives of the people who'd grown the hair they'd wear on their heads? As if to answer my question, music filled my ears, and a pair of extensions started moving—waltzing off the wall as if to communicate. They shimmied and moved like cobras rising out of a snake charmer's basket, pirouetting as if to confirm my suspicion. Suddenly, the locks on a wig lifted up off the Styrofoam head, defying gravity and cascading upward in a lyrical spiral. Another set of braids shot out in all directions as if electrocuted. Elsewhere, permanent curls rolled and unrolled rhythmically as if someone were curling and uncurling the strands with an invisible flat iron. Talk about hair-raising. Hair was literally standing on end, and it was breathtaking.

"Do you hear the soundless sound?" It was Goldy, silently signaling me from a different room.

"Yes." I said without a word.

"Do you understand the test?" Goldy spoke into my head.

"I see the lives of the hair. Is that it?" I asked.

"No."

"Then I don't think I understand." I looked around, catching my reflection in a mirror on the wall and seeing my uncertainty. I had no idea what was expected of me. Yet again.

I studied every wall of the room. The hair and shadows had stopped moving, leaving me alone with my thoughts and my fear.

"What is it? What is it?" I was drawn toward the wall of Polaroids. Dozens of faces, proudly modeling their new locks. I squinted to go deeper, and the photos became magical animations: before-and-after portraits in reverse. The "after" images with wigs winked into "before" shots sporting little or no hair. The curtain between their pain and their joy rose and fell for me. Some of the images spoke to me, talking about themselves and talking to each other as they hung on the wall. Slowly their words became a soft chant, and they were all pointing at me and speaking simultaneously "Look. Look. Look." I moved toward my reflection in the mirror, drawn in.

"What is it, Beth? What's the test?" I gazed deeply into my own eyes and couldn't believe how slow I'd been.

My heart fell. I'd lost all my stuff. I'd lost Richie. I'd lost everything. My hair was all I had left. I didn't want to lose that, too.

I was biting my lip to stop the tears, when my hair started moving. Strands began unbraiding and waltzing out in all directions. Pieces reached for the walls, the ceiling, the back of the room. Fibers swirled, snaking into beautiful patterns around my skull. It appeared that my hair wanted to stay. My hair wanted to help. It would grow back. After all, my hair wasn't me. It was just stuff.

"Yes!" I said, getting it. My heart was pounding as I brushed it all smooth, pulling it back into a tight ponytail and carefully braiding it. I picked up a pair of cutting shears and held them up to my braid, frantic suddenly. "Is this it? Is this the test?" I wanted to be sure.

A voice inside myself answered, as clearly and loudly as I'd ever heard it. *Are you ready to listen?* it asked.

Yes, I thought. *I've been through too much not to listen anymore. It's not worth it.* I meant it. *Yes.* I waited for an answer.

Your hair is the price, my inner voice said sweetly. *Cut it.*

I picked up the shears and cut off my ten-inch braid without hesitation. The remaining locks seemed to sigh with relief, stretching into the air before falling into place around my face. If my hair was the price, I understood why listening to your inner voice has a cost. I'd finally paid my inner tuition. My intuition.

Goldy returned to the room with a big smile on her face and a fat, gold envelope in her hand. I handed her my braid as she passed me the envelope and put a merciful hand on my head. "You look incredibly beautiful." We said good-bye, and as I walked out of the chamber of dancing wigs toward destinations unknown, I knew it was true.

CHAPTER 32

EW YORK CITY WAS ALIVE WITH ENERGY AS I RACED to my next test: an address on 17th Street. I felt light-headed with the shorter hair, and I couldn't stop touching it. It was totally freeing, and I marveled at my new look in every reflection I could catch myself in. Sometimes doing a double take, as if seeing my long-lost twin for the first time.

When I arrived at 17 East 17th Street, I did a different kind of double take. The kind you do when faced with identically dressed identical twins. They were heart-stopping beauties wearing skinny jeans, amazing sneakers, and the sickest tracksuit jackets I'd ever seen. They were like hip-hop mirror images of each other, with similarly braided hair and slightly different colored eyes. I was unsure which one I should give the final card to, but they simply nodded to me and said simultaneously, "Choose."

"May I touch each of your arms first?" I asked. They shrugged at each other and extended their limbs willingly. While feeling their skin, images exploded to life: Indiana? Michigan? Turntables? Microphones? Record stores? The mashed-up jumble overwhelmed me, and I pulled back, staring into their eyes. Without thinking, I picked the one on the right and handed her the final card: the Lovers. The one on the left kissed her sister on both cheeks before hopping into a waiting gray sedan.

I followed the twin into the building, my heart palpitating from the day. Between my tattoo, my stuff pyre, the pole dance, and my haircut, I'd faced everything. I'd been scared, but it hadn't stopped me. The visions taught me about myself through other people, I guess; today I'd learned about me. I wasn't my grades; I wasn't the labels: daughter of Jan Michaels, graduate of New Glen High, best friend to Shirl. I wasn't Richie's crush, and I wasn't my story. I was someone capable of doing things I'd never imagined I could do. There was a lot more to me than I thought.

After ten minutes of twists and turns through the endless

corridors of the building, we arrived at a large door marked FIRE EXIT, complete with alarm warnings. Twinster smirked at me before opening the door, setting off the alarm. I followed her through another maze, complete with blinking red lights and sirens. She pushed open another door, revealing a night-club with a dance floor that was very much alive. She led me through a maze of sweaty bodies grinding to the music. A DJ booth was perched high over the throbbing mob, and the twin led me up a steep, narrow staircase toward the turntables. My body throbbed with bass as we ascended twenty feet or more. A previously nonexistent fear of heights began to kick in as we wobbled higher and higher on the super-shaky scaffolding. The lights, smoke, and sound created a nerve-racking nausea. I was dizzy, and my lack of food was starting to catch up with me.

Waiting for us at the top was none other than . . . the other twin! She winked at me as she jockeyed the ones and twos with finesse, alternating between vinyl and laptop with total fluidity. Her handiwork was so nimble I almost forgot we were a good story above the crowd. Twinster leaned in to my ear and asked the following question.

"Who do you need to forgive?"

"Who do I need to forgive?" I yelled back, and she nodded emphatically.

I flashed on my mother and Shirl, on Richie Mac and everyone I'd ever been mad at. My mind raced through every hurt, every slight, every blame I'd ever cooked to a crisp inside of myself. I thought of how confusing the visions had been and of the countless moments where I'd blamed myself. All the times I'd asked: *What have I done to deserve this? Why am I being punished? Why am I so alone? Why is the universe out to get me?* There were so many people I needed to forgive: Shirl, Richie, but especially my mother. Before I could do that, I needed to forgive myself. Really forgive myself. I hadn't done anything wrong. I'd done the best I could. They'd done the best they could. I didn't want to resent anyone anymore.

I felt a hand on each shoulder, a twin on either side of me. "Are you ready?"

For what? I wondered, as Twinster grabbed the microphone and started beatboxing to her sister's track. The crowd went wild, their hands upraised, bodies pumping up and down in unison. DJ handed me a gold envelope, with a look that said, *It's going to be okay.* My stomach dropped in fear of what the card would say. My fears were borne out as I read the following words:

Let go.

Did they want me to kill myself? Was my life the one that was in danger? Was I the somebody who might die after all? As if reading my thoughts, Twinster climbed over the scaffolding and handed her sister the microphone, waving me to her side. No way. Not one cell in me wanted to do this. At all.

"You want me to fall into this crowd?" I screamed over the noise.

"Yes." She twinkled. "Have faith."

I was tired of being scared. I was tired of hesitating. I was tired of my negative thoughts that always assumed the worst. Maybe it was time to have faith. Then I heard my inner voice say, loud and clear: *Leap. And the net will appear.*

"Okay," I said, as I threw my leg over the guardrail and stood with my back to the crowd.

DJ Twin grinned and said, "On three, everybody, I want you to catch my soul sista here. Are you with me?"

I heard the crowd roar with approval. "ONE! TWO! THREE!"

And without a net, without a bungee, without a wing, without a prayer . . . I fell backward. In that instant a flashing strobe made the room pulsate, flaring off the mirrored ceiling. The sudden blast of searing light scalded my eyes. And time slowed to a virtual halt. My reflection above me, the crowd underneath me, all stopped. I appeared suspended, covered in the mercurial grooze I'd seen earlier. I stared in wonder and took a breath. The light pulsed again, burning away all that was false, and made clean my field in a spectacular burst of white. The grooze exploded and dissolved into dust around me, brightness scorching my eyes like suns. I had to squint from the brilliance, seeing my likeness as if for the first time. The energy around me dulled, then sharpened with an audible sigh. I saw myself, my entire self, for the first time. Movement jostled all around me, casting incandescent flickers onto every surface in the room. Downy white flutters were waving behind my head, pressing against the walls. Oscillating flutters kissing, embracing, and caressing me. Alive. I searched my reflection for the answer and heard myself say two words: "My wings." I burst out laughing and felt lightness in my chest and heart. It was absurd. It was ludicrous, even. Me? Wings? This was not possible!

"Don't get carried away," Sister Mary's voice suddenly sassed in my mind. "Everyone has them. They just don't use them. For some people, not using them will hurt more. You are one of those lucky few." And like that? The wings disappeared. "You haven't earned them yet, my dear. That was just a sneak preview, but make no mistake: You must earn them." The image and Mary's voice vanished.

Then gravity returned, speeding my descent and wrenching me into real time. I watched as the twins grew smaller, and my body jerked to a halt as dozens of arms, hands, heads, and elbows caught me. Strange hands buoyed me above the ground as tiny feathers floated through the air, lending more support than I'd ever felt in my life. Random arms and hands hugged me, high-fived me, and embraced me. And then gently set me down. On my own two feet.

CHAPTER 33

HEN I WALKED OUTSIDE, IT WAS DARK. A CHAUFFEUR stood outside a gray sedan, holding the door open for me. I climbed inside to the smell of burritos. Food had never tasted so good. I relished every bite as the car brought me to an address on Fifth Avenue. The chauffeur opened my door and escorted me inside the building. "Seventh floor," he said. When I arrived upstairs, there were no signs, only a small pair of red velvet curtains hanging on a wall. When I pulled them away, I saw that the shiny brass plaque underneath was engraved with three marks I knew well without knowing at all: 7RI. I blew out some nervous air, realizing that I still didn't know what it stood for.

The door was ajar. I pushed it open. And there they were. Six young women sitting in six chairs: Dreads, Dolly, Peacock, Goldy, and the twins. They all smiled, each young woman more beautiful than the next. As they began standing up and extending their hands to shake mine, their unusual eyes refracted the light in the room, resembling jewels. Peacock went first. "Hello again, Aleph. Or do you prefer Beth? I'm Hen."

"Either one is fine, to be honest." It felt wild to be called by a new name, and I had to admit something to myself: I really, really liked it.

"I'm Gimmi." Dreads winked. "How's your back feel?" I assured her I was healing nicely.

"Hey, Beth." Goldy embraced me warmly. "I'm Va-Va."

"As you know, I am Dolly." Dolly's hair went all the way to her waist. Without sunglasses on, her Eurasian eyes were a dazzling shade of green.

The twins were the last to introduce themselves. I still could not tell them apart, and I realized the only difference was the staggering shade of purple in their eyes.

"I'm Zara." The purplish-pink shade of her eyes was bananas.

"I'm Innee." Innee's violet lenses studied me intensely. She had a bit more attitude than Zara, but beyond that? Their resemblance was uncanny. And of all the young women here, they were clearly closest in age to me.

I noticed a seventh chair was empty at the end of the row, and it reminded me of my dream back in the attic.

"You might want to sit down." Hen pointed to it, and I sat in my déjà vu. Seven chairs, but no blackboard.

A woman in a nun's habit walked in and stood in front of us. It was none other than Mary, wearing the same little brown shirt, brown skirt, and orthopedic shoes. Walking over to a small MiniDV camera on a tripod in the corner, she turned it on before speaking. We were being recorded.

"Is that necessary?" Hen asked, annoyed. They seemed to know each other.

"You know it is." Mary was emphatic. "Shall we?" Off of Hen's nod, Mary continued. "Welcome to 7RI, the headquarters of Seven Rays International. I want to thank you all for coming. My name is Sister Mary. I am the executive director of the 7RI Trust, and I am in charge of maintaining the archive. I have been interacting with each of you for various lengths of time, and you've all undergone various verification protocols."

Sister Mary took the camera off the tripod. "Please remove your left shoe and any hosiery you are wearing." We each took off one of our shoes. "Would each of you please straighten your left leg and flex your left foot?" She lowered the camera to foot level, filming each foot while zooming out, zooming in. Face with foot, then foot, then face, zooming in on something.

"There are small red dots on the soles of your left feet." Mary placed a magnifying glass over each foot. "The mark on your foot is a small tattoo. To the naked eye it appears to be a simple red dot. The dot is actually comprised of an intricate design, visible only under magnification."

Gimmi whispered to us, "I can't believe I never noticed it before."

"Thank you." Sister Mary put away her gear. "You may put your shoes back on. Now, each of you must consent to go through one last procedure before your first assignment."

"What assignment?" I asked, as all six ladies looked at me. They had no idea either.

"Are the tests ever going to end, Mary? It's starting to feel a little ridiculous." Gimmi had her own history with Mary, I guessed, and from the way she was sucking her top lip with her teeth, I gathered it wasn't all peachy.

"All your questions will be answered in the appropriate time. Please remove all your clothes except your underpants. Thank you."

Nothing like getting naked in front of complete strangers. The others didn't argue, and although I was self-conscious, I wasn't about to protest. I laughed in the knowledge that Shirl and my mother wouldn't recognize me. If this had happened two years, two months, or two weeks ago? I would've freaked. I wondered where and how Richie was, and just sent a hello out to him via the universe: *I really need you again, Richie. I hope you're okay.* I missed him and still wanted to be near him, but the day's tests helped me find a way to make it alright. Even in my underwear in front of complete strangers.

"I'm sure he got the message." It was Va-Va, broadcasting to me telepathically with a smile.

"You think?" I silently asked her, and Va-Va nodded. "Nessa sends her love too, you know—" she added, and my heart filled up. I really missed that cute mute.

Sister Mary flipped a switch on the wall, and the room turned into a blackish purple playground. I heard a gasp and looked around. We all had glow-in-the-dark markings on our skin. Gimmi pointed out the location of the UV black-light tattoos for Sister Mary, who continued recording our tattoos. I was dying to know what mine said! "Your tatt reads 'Y-V-H-V,'" Gimmi replied to my thoughts. "Your tattoo is four letters. Y-V-H-V."

"Wow. That's exactly what I wanted! How'd you know?" I joked aloud, and she laughed. I'd barely glimpsed the other tattoos before the regular lights were switched on.

"None of us had a choice in design, if that makes you feel any better," Gimmi said.

"Who did your tattoo?" I asked.

"I did. But that doesn't mean I chose the design." Off my look of surprise Gimmi whispered, "What? You think you're the only one who's special? Get in line, kid."

"But what's it mean?" It was the most I'd gotten out of anyone.

"It's another language," Gimmi said sympathetically. "You'll understand when you're ready to. You just don't get to know when that is." I felt a flush of excitement, and I realized that I liked not knowing the answer. I'd grown up learning to know the answer. Specializing in knowing the answer. But at that moment? For the first time ever? I don't know why, but I was loving the mystery.

"You've all passed inspection. Put on your clothes and follow me. There isn't much time." Sister Mary packed up the camera and led us out to a waiting van.

We were transported by SUV to All Saints Hospital. It was a relatively small three-story building, and we were ushered up to the top floor, where a woman in the intensive care unit was hooked up to three machines and several IV drips. I looked at the name on her chart: Sarah I. David. I closed my eyes and squinted into my Sight. The tangle of energies was so intense it took a minute to clarify what I was seeing. Ropes pulled from every angle toward her small, shriveled body. They weren't all knotted, but they were absolutely there. Dark blobs clung to her periphery, each one containing a movie, so I focused on the brightest one. It showed Sarah, months earlier? Years earlier? Healthier but still in the hospital. The image pulled wider for me, an overhead view of the hospital wing as if the roof had been removed and I could see into every room, see all the energies dancing and lodging amongst the cancer patients. Cancer burnished with brown tone, sepia globules pulsing like living balloons, tethered by some invisible string and cleaving to their patient, their carrier.

But time twisted in Sarah's picture, reversing backward, revealing her admission into the ward and speeding up so I could see the impact of her arrival. The brown blisters began tugging in her direction, becoming unfastened from their owner and gravitating toward Sarah's room. Her energy would absorb the globule, pop it, and vaporize it. After the bubble burst, an appendage of light would extend from Sarah to the patient it had come from, scaling any remaining hole in their body. On a lung, a breast, a pancreas, a brain, or all over—wherever the cancer had been would get gassed up with a luminous substance. Once the hole was filled, the tentacle retracted back into Sarah, as another brown ball made its way toward her. Funky, round football players, continuously rushing her room for the tackle. Cancer pirates, stealing her healing booty.

Speeding and slowing the movie revealed another phenomenon. Once the globules had been absorbed by Sarah and the tentacles had retracted, the patient got well. Patients would get up and leave that day or the next. It was an exodus of healing in high speed. It wasn't treatment that explained the success rates of the hospital. It was Sarah. She was absorbing and eating the cancer of the entire ward. And it was killing her.

Each of us took a turn assessing Sarah's condition. After a minute Sister Mary cleared her throat. "This situation demands that you listen to me and follow my directions explicitly." She studied all of us. "Am I making myself clear?" We nodded. "Normally, you would undergo a rigorous curriculum that would teach you the following technique. But due to circumstances, there is no time.

Do I have your promise that you will listen to me and follow my instructions precisely? This is very dangerous, and you need to maintain willingness at all times. I need seven yeses, please." We were all willing, and each one of us spoke the word: "Yes."

"Position yourselves around Sarah in the following configuration, please. Hen at the midsection, Gimmi next by the heart, Va-Va by her brow, Dolly near the throat, Zara next to the solar plexus, Innee to her left. Then Beth will stand between Innee and Hen, finishing the circle to Hen's right." We formed a ring around the bed while Mary positioned the digital camera, then carefully removed all Sarah's IVs and monitoring devices, leaving only the breathing tube and heart monitor in place. Afterward, the tiny nun carefully wrapped an odd copper and wire strap around her small wrist.

"Wait!" Dolly blurted. "What if someone interrupts us? Is the door locked, or—" Mary held up her hand. "If 7RI didn't own this hospital, I might share your concern. I assure you, we will not be bothered." Mary positioned herself and cleared her throat, deepening her voice.

"Place your left hand up, please. Place your right hand over the patient. Now take your left hand and hold it under the right forearm of the person to your left. Like so." Mary demonstrated and we obeyed.

Within seconds a pulse of white light flashed between us. An enormous jolt of lightning cracked the ceiling and blew out the fluorescents, sending lightbulb glass flying, thrusting all of us off balance. Zara and Innee were hurled to the floor.

My skin was singed, as was Hen's hair. The smell of burning hair and scorched wires filled the room. My throat and lungs choked shut from sheer panic.

Gimmi leaped up and raged in Mary's face, "Are you positive you are giving us the correct instruction? This is scary, Mary!" Grunts of assent popped up around the room. Mary held her ground, unintimidated by Gimmi's proximity.

"I warned you that this was dangerous, and I need you to stay calm. We're going to adjust the frequency now. You must touch at the same time, remembering to direct the intention and energy toward the patient. Not toward each other." Mary climbed onto a nearby chair, securing the video camera to the chair legs with a bungee cord for reasons that were beyond me. "I will cue you. Please breathe and ground the energy through your feet. There's not much time." Sarah's heart monitor was going bananas, and clearly we'd compromised her already fragile system.

Sister Mary was vigilant with the video camera, leaving one foot off the chair to avoid electrocution. And flying bodies.

"This is about right timing and right intention. Repeat one word and one word only in your mind as we proceed. That word is 'love.' Say it repeatedly, lest any other thoughts enter your mind. On the count of three, please put your right hand on the patient without touching each other. One, two, three."

We did as we were told. I focused on my breathing and on Sarah.

"On the next count of three, you are going to place your

left hand under the right forearm of the person to your left. Once you have done so, you will create a circuit, sending the electricity through your right hands into Sarah's body." She took a deep breath and paused. "Whatever you do, you must not remove your hand until my command."

"What's the command?" It was Va-Va, who clearly disliked the nun.

"I will say: 'Khet.'" It sounded like the word "hat" but with an *e* instead of an *a*. "Are we clear?" We all nodded, even though I'd never heard that word before and had no idea what it meant. "Now, on three, place your left hand into position. One, two, three."

We each grabbed a forearm. I felt my right forearm get clasped on cue, voltage coursing through me, through each of us in a circuit. The taste of metal filled my teeth and the hairs in my nose; a snapping sound clacked in my ears. The feeling of sharp rubber bands snapping against my forearm hurt the skin, and I gritted my teeth to keep from screaming. I squinted through a blinding glare to see what was happening. Light was pouring out of everyone's eyes, ears, and noses, but that was nothing compared to our fingers. Electricity gushed out from our palms and into Sarah, convulsing her body into violent spasms. Her frail body raised off the bed, legs kicking reflexively into the air and arms flailing, as we struggled to keep our hands on her.

"Hold on!" Mary yelled, but I could barely hear her from the *click-clack* zapping in my ears. Sarah's movements were quickly escalating and overpowering the group, her oxygen tube yanking out and heart monitor crashing to the floor. Mary's video camera flew out of her hand, snapping wildly from the bungee. I held on for dear life, but I wasn't sure I could sustain the intensity for much longer. It was becoming unbearably cold: The force of the heat coming out of us was freezing us. My hands were turning to ice, and my teeth began chattering uncontrollably. The room was in a whiteout. I heard some groans and guttural strains from the circle, and when I felt like Sarah's body would catapult through the ceiling and kill us all, I heard Mary yell, "KHET!" and we all let go, collapsing to the floor, shivering.

I'm not sure how long I lay shaking there, exhausted, frozen, and thirsty. Mary quickly tossed blankets over each of us. As I lay there, my mouth was filled with the alarming sensation of burned tongue and sandy ice. My eyelids stuck to my eyeballs, and my lips felt chapped. I looked at my hands. My fingernails and cuticles were covered in frost. I touched my face and had no sensation at the tip of my nose. Mary sat me up and inserted a straw into my mouth. I sipped a small bottle of cherry-flavored liquid as she swabbed a balm onto my lips, tilted my head back, and quickly squeezed drops into my eyes. "Sit up, Beth. Take a chair. See what you've done." I was drinking electrolyte solution, and my body absorbed it like a sponge. Sitting up, I surveyed the room. Each girl looked like she'd been in a snowstorm: tiny icicles on hair and a snowy dust across lashes and cheeks. Mary gave me some warm water and repeated this procedure around the room till we were each tended and upright. We looked like rescue victims from an avalanche, shivering as our body temperatures returned to normal. Snowflakes fell softly around the room.

We all eyed the bed nervously, because Sarah didn't move. Sarah, in fact, looked dead. That didn't stop Mary from reinserting all the monitors and IV drips into the lifeless body. As I looked around at these strangers, I wondered: Had we trusted too blindly? Would we now be in trouble for following the ramblings of a crazy nun? Va-Va mentally talked to me first. "Don't worry," she said. "I will get us out of this."

Hen rose and examined the EKG machine, checking the connections and tapping it. She checked Sarah's wrist for a pulse. "Nothing. I'm sorry, Mary. We tried." Hen was compassionate, but also clearly concerned for our welfare.

"I'm leaving," Gimmi declared, but as she opened the door, the EKG beeped to life, and we turned to watch this stranger do something even stranger.

First was the skin: dry cells flaking off like dust blown into air, revealing fresh skin underneath. Mary pulled the cap off of Sarah's bald head. A layer of fuzz blew out of her scalp, wisping out and off the follicles in clumps. Visible strands of hair followed, piercing her scalp like fast-growing stubble. The hair extended like a time-lapse photo, lengthening and thickening until reaching four or five inches. Color bloomed in Sarah's cheeks, as fingers and toes began subtly moving, stretching and flexing almost imperceptibly.

Sarah's fingernails became flush with pink as they developed, extending past the edges of her fingertips. A loud "aaaah" sound poured out of her mouth as her lungs enlarged under her rib cage, her organs visibly reanimating beneath the dermis. Blue and red lines of her vascular system pumped blood in Technicolor.

Mary whipped opened her kit, quickly massaging Sarah's hands and legs with a licorice-scented spray, softly whispering over her body. I got up in time to see Sarah's eyes just as they blinked open. Mary dropped eyedrops into her squinting lids, placing a straw into Sarah's mouth. Sarah downed the entire bottle of water in one gulp, and Mary gave her another one. And another. And another. We all looked at each other uneasily, unsure of what to say to this woman or how to convey the magnitude of what had just happened. Sister Mary elevated the bed so Sarah could sit up. It was clear that Sarah had something to say.

"Do you have the energy to talk?" Mary asked her.

"Yes," Sarah whispered softly, and nodded, coughing lightly to clear her throat. She beckoned us closer to her bed, her vocal cords no doubt dry from the ordeal. Something in her eyes looked familiar to me, and as she gathered the energy to speak, I watched as the seven of us—seven girls of every color, style, and stripe—leaned in to hear what this woman had to say. I felt incredibly dizzy still, but my adrenaline kept me upright. It was miraculous, but there were no words.

"Thank you." It was the most loving, grateful tone I'd ever heard. "I am—" She paused, looking at each of us and beaming with—was it pride? Gratitude? Humility? She seemed dazzled by us, all of us, even in our dazed and disoriented states.

"It's so nice to meet you. Each of you." She paused, looking at each one of us and closing her eyes and nodding. With each nod she took a deep breath, her color getting better every second. I could not believe we'd resurrected this woman from the brink of death.

"I've wanted to meet you all for so long. Although these conditions are not ideal, I am still quite happy." Was she tearing up? She started weeping. Sister Mary started crying too.

"Don't cry," I said. "It's alright."

"You must be Aleph Beth," she said to me, before looking at all of us. "And you are Gimmi, Dolly, Hen, Va-Va, and Zara and Innee.

"I have wanted to meet you all because I am—" She wiped her eyes and took a deep breath. "I am . . . your mother."

"What?" we said, and looked at each other, uncertain as to whether her brains had been fried beyond use or not.

"It's true," Sister Mary added.

"We all have the same mother?" I said in shock.

"Yes. You are all sisters." Sarah smiled. "Half sisters, most of you, except for Innee and Zara, but sisters nonetheless."

Our reactions were as different as we were. Gimmi and Va-Va stormed out of the room. Dolly and Hen embraced. Zara and Innee took turns looking at Sarah and then each other. I stood there in disbelief, realizing she was the mother who would've died if I hadn't come to New York.

"How are we all sisters?" Innee asked. "We're so close in age, aren't we?" Mary managed to get Gimmi and Va-Va back into the room.

"It only takes nine months"—Sarah coughed—"to make a baby. I was very busy." She smiled on the word "busy" and started nodding. "Gimel Electra Ray was born in Shigatse, Tibet, some twenty-six years ago." I gathered she meant Gimmi, but I didn't want to interrupt. None of us did. "Daleth Alcyone Ray was born in Château de Liberté, France about twenty-four years ago. Heh Maia Ray was born in Luxor, Egypt, of course, less than two years later. Let's see, Vav Taygete Ray was born in Crete eighteen months after that. My little twins, Zayin Celeano Ray and Asterope Ray, debuted in Lebanon very shortly after that." Sarah nodded sweetly and took a big sip of water and a deep breath. "Last, but certainly not least, was my Aleph Beth Merope Ray. Born in Transylvania, Romania."

"Romania?" I blurted. "I thought I was born in Michigan or New York!"

Sister Mary interjected, "Many of your birth certificates were altered for your protection. Zara and Innee were given different names for similar reasons. Worry not. The originals are safely in our archives."

"You certainly must've slept with a lot of different guys," said Dolly, stating the obvious.

"Please do not confuse the sacred with the profane!" Mary instructed Dolly. "I will not tolerate disrespect."

Sarah nodded at Dolly with forgiveness in her eyes. "Yes.

With the exception of Zara and Innee, you all have different fathers, specifically chosen for particular reasons involving their cultural, religious, and genetic heritage."

"Which is what?" Hen asked, quite insistently.

"You are all one blood, and that's all that matters," Sarah offered.

"She deserves an answer. She wants to know about her father," Gimmi urged.

"In no particular order"—Sarah halted, clearing her throat, and sadness flickered across her face—"your fathers are Hindu, Muslim, Buddhist, Catholic, Protestant, and Jewish."

"But why give us all up? Why keep having children only to give them up?" Zara was confused, her brain moving a mile a minute.

"There is an explanation for everything. There was another plan for your initiation, but I became ill and plans had to change. As Gimmi and Dolly can attest, all initiations were triggered on your eighteenth birthdays. Tests were administered on an explicit timetable under extreme secrecy. The oldest have been waiting the longest for this final initiation, and for that I want to thank them." Gimmi and Dolly nodded with understanding, although they didn't exactly look thrilled.

"I've waited for this for almost eight years," Gimmi said to all of us. I'd barely lasted the past few weeks, and I felt insane. I wondered if they knew what they were waiting for, when Va-Va said as much.

"We knew we were waiting for something, Beth." She

smiled. "We just didn't know it was you." The six girls all nodded in agreement. Mary pulled a dossier out of her bag and handed it to Sarah.

"Ladies. If I had died, this would have been your inheritance," Sarah offered quietly. "But since you've saved my life? Consider it a gift." Seven gold envelopes were dispensed around the room. As the envelopes ripped open, I heard Zara gasp and Innee squeal, followed by a "holy crap" from Hen and some sobs from Dolly.

"Why?" Innee asked.

"One tree. Many branches. No strings." Sarah was clear. "You all have important work to do, and you will need resources to nourish and protect that destiny."

"What is this? What if I don't want it? What if I just want to live my life as I choose?" Gimmi was insistent, rebellious.

"There are no strings. You have free will. You have choice. But you are the Seven Rays. The fact that you healed me is living proof of your power, testament to the seven spiritual gifts you offer: Healing, Miracles, Tongues, Prophecy, Discerning of Spirits, Knowledge, and Sight. My gift to you is the assurance and the knowledge that the gifts you possess are all quite real. None of you are crazy." I looked around the room and saw those words resonate for every one of us. We'd all believed it about ourselves at one time or another; I wasn't alone. "Hide the gift or share the gift, but use your talents for good. Or they will destroy your lives and burn you beyond all recognition." These last words landed in the room like an enormous thud. None of us doubted her sincerity.

"Is that a threat?" Gimmi asked.

"Simple truth," Mary responded.

"You may need these resources to shield yourselves from those who would take advantage of you." Sarah's cheeks burned rose with the intensity of the moment, but she was beatific. "I hope you will accept them."

I couldn't process everything, so I just opened the envelope. Inside was a crisp cashier's check. Made out to me. I noticed it had a helluva lot of zeroes. Seven zeroes. Followed by screams. I was happy to discover that the screams of joy and the zeroes? Were all mine.

CHAPTER 34

I LOOKED AROUND THE ROOM BEFORE WE WERE transported back to 7RI. Our responses to the news were as varied as our hairstyles, and it was clear that our questions far outnumbered the answers. We said our good-byes to the resuscitated Sarah David and left the site of our first miracle.

Once outside, flurries of snow appeared around all of us in an orb. As we walked toward the van in our own ecosystem, we had no problem clobbering Mary with our collective quest for information.

"What the hell are the Seven Rays?" Gimmi wondered.

"I think it has something to do with the constellation Pleiades," I offered, "but I'm not entirely sure."

"Where did she get all this money?" Hen was dazed from the zeroes and I couldn't blame her. We all were.

"The David family is an empire unto itself," Mary explained quietly. "Sarah was one of the last remaining heirs of a legacy that is thousands of years old. That is, until all of you were born. A family covenant required that she . . ." Mary trailed off. "I've spoken out of turn. Much was required of your mother. I hope you will grant her the opportunity to share her story with you." The edginess of all these unanswered questions vibrated palpably amongst the group. It was simultaneous information overload and underload.

"What are we supposed to do? Who is after us?" Dolly seemed genuinely concerned. "How do we protect ourselves?" she demanded. "Full-time security? Armored cars? What?"

Mary took a deep breath, calmly absorbing the verbal bullets from every direction. They were pointed questions she was unwilling to answer.

"Who exactly are our fathers?" Gimmi and Hen demanded.

When Mary did not answer, Innee's eyes rolled back into her head, and she began rhyming in jibberish, speaking in tongues. Zara snapped to and closed her eyes, patiently translating Innee's inscrutable language aloud:

"The fathers that live? The ones that are alive," Zara whispered, "do search for you. But there is one man—" But Zara couldn't finish. Innee was speaking too quickly.

"What? Zara, what?" Va-Va urged her to continue, looking to Mary for help. If Mary could complete the sentence, she refused. Innee's ramblings filled the van. Zara listened intently.

"This man," Zara continued, "controls men, who want to control you." We all looked to Mary for confirmation of this. It was written all over her face. It was true.

Zara then began ranting in some foreign tongue, *"Hou elkaars handen vast!"* She paused and changed accents: *"Dastemunoo begereem!"* And again, *"Emsick yedee!"* Instinctively, we all grabbed hands.

Mary shrieked reflexively, "No! No! Do not hold hands! Do not touch each other!" Then to the driver, she wailed, "Pull over! Now!"

But it was too late. As our hands clasped, a blast of light blazed through the entire van. We were suddenly pummeled into a centrifugal force that seemed to pin us against the walls of the van. It was as if we were spinning on a ride where the floors drop out. The van hadn't changed course, but we had.

Before our eyes, the flash of light shape-shifted into a revolving sphere. It took over the space inside our impromptu circle, flickering with images like a movie screen. The globe began projecting footage of Gimmi. There she was, climbing up a steep incline, methodically spraying something onto a massive surface. Our vantage point pulled far away as if on a satellite, and day time-lapsed into night. Gimmi then perched herself atop the Great Pyramid, now covered in ultraviolet hieroglyphics.

Suddenly there was a flash, and the orb filled with ultraviolet light. It scorched our eyes as Zara's and Innee's figures filled the sphere. An image flashed onscreen in time-lapse of the twins emerging from some tropical surf in bikinis, wearing large packs. They were running down a beach, dripping ocean water as they pulled what looked like heavy, bulletproof vests out of their bags and over their bodies. Sand kicked up as they picked up speed, pulling full-length black garments over the vests. They were sprinting. In burqas.

The image disappeared in a flash of white. Inky strands covered the white space, as flowing black hair filled our van-sized crystal ball. Dolly's terrified face blew into view, as men in black hats and long black coats were chasing her down a narrow street. The men were screaming at her, pointing guns in her direction. Time slowed down, revealing glittering fragments falling onto the ground in slow motion. Diamonds. Diamonds tumbled out of Dolly's pockets as she outran the angry mob of bearded men. The image darkened to black.

I looked around the van, trying to see my half sisters, when a bright, pink light shined inside the orb, blasting our field of vision. The power emanating from the circle of light was too strong. Suddenly Hen appeared inside the sphere. Her striped hair was peeking out of a hard hat, and she was digging with high-tech instruments. Hen's excavation continued until her image disappeared behind an enormous pile of displaced earth. Her figure was dwarfed by the giant stone paw of the Sphinx. The screen was filled by a dust storm so realistic, I could practically feel the dry wind whipping against us.

Then it got quiet, as an orange sunset began glowing inside the movie ball. A bird's-eye view swept onscreen and revealed Va-Va asleep atop a giant ginger rock, ovals of light twice her size engulfing her, dancing and pulsing around her body before launching into the atmosphere like missiles.

The screen went black. It was time for my face to appear in the community crystal ball. There I was, panting and breathing harder than I'd ever seen myself breathe. Sweat was pouring down my face. I was screaming in agony. I was scared. Finally the word "ENOUGH!" screeched inside the van. Mary's nails were digging into my arm, ripping my hand out of Zara's grasp. As our clasp unlocked, the image ball vanished, leaving seven stunned zombies in its wake. The van was no longer moving, though it felt like we'd been careening at more than a hundred miles per hour. I shivered. Small frost crystals sparkled at the end of the tiny hairs on my arm.

"Let's take a breath, shall we?" Mary's voice creaked. "Sarah will share as much or as little as you want to know. When the time is right. I suggest you not overanalyze the images you just received. Or pursue answers to your questions in unsavory ways." Mary sat in front as the driver resumed his journey. We rode in silence, brushing the frosty crystals off of our chilled skin, and no one said a word.

At 7RI headquarters we didn't make plans. We knew— telepathically—we would stay in touch. We were all reeling far too fast to speak.

I stood in front of the building in a daze, unsure of what was next. My mind raced about whether what I'd done and seen made any sense, and whether I'd use the money and go to college, not to mention the more immediate stuff, like where to sleep that night. Sister Mary offered me the keys to the David penthouse on Park Avenue. I didn't want to be alone, but I was too shy to ask these relative acquaintances for help. They all offered me a place to crash, but I declined for some reason. As my sisters went their separate ways, Dolly tapped me on the shoulder and pointed to her temple across the street. "Call me tomorrow. But I think somebody wants to talk to you right now." I turned around, and my questions were answered. There stood Richie Mac.

We stood there for a long while, just looking at each other from across the street. When a smile finally crossed his face, something happened. Beautiful energy was flowing around him. Shafts of light moved and swayed around him like his own red-carpet premiere. It was the first time the Sight had worked with him in ages, and I could see it all so clearly: Richie Mac loved me.

He walked toward me. "I'm so sorry. I'm so sorry for every- thing I said and anything I did that hurt you. I didn't mean it." He paused and stood a few steps away from me, and knotted ropes flashed in and out of my field of vision. "Can you forgive me? I was scared, but I didn't mean it, Beth. I didn't mean those things I said." He was telling the truth, and suddenly ropes were untying between us and dissolving with every apology.

"I can't be without you. I can't live without you. Whether it's for one day, one week, one month, or one year. Whatever it is, I'll take it." He came closer, needing me to understand something. "But I couldn't take it if you thought that I didn't care about you." He held my hands, and there was no jolt! Just incredible warmth. "I love you more than you'll ever know." He dragged out the last few words, making sure I heard them. I heard every syllable. My heart lit up like a brush fire.

"By the way? There's nothing to forgive," I said. I meant it.

He laughed and touched my face gently, and I remembered we'd never actually had a second kiss. I smiled at the thought, and he said, "It's the only thing I've been thinking about."

I put my cheek close to his. Richie held my face in both hands and slowly, tenderly kissed me. The electricity threatened to shock us at first, but we willed it into submission, harnessing it and focusing it. Together we rode the voltage with our mouths. A ball of light formed between our lips as we dove into the longing that had been consuming us. The charge of the kisses escalated as we moved this light back and forth, a game of catch with tongues and mouths. Passing this beautiful substance—what was it?—drinking it in, and then returning it. In the corner of my eye I saw our reflection in a car window. A figure eight of light shimmered between our heads, dancing on the windshield. He held my lips on his for one long, precious moment and pulled back slightly. Richie caressed my face with both of his hands and gazed into my eyes again, all love. "I just wanted you to know that."

Without a word Richie Mac and I got into his ugly green station wagon and drove toward things I didn't understand. I wasn't even sure I wanted to. But I knew it didn't matter whether I understood them or not, because I saw them with my very own eyes and felt them with my very own heart. I knew that seeing was believing. Because there are some things you can't unsee.

–End–

ACKNOWLEDGMENTS

I WOULD LIKE TO THANK MY BESTIES, Bobby Lavelle, Jacqueline Cronin and Helen of Cavallo, TR Pescod, and Tina Fischer. But much love to my loyal true blues: Sheila Roche, Lara Harris, Jim Hecht, Adam Vetri, Brian Gattas, and Joy Gorman. You all kept me going in so many ways, and I adore you for that.

Much love to my mom, Christine Bilonick, for all the love, appreciation, and faith she sends my way. Much love to my dad, Bruce Bendinger, for encouraging my sense of humor, and for those typing lessons!

I am grateful for the kindness and compassion of numerous smart brains, wise eyes, and kind hearts throughout the writing of the book: Martina Broner, Gitty Daneshevari, Gail Lyon, Nancy Weiss, Howard Wills, the Tully Family, Polly DeFrank, Marty Scott, Lee Konecke, and Mark Feuerstein (my coffee klatsch!).

A loving squeal for my enthusiastic and insightful editor, Emily Meehan! More squeals of thanks for Courtney Bongiolatti, Julia Maguire, and Stephanie Abou.

An over-the-top salute to my McKnight in shining armor, Gregory McKnight, my brilliant and spectacular agent who believed in me from day one. Much respect and thanks to Craig Jacobson, Jessica Matthews, Maha Dakhil, and Sally Wilcox.

An enormous shout-out to some very worthy people and places who have helped me along the way: Cheebo, Chateau Marmont, Hoffman Institute, Mindi Schumacher, Barry Michels, Dr. Elba Olivares, Dr. Catherine Veritas, Lisa Sutton and Amy Lafayette, Mike Bulger, Scott Cunha, Justini Conlan, and Gareth Monks. Giant hugs to my many friends at the Henson Lot—you all have a big place in my heart.

Massive thanks and props to Jason Falk for his extraordinary and tireless efforts on the brilliant cover design.

To super sweetheart Sara Lindsey! I am so grateful for your constant patience, dependability, and loyalty. I couldn't have done this without you. Thank you a million times.

Last but not least, my biggest and deepest thanks goes to Rebecca Hobbs. Thank you for blessing my life and this book with your dedication, commitment, energy, and love. You are an angel.

A sacred oath,
a fallen angel,
a forbidden love

YOU WON'T BE ABLE TO
KEEP IT *HUSH, HUSH.*